Readers love
STEPHEN OSBORNE

Dead End

"I love Stephen Osborne's Duncan Andrews Mystery series… this latest installment was a winner. In fact, this was probably my favorite book in the series."

—Boys in Our Books

"*Dead End* was my favorite book of the series… I'd certainly read whatever else this author writes in this universe."

—It's About The Book

"Osborne's wit and clever writing are there, as is the cast of characters we've come to know and love…"

—Prism Book Alliance

The Scarlet Tide

"The investigation part of the story flows well, is interesting and gives the plot plenty of action and danger."

—Literary Nymphs

"I'm a fan of this series… the love story is so good!"

—Live Your Life, Buy the Book

By Stephen Osborne

Cuddling (Dreamspinner Anthology)
Pop Goes the Weasel • Rat Bastard
Speaking of Dreams
Temporal Driftwood
Wrestling with Jesus

Duncan Andrews Thrillers
Pale as a Ghost
Animal Instinct
The Scarlet Tide
Dead End

Published by Dreamspinner Press
www.dreamspinnerpress.com

Speaking of Dreams

Stephen Osborne

Published by

DREAMSPINNER PRESS

5032 Capital Circle SW, Suite 2, PMB# 279, Tallahassee, FL 32305-7886 USA
www.dreamspinnerpress.com

Speaking of Dreams
© 2015 Stephen Osborne.

Cover Art
© 2015 Anne Cain.
annecain.art@gmail.com
Cover content is for illustrative purposes only and any person depicted on the cover is a model.

ISBN: 978-1-63476-586-2
Digital ISBN: 978-1-63476-587-9
Library of Congress Control Number: 2015942998
First Edition October 2015

Printed in the United States of America
♾
This paper meets the requirements of
ANSI/NISO Z39.48-1992 (Permanence of Paper).

*Dedicated to the memory of David Woods
and the memory of Andrew Ruiz*

CHAPTER ONE

FORTY-FIVE.

Forty didn't bother me so much. I'm not sure why. Maybe because I had a lover back then. Getting older isn't such a bad prospect when you've got someone to grow old with. But forty-five and single… you might as well hang it up. In the gay world, forty-five is ancient. Forty-five means you must have been around to see what happened to the dinosaurs. Forty-five and you could have been around to wave farewell to friends sailing on the *Titanic*. Forty-five and…. Well, you get the picture. It's old.

Not that I felt old. Or looked it, in my humble opinion. Believe me, I took a close look in the bathroom mirror when I was getting ready for my birthday bash, and I wasn't horribly concerned with what I saw. Okay, maybe there was the hint of crow's feet around the eyes and a few—but not many—gray hairs nestled amongst the blondish-brown. Slight sagging of the cheeks. There were exercises you could do to help correct that, weren't there? Or creams. Or plastic surgery. Hey, if it was good enough for the late, great Joan Rivers, comedienne extraordinaire, it was good enough for Frank Hunter, artist and waiter for a catering firm.

I was still in good shape. While I can't say I often saw the inside of a gym, I did a fair amount of walking. Every morning, rain or shine, I took my dog for a walk around the neighborhood. If this doesn't sound like much of a workout to you, you haven't met Fantine. Fantine is a border terrier and a bit of a diva. She likes her walks and grumbles if I try to cut them short. She has a path that she likes to follow and doesn't deviate from it much. When we get home, I feel like I've had a good workout and deserve a cup of tea. She's ready to go again.

Thank goodness for Fantine. She gives me someone to talk to when I come home from work. I used to talk to Jason, but the silly bastard went and died. I wasn't there. He was visiting relatives in Virginia and, as far as anyone can tell, got really drunk one night and fell off a pier and drowned. The drowning part is fact; the drunk part I'm assuming. His family won't say. In fact they don't like to talk about that night at all, especially with me. But I can see the whole thing in my mind. He probably got angry with his brother or with his mother or his father and started hitting the rum. Jason loved his rum. I can see him staggering out of the house late at night, clutching the bottle in his hand, as clearly as if I'd been there. I have no doubt he was muttering to himself as he walked down to the pier, cursing whoever had angered him. He liked to curse almost as much as he liked rum. And then—a slip, a splash, and....

And nothing. No more Jason.

I talked to him even after that. Had whole conversations. I'd come home from work and ask him how his day went and then I'd tell him about mine. This went on for months, until I decided to get a dog so that if someone overheard me talking to Jason, they wouldn't think I was crazy for talking to a dead person. They'd just think I was crazy for talking to a dog and asking her how her day went.

Where was I? Oh, yes. Turning forty-five.

Turning forty-five sucked almost as much as the gin and tonic I was drinking, which I'm pretty sure they made with paint thinner instead of gin.

"You're thinking about Jason, aren't you?" Zach asked.

Zach was my best friend. Every now and then someone just fits a stereotype, either by accident or design. Maybe Zach was as butch as anyone when he'd been young. Somewhere along the line, though, he put on this act to become a flaming queen. Maybe after a while it was impossible to tell where the act left off and Zach began. Or maybe he'd always been effeminate. Maybe being a drag queen just brings out the diva in you. Who knows? All I knew was that I loved Zach Schubert as a brother. He was a big black man. Not obese. Just stocky. His drag name was Hetty Suxual. Yeah, I know.

I smiled. "How could you tell?"

"Honeychild, whenever I see you go all puppy dog eyes, I know you're thinking about Jason. How long has it been?"

"Four years, seven months, and eight days."

"Not that you're keeping track or anything."

I shook my head. "God forbid."

"How long since you've been on a date?"

That was from Shawn Watson. Shawn's an accountant, although he doesn't look like one. He looks like a professional tennis player or something. You know, tall, with wavy blond hair and teeth that are just a little too white.

"Darling, Frank don't date," Zach answered for me. "You know that. He keeps thinking that Jason is gonna walk through that door and everything is going to be all hunky-dory again."

We were celebrating at a bar called Dixon Street, so named because, well, it was located on Dixon Street. It was a pretty big place, with three bar areas. There was the main one, with a huge dance floor and even a stage. Then there was the upstairs bar, which was supposed to be a quiet place where you could go and actually hear what someone else was saying over the blaring music. Lastly there was the show bar, a room off to the side with loads of tables and another stage, a little smaller than the one in the main room. This was where they usually had the drag shows, where Zach performed. Tonight, though, was Tuesday. No drag shows on Tuesday, generally because the crowds weren't big enough to warrant a show. We were practically the only ones in the show bar, the five of us. At another table two young studs held hands and gazed longingly into each other's eyes. And then there was Benny, the bartender. Slow night.

"You should," Gene Ross said. "You're not getting any younger."

I made a sour face. "Thanks, Gene. I wasn't aware of that. I thought all the birthday cards with tombstones on them were sent to me by mistake."

I wasn't really mad at Gene's remark. Gene was the youngest of our little group, not even having hit thirty yet. Gene was short, and I mean really short. Maybe five foot two. God may have shorted him on stature, but he made up for it in looks. Gene was, quite frankly, fucking handsome. Thick black hair, a killer smile, and dark brown eyes that made your heart melt. If he wasn't straight, I'd date him. If he wasn't so young. And if I dated.

Sitting next to Gene was his best friend, Marril Leblanc. If you didn't know Gene was happily married and had a bevy of kids, you might think he and Marril were lovers if you saw them together. Marril and Gene had grown up together, and if Gene had been bothered when his best friend started working as a drag queen at Dixon Street, he certainly never showed it. The two sat close together, actually touching shoulders and occasionally leaning into each other. They were a textbook bromance.

Marril sipped at his cosmopolitan and batted his long and very fake eyelashes at me. "I think we need to look to Frank's future, not his past. Whether he wants to throw himself back into the dating pool or not is his business. Doesn't matter. What matters is that he's got us. Friends are what really matter. Lovers are just the icing on the cake."

I lifted my glass. "Hear, hear," I said.

We all clinked glasses. Well, Gene had a beer bottle, not a glass, but it clinked just as well. I drained the rest of my gin and tonic. It tasted better now that it had killed most of my taste buds.

Gene's bottle was empty, and Zach's screwdriver was nearly gone. "I think," Gene said, "another round is called for."

"I'm good," Marril replied. His cosmo had barely been touched. Not one of your drinkers, our Marril.

I started to get up but was met with violent gestures and tutting sounds. "It's your birthday," Zach said. "You're not allowed to buy."

Eyebrows raised in mock admonishment, I said, "I was going to hit the restroom. Calm your ass down."

"Huh," Shawn muttered. "Generally it's Gene who runs off to the john whenever it's time to buy a round."

That was mean of Shawn, although if it bothered Gene it didn't show. Gene worked at a factory that made plumbing supplies, and he wasn't doing badly. Well, he wouldn't be if he didn't have a wife and three kids to look after. It wasn't that Gene lacked cash, more that nearly every cent he had went to his family, which was perfectly understandable. Unless you're a snarky bastard like Shawn.

Everyone ignored Shawn's comment, maybe hoping he'd take the hint and tone down his sarcasm. I don't know why we expected this. It never worked.

I don't really dislike Shawn. I'm just not sure I like him.

"Remember where it is?" Marril asked, the joke obviously referring to my inability to hold my liquor. Two drinks for me is plenty. Three and I'm tipsy, if not actually drunk. I've only made it to four a couple of times, and one time I wound up sprawled in the snow clutching a fire hydrant, telling the cold metal fixture I loved it. Pretty sure I thought it was Fantine.

"I can still walk and chew gum at the same time," I said.

I made my way to the restroom, which was off the main bar. There weren't many people there either. A few people were clustered around the bar itself, and a few were dancing. Whoopee! A Tuesday night at a gay bar in Indianapolis is definitely not party central. Still, I was glad my birthday had landed on a weekday. On a Friday or Saturday, Dixon Street was so packed you could hardly breathe. Not my idea of a fun time.

Another plus: since the place wasn't busy, the restroom was relatively clean. No one had pissed all over the floor. No one had thrown up into the sinks. No one was fucking in one of the toilet stalls.

I stepped up to one of the urinals and unzipped. I'd thought I was alone, but someone must have come in right after me because he chose the urinal right next to mine. He was Hispanic, if I was any judge of ethnic types, and young. I guessed twenty-two, tops. Smallish and darkish and all black Muppet hair. As one does, I tried to ignore the fact that he chose to stand right next to me, when there were four other urinals he could have chosen, and went about my business. The stream had just started flowing when out of the corner of my eye I saw the guy lean over and check out my junk.

"Nice," he said with a smile.

I blinked. Holding back my ire, I said, "Did you just look at my dick?"

"Sure. Did you think I was complimenting the urinal cake?"

Flustered, I stuttered a little. "You're... you're not supposed to do that! It's just... not done!"

He shrugged. "Then why do they put them close together with no barriers in between? I'm pretty sure you're supposed to scope out the other guy's package." There was just a hint of a Spanish accent when he spoke.

Part of me wanted to just walk away, which wasn't possible as I was in midstream. And I knew I should be really angry, having someone blatantly checking me out like that, but the young man had such a disarming smile it was hard to be mad. He was just having some fun. Still, I tried to sound cross when I said, "It's a tacky thing to do."

"Hey, I said it was nice. And that's not even seeing it at its best." He reached out his right hand for me to shake. "I'm Donny."

I glared at the hand as if it had been a venomous snake. "Um...."

"It's okay," he said. "I didn't pee on it."

I finished urinating and tucked everything away after giving it the old obligatory tap-tap. "Maybe we should wait until we've washed our hands."

Donny shrugged again. "Up to you."

Moments later he joined me at the sinks. I was rinsing the soap off my hands when he turned on his taps and squirted a lavish amount of soap out of his dispenser. "Gotta get all the nasty germies off my hands," he said, flashing me a cheeky grin.

I couldn't figure out if he was just having fun or actually flirting with me. Surely not. I was ancient, and he was just a fledgling. I have to admit, though, that my heart wasn't disliking the possibility of some youngster finding me attractive.

The restrooms at Dixon Street didn't have towelettes to dry your hands off. They had those awful air dryers. I was standing before one, letting the hot air do its thing, when Donny stepped up to the one next to me. He smacked his elbow against the button to start his up, then rubbed his hands under the nozzle. "Nearly ready for that handshake now?" he asked.

I chuckled. He really was cute. "If you insist." I stuck out my hand.

Suddenly Donny thrust himself at me, throwing his arms around my neck and planting his lips firmly against mine. Shocked, I stumbled backward until my backside hit the sink counter. I tried to pull my lips away, but the kid had a good grip on my neck. I finally put my hands on his shoulders and pushed him away. His eyes were sparkling and his grin went nearly from ear to ear.

"Much better than a handshake, wouldn't you say?"

I didn't know what to say. No one had kissed me on the lips since Jason. I'd forgotten that the simple act of someone pressing their mouth against yours could send jolts of electricity down your spine. Eventually I found my voice. "I'm nearly twice your age, kid."

Another shrug. "So? You're cute. It's not like I turned you around, bent you over that counter, and pulled your pants down so that I could fuck your—"

"Whoa!" Brazen little bastard! Still, he said I was cute. I hadn't been called cute in decades. Hell, Donny might not have even been born the last time someone called me cute. Other than Jason, that is.

Donny slipped his arms around my waist and pulled close to me, grinding his groin against me a little. "We can, if you like. I don't think anyone will disturb us."

Again I pushed him away. "I'm flattered," I said. "Really, I am. And I understand that there are slim pickings tonight. But you're much too young for me."

"You got a guy?" he asked. He was giving me his best sexy face. At least I hoped it was his best. If he had one better I doubt I could have resisted. My God, he had the most gorgeous eyes. And he knew how to use them.

"No, I… I don't."

"Then what's to stop us having some fun? You might find that you like having a younger guy in bed with you." His eyebrows twitched bewitchingly. "You know, young guys have tons of energy. I bet I could make you really, really happy."

He got closer again. I would have backpedaled, but I was already against the counter. "Look, kid, I—"

"Donny. Donny Rodriquez."

"Donny. You're really cute, and as I say, I'm flattered. Especially as today's my birthday and I was feeling—"

His eyes lit up. "Your birthday? We should celebrate! I could be your present!"

I put a hand on his chest to stop any further encroachment on my personal space. "Nice as that sounds, I've got friends waiting for me."

"So do I," he said dismissively.

It didn't sound like he cared much for the people he was with. Now that I had a good look at him, I recognized him as one of the few who had been out on the dance floor, flailing about to the beat. He was wearing a white T-shirt with some design on it in black and tight, tight jeans. I couldn't help but notice that there was a prominent bulge in the crotch. The kid was horny, but I really didn't need to see the bulge to figure that out.

"I can ditch them, though."

Okay, it had been four years and seven months since I'd had sex with another person, and I'd kind of gotten used to the idea that it would never happen again. And I thought I was okay with that. I'd have the memories of Jason. But now there was this hot little number standing in front of me actually *wanting* to hook up with me. Part of me really wanted to say yes. Yeah, he was young, but we weren't talking commitment. And if it didn't bother him….

But it bothered me. A little. Enough. "Sorry," I said, gently pushing him farther away. "I'd better get back to my friends."

He looked disappointed. "You haven't told me your name."

I almost didn't tell him. After all, what did it matter? We'd never see each other again. But I couldn't resist those eyes. "Frank," I said. "Frank Hunter."

Donny pushed my hand aside—I hadn't even realized I'd left it placed against his chest—and stood on his tiptoes and kissed me again. This time the kiss was sweet and gentle, not the desperate, horny first kiss. I found myself closing my eyes and wishing—despite my better nature—that the kiss would go on and on. Maybe forever.

He broke it off much too quickly for my liking. Beaming, he said, "Happy birthday, Frank Hunter."

And then he turned and left the restroom, leaving me still leaning against the sink counter.

CHAPTER TWO

I OFTEN have weird dreams.

That night I dreamed I was in a big dance hall. Everyone was dressed like it was the 1940s, maybe right after the war. There were lots of guys in uniform, and the women had colorful hats on. The orchestra played "In the Mood." I was dancing with Jason, who wore a sailor's outfit. Jason had never been in the service, but as he'd died in water, I guess the Navy made some sort of sense.

"I love this song," I told him as we moved in time to the music.

Jason was uncharacteristically silent. He seemed to be thinking hard, like he wanted to say something but couldn't come up with the proper words.

Finally he shrugged and said, "I like it too."

I went to kiss him, but before our lips met I felt a tap on my shoulder. I turned my head to find Donny standing there in his white T-shirt and tight jeans. "Mind if I cut in?" he asked.

"I'm dancing with—"

But I wasn't. Jason had vanished. So had everyone else in the room, save the orchestra, who finished "In the Mood" and went into "Begin the Beguine."

"I guess so," I said, feeling somewhat sad that Jason had left me.

But Donny wasn't there any longer. I was alone on the dance floor, listening to the old Cole Porter song.

ZACH NEVER walked into a room. He made an entrance, even when the room was my living room and I was the only person to appreciate the spectacle. Somehow, even when wearing men's clothing, Zach seemed to be in drag. Today he was wearing a button-down blue shirt and tan slacks, but you'd swear it was a blouse covering his chest. Or maybe it was the eyeliner that conveyed the impression that he was only a step away from becoming Hetty Suxual.

I sat at my desk and tried to close my laptop before he saw the page I was checking out. Zach snaked out a hand and prevented the action. He stared unbelievingly at the screen.

"An online dating site?" he asked.

"I was just looking," I replied, a little defensively.

Zach's eyebrows arched. "Seems little Donny awakened your libido. If we ever run across the tyke again I'll have to thank him."

After I'd returned to our table, I had, of course, told everyone about my encounter with Donny Rodriquez in the restroom. Jokes ensued the rest of the night, mostly referring to me robbing the cradle, and included one suggestion that we cruise high schools over the weekend so that I could find another young date.

My cheeks were red, I was sure, as I replied, "Maybe he did. I mean, I know he was probably drunk and it's not like there was a big crowd last night, but he really seemed interested."

"Well, why wouldn't he be, darling? You're a catch! You're like a young Robert Redford with just a little Roddy McDowall thrown in for good measure."

"That's an odd combination."

"I took a gander at little Donny when we left. He was the one out on the dance floor, wasn't he? The one wearing jeans so tight they left nothing to the imagination?"

"That was him."

"He was pretty."

"And awfully young."

"So? He was legal. Barely. You know what's great about boys his age? They're like Bic pens. You use 'em, abuse 'em, and when they're used up you just toss them away!"

I chuckled. "That's awful."

"But true. Now, who are you looking at here?" Zach squinted to see the screen. "Oh, no. Not that one. I think things are living in his beard. Besides, he's into leather."

"It doesn't say that."

"You can tell. Something about the eyes. No, honeychild, you hook up with him and you're going to end up with your ass in a sling and him standing over you with a cat-o'-nine-tails. Who else you been scoping out?"

Zach ended up pulling up a chair, and together we went through a couple dozen prospects. Zach put the kibosh on most of them, finding them lacking in some way. We finally narrowed the field down to three.

"How do we get more information on them?" Zach asked.

"I'd have to join the site. You don't get contact info unless you join."

"Well, join, honeychild, join! If you don't want that blond one with the dimple, I might have to snatch him up!"

"I'm not sure I'm ready to take the plunge."

Zach grunted. "Well, you can always come to the show tonight. Maybe Donny will be there."

"Pass."

"I don't think I've ever seen him before," Zach said. "He might be a newbie. Or maybe he just never comes to the show bar. You know, one of those dance floor bunnies who never venture into the darker corners of the bar." Zach made it sound like parts of Dixon Street were akin to Dracula's castle. "Seriously, though, you should come out. If any young kids try to make out with you, big bad Uncle Zach will smack them."

I pondered going out. I didn't have a catering gig until Thursday night, and I could use a break from my art projects. I had a small showing coming up at a local gallery, but it was over a month away, and there was plenty of time to get ready for it. And I hadn't seen Zach's show for quite a while. "Maybe," I relented.

Zach took that as a yes and went on to other subjects. "Did you finish that painting? The one with all the blues and the ghostlike thing reaching out?"

"Finished it last week." It wasn't a ghost, but I didn't tell Zach that. I always have had a hard time explaining what my paintings meant, thinking it was best for the viewer to make up his own mind as to what it was about. If Zach saw a ghost, fine. To me, though, it was the soul of man, reaching out for meaning in the cosmos. The dark blues were supposed to give a mood of desperation, of longing for something unattainable.

Or maybe it was just a lot of blue with a humanlike white blob in the center.

"I do have something I'd like you to see, though. A new piece. Not a painting. I was thinking of adding it to the art show."

"Let's see it."

I led Zach out to the garage, which was located slightly behind the house, off to the side. When my dad retired, for some reason he and Ma decided to move to a smaller place in Kokomo, and they left me their house. For anyone else, the two-story farmhouse might have been too large for just one person, but most of the rooms had been converted to satisfy my art obsessions. One was a painting room, one was a sculpting room, and the garage was for larger projects. The weather was fine for early May, and we didn't need to pause to put jackets on, although there was a slight breeze. I opened the side door of the garage and ushered Zach inside, snapping on the light.

Some people keep a car in their garage. Mine had four toilets right in the center. They weren't hooked up or anything. One was painted a baby blue and was decorated with a kid's mobile and had things like pacifiers and teddy bears glued to it. The second one was painted green and had a college cap positioned at a jaunty angle over the tank. There were pages from textbooks glued all over it, as well as a few pens and an old cell phone. Number three was red and had a box of half-eaten chocolates covering the seat. All sorts of valentines were glued to the surface, on one side pristine, the other torn and dirty. The last toilet was black and resembled a tombstone, even to having a name—John Doe— etched on it, along with his birth and death dates.

Zach walked around the toilets, eying them carefully, chewing on a fingernail as he tried to make up his mind about them. Finally he stopped by the tombstone toilet. "Well," he said, "it's easy to get the theme of this little exhibit."

I wondered if he was right. "And that is?"

"Life," he said, "is shit."

Right the first time.

AFTER SUPPER, I got a call from Connie, who ran the catering business. She informed me that the gig at the Veterans' Hall on Saturday had been canceled but that we were now doing a private party at a house on Meridian Street. "One of those huge houses," she said, not holding the disdain from her voice. "Very rich bitch. I can't be there, so you'll be in charge. I'll e-mail you the details."

I thanked her and hung up after we switched from business to a few lines of small talk that neither of us had our hearts in. Connie was all right, but she wasn't a friend. Just a boss, a good one. But other than serving food to people, we really didn't have much in common. I checked my e-mail to make sure the promised missive had arrived, then put on an old shirt and went upstairs to the attic, which was my painting room. Fantine followed me up, but once we entered the room and she saw that I wasn't going to play ball with her, she curled up in the corner and was soon snoozing, dreaming of rabbits to be chased and Frisbees to be caught.

Earlier I had stretched a canvas and had it set up on an easel by the big picture window, but it was blank and I was sure it would stay that way for a week or two. I really didn't want to get started on another project with the art show coming up. Sometimes, when I really got into creating something, the real world just didn't exist, and I couldn't afford to be distracted. So I sat down at my work table and opened up one of my sketchbooks. By my elbow was a remote control for the stereo. There were six CDs in the machine, and I hit Random. "Falling Slowly," a song from the musical *Once*, began to play. A slow, melancholy song.

I began to draw, letting my mind go. I started off with some clouds but quickly turned a page. I started again, this time drawing a figure standing in a cloud of dust and debris. "Falling Slowly" finished, and "So Anyway" from *Next to Normal* came on. Christ, didn't I have any happy songs? Time disappeared and my hand took on a life of its own, as it sometimes does. After a while I blinked and came back to reality, only to realize that the figure I'd drawn was Donny Rodriquez, complete with T-shirt and tight, tight jeans.

Holy Mother of God, what was wrong with me? I nearly crossed out the drawing, but something stayed my hand. The sketch, incomplete though it was, wasn't bad. The figure was standing with his hands in his pockets and exuded a cocky attitude. You couldn't see much of his face; he was all hair and eyes. Just like the real Donny.

Suddenly I knew whose likeness had to be captured on my new canvas. I even had the title.

Youth.

CHAPTER THREE

I'M NOT really mad at Jason for drowning himself. Not anymore. Well, sometimes I am. When I see something that reminds me of him and I think of how he's cheated me out of the rest of his life. Like on Wednesday, when I saw someone wearing a Rasta hemp belt of green, yellow, and red. Jason nearly always wore a Rasta belt. I think it was the only one he owned. Once we were going to the funeral of a friend of ours, and while he was getting ready he started to put on his Rasta belt.

"You can't wear that to a funeral," I told him.

He seemed surprised by this. "Why not?"

"It's too colorful."

Jason grunted a little at this comment. "Times have moved on. You don't have to wear only black at a funeral nowadays. Allison wouldn't have objected. She always liked color."

"Yeah, but her parents are very conservative. They're going to expect a more…." I searched for the words. "Traditional turnout." It wasn't exactly what I wanted to say, but it was as close as I was going to get.

"Fuck Allison's parents," Jason said. But he borrowed a belt from me to wear that day.

I was at a Starbucks on the north side of town, and the barista was wearing a hemp belt that could have come right out of Jason's closet. I sat down with my cafe latte, sipping every now and then as I went through my e-mails on my phone. My mind, however, couldn't let go of the belt. What would our life be like now if Jason hadn't died?

Well, I'd be happy, for a start.

Maybe we'd have adopted a kid. I doubt it, because even though Jason always said it was something he'd like to do one day, he was the world's best procrastinator. Plus, he was pretty much a big kid himself. Even though he was in his thirties, he still dressed like a college kid. The hemp belt. Black canvas Converse shoes. And I rarely saw him in jeans that didn't have a rip in them somewhere. He also colored his hair and wore it long, thinking it made him look younger. I don't know if it really did, but we both liked his hair dark and long so I wasn't about to complain. Jason was, though, obsessed with looking younger.

Well, we all have our personal demons.

I loved him. Still did. I loved him despite his penchant for getting too drunk. He smoked a lot of pot too, something I could never get into. Always made me cough, and I mean really cough. Like a lung was coming up. Jason always laughed at that, which didn't help because it would make me laugh. Laugh cough laugh cough.

E-mails. Supposed to be reading e-mails. Not thinking about the past.

I brought up one e-mail on my phone and started to read through it, but even before I'd finished the first sentence I found myself looking over at the counter and watching the baristas at work. The one with the Rasta belt was tall and had close-cut blond hair. He was probably a college student, going to IUPUI or Butler. Working with him was a black woman, maybe a year or two older than him. They were laughing and joking in between customers. They seemed to be flirting with each other, he a little more seriously than she was. I wondered if anything would come of it.

And thinking of flirting brought up an image of Donny Rodriquez. I wasn't even sure what he had done could be considered flirting. It was more of an attack. Still, he stirred something in my brain if not my groin. Maybe I was ready.

Then I caught sight of the barista's belt again and I wasn't so sure. How could anyone live up to Jason? What if I started dating someone, went to bed with them, but all I could think about was Jason? Jason had been so hot in bed. I shivered a little, thinking of how he used to nibble on my neck, knowing that was one of my erogenous zones.

Damn him. Why did he have to go visit his parents that week? Why did he have to fall off that stupid pier?

The e-mail was from the gallery. They wanted to confirm some of the details. Important stuff, but I couldn't concentrate. I glanced around the room, checking out the guys to see if there was anyone I would consider dating. Hypothetically. Not the barista, for sure. Straight, and not with that belt. Plus he was too young.

There were two guys at a nearby table. One wasn't too bad. Had a nice smile. I hated his tie, though. Good God, who let that man go out in public wearing a red, white, and blue striped tie? Patriotism is one thing, but this was carrying it too far. I bet he listened to Rush Limbaugh and thought Sarah Palin was a misunderstood woman. I didn't even bother looking at his companion. Anyone who would sit at the same table as that tie was guilty by association.

Across the room a guy sat on his own, reading a book and sipping his coffee. An actual paperback book. One of James Patterson's, I saw by the cover. Could be worse. I tried to guess his age. He looked young, but there were lines around his eyes. Thirty? Thirty-five? He was a theoretical possibility, at least. He looked like he might enjoy Broadway musicals. He had light brown hair, not long and not combed—possible sign of an artistic type!—and glasses with black frames. He hadn't shaved in a day or two. I liked that. More concerned with enjoying his coffee and plowing through an old James Patterson than his personal appearance. Suddenly in my mind he was a combination of d'Artagnan, Sherlock Holmes, and Jean Valjean.

Bear with me here. D'Artagnan, a sense of adventure. Sherlock Holmes, analytical. Okay, that was probably due to the glasses. Jean Valjean, well, he had to have a sense of the tragic about him, didn't he? Otherwise why would I be attracted to him?

I set down my iPhone and got up. Slowly, I approached his table. He looked up from his book questioningly.

"Pardon me, I don't mean to interrupt your reading," I said, "but something told me I had to say something to you, that we were destined to meet. I'm Frank Hunter, by the way."

"And I," he replied, pushing his glasses back up his nose, "am intrigued."

Well, that's the way it would have gone if I wasn't too scared to get up out of my seat. Unfortunately, before I could move my butt, he closed his paperback and got up to leave.

How many possible relationships do we miss out on in life because we're too afraid to walk across a room and make an ass out of ourselves?

LATER I was at home, making another sketch, with Fantine curled up at my feet. This was a more detailed version of what was forming in my head. The figure (Donny?) was still the focus, but now there was an explosion happening right under his feet. Maybe he even caused the explosion, just by the nature of his personality. Certainly it didn't affect him. He was oblivious to the destruction around him. Pieces of wood and debris were flying everywhere, but he was calm, his hands in his pockets, all cheeky attitude and spark. Full of that feeling that when you're young, nothing bad can happen to you. You can survive anything.

Even your lover falling off a pier.

I wondered if I found Donny again, would I have the nerve to ask him to pose for the picture. Maybe that wouldn't be a good idea. Maybe I should find someone who looked a bit like him, a Donny substitute. Having Donny up in my painting room day after day might not be safe. For me, anyway.

I sighed as I made an adjustment to the hair falling over the figure's forehead. I decided the arms weren't right. The hands shouldn't be in his pockets; they should be outstretched. At my feet, Fantine let out a sigh of her own. From the stereo speakers came the voice of John Barrowman singing "I Am What I Am" from *La Cage aux Folles*. My stomach rumbled, and I realized I'd skipped lunch. Too late now. Just have to wait for dinner.

My phone rang. I was somewhat surprised to find that the caller was Marril Leblanc. While a good friend, Marril rarely called me. He usually got in touch with me through Zach. "Yo," I said as a greeting.

His tone was solemn. "Frank, honey, something has happened."

I quickly glanced at the clock. It wasn't quite five o'clock, but Marril was probably at the bar, along with Zach, getting ready for the night's show. They liked to arrive early so they could ensure their outfits were just right, their hair just right, and their gossip caught up with. Had something happened to Zach? "What's up?" I asked.

"It's Shawn. He didn't show up for work today."

I breathed a sigh of relief, although I felt a little guilty about it. At least Zach hadn't fallen off his heels and nearly killed himself or something like that. "Well, I don't—"

"One of his coworkers tracked me down. They're worried about him." I could hear panic rising in Marril's voice. "*I'm* worried about him. Gene and I had breakfast with him this morning, and he was very depressed. Seems he just got dumped."

"I didn't know Shawn was dating anyone."

"No, we didn't either. I don't think he wanted us to know, not just yet. You know how you have to wait to make sure it's the real thing before you introduce your guy to your friends, 'cause if the friends don't like him, baby, it's all over. Maybe it was like that. But I guess Shawn was really into his guy, and he was devastated when the guy broke up with him."

"Maybe he just took a day off to—"

"No, I called him. Finally got him to answer. Frank, he's taken some pills, I think. He was barely coherent. Can you go over and check on him? Gene will go with you. Zach and I would go, but…."

"Yeah, you've got your show. No worries, I can go with Gene. Don't worry. I'm sure it's nothing."

"I hope so," Marril said. "Shawn's pretty fragile, you know, when it comes right down to it."

Shawn? Was he talking about the same Shawn? Shawn Watson, he of the barbed tongue? Granted, Marril knew Shawn better than I did. In fact, Shawn had joined our little group because of his friendship with Marril. But Shawn? Fragile? To reassure Marril, I said, "Don't worry. You just put on a good show tonight. Gene and I will take care of this."

"I hope you're right and that he's okay." Marril clearly was next to frantic.

"We'll text you guys as soon as we know anything. Don't worry."

Telling Marril not to worry was a bit like telling a dog not to sniff butts, but it seemed like the thing to say at the time.

Chapter Four

GENE RAPPED on Shawn's apartment door. "Shawn, you in there?" he called.

After several texts and a short phone call we agreed that Gene would pick me up in his car and we'd drive out to Shawn's together, partly so that we'd arrive at the same time to tackle the problem and partly because I didn't know where Shawn lived. Turns out it was one of the old buildings downtown that had been converted into apartments. It was a four-story brownstone several blocks north of Monument Circle, and of course Shawn lived on the top floor and the elevator was out of order. I was puffing by the time we got to Shawn's door. Gene seemed unfazed.

There was no response to Gene's first entreaty, so he tried again. "Shawn, open up!"

We heard some rustling from within. Finally a muffled voice said, "Go away!"

Well, we knew now that he was alive. The voice did have a slurred quality to it, though, that bothered me. Maybe he was just drunk, but I had a vision in my head of Shawn sitting in his living room dressed only in his underwear, washing down a bottle of pills with a bottle of whiskey. I have a habit of imagining the worst.

"We're not going anywhere until we talk to you," Gene said, raising his voice to show he meant business.

"Fuck off!" Shawn shouted.

I could see the muscles in Gene's jaw tighten. "Shawn, I'll fucking break this door down if I have to. Let us in!"

Another picture in my mind, this time of little Gene—who I'm sure was much stronger than he looked, but still—dislocating his shoulder by ramming it into the door and my having to call paramedics for both him and Shawn. See what I mean about imagining the worst?

The two of us stood there listening. More shuffling sounds came from inside, and finally we heard the sound of the door being unlocked. Before Shawn could even open it, though, Gene pushed his way through. I followed.

The place stank, maybe because of the pool of vomit we could see in the hallway, just outside of what I assumed was the kitchen. Some of the puke had splashed up onto the wall. It was partially dried, so the upchucking hadn't just occurred. To make it worse, it looked like Shawn had trailed through the pile of sick as he approached the door.

Shawn himself was naked except for a sheet he had wrapped around himself that looked like he had pulled it off his bed. His normally pristine hair was a mess, and his eyes were heavy-lidded and had a dull sheen to them. As soon as we had shut the door behind us, Shawn turned his back to us, as if he couldn't bear to have us see him in this state.

"I told you to go away," he mumbled.

"We're worried about you," Gene said, following after Shawn, who was heading down the hall, once again treading in the spew. Gene and I carefully avoided it.

We found another pile, this one even more aged, in the living room. It looked like Shawn had been lying on the couch and had just turned his head to retch onto the carpet. Lovely. Shawn had the blinds drawn, so the apartment was darkened, not that I really wanted to have a good look at it. There might be hidden pools of vomit everywhere. Shawn pulled the sheet tighter across his shoulders and plopped down on the sofa.

Gene stood over him, noting a near-empty bottle of Jack Daniel's on the coffee table. A prescription bottle stood next to it. "Shawn, did you take any of these pills?" When there was no reply, Gene picked up the bottle to read the contents. He looked over at me. "Sleeping pills."

"Shit," I said, fishing out my cell phone. "I'll call 911."

"You're not fucking calling anyone!" With speed I wouldn't have thought possible in his state, Shawn flicked out a hand and knocked the phone out of my grasp. Of course it landed in the vomit. "I don't need anyone," he moaned. "Leave me alone!"

"Shawn," Gene said, his tone calm and reasonable, "no one is worth this. You're not going to let this guy think he got to you, are you? Come on, buddy." Gene sat down on the couch next to the now-shivering hulk under the sheet. "We need to make sure you're okay."

Gingerly, I plucked my phone off the floor. Luckily, it wasn't too upchuck-covered. I looked around for something to wipe it off but didn't see anything suitable. It seemed crass, but with no other option I leaned over and grabbed an end of Shawn's sheet and used that. He didn't seem to object.

Shawn began to cry, softly at first. In moments, though, the floodgates opened and he was doing the whole wailing and shoulders-shaking thing. Gene nodded at me. "Go ahead and call."

I tried to ignore that fact that my phone now smelled like a combination of whiskey, vomit, and—strangely—Arby's.

GENE AND I were sitting in a waiting room at Methodist Hospital. We talked little. There didn't seem to be much to say. Plus, there's that atmosphere of gloom that permeates any waiting room. There were a few people still cooling their heels, not having been summoned into one of the examining rooms yet, one guy cradling an obviously painful arm injury. Others were sipping colas or munching candy from the machine, hoping soon for word of an injured or sick loved one.

We sat quietly for about an hour, every now and then muttering some mundane sentence just to make sure our vocal cords still worked. Gene leafed through a *Sports Illustrated*. I scanned a month-old *Time* magazine without actually reading anything other than advertisements.

"Think he'll be okay?" I asked, not looking up from an ad for toothpaste.

Gene grunted. "With all the puke in his place? My guess is that anything dangerous has already left his system. Still, it pays to be careful."

That seemed to use up all the words we had in us. I flipped over a few more pages. I found an article about the terrorist group ISIS. I didn't want to read it and was contemplating getting a Snickers bar to satisfy my rumbling tummy when a young doctor came through the swinging doors and approached us.

He consulted his clipboard. "You guys brought in Shawn Watson." It was almost a question.

We stood, and Gene nodded. "How is he?"

The young doctor—who scarily resembled Zach Braff from *Scrubs*—gave us a reassuring smile. "Mr. Watson should be just fine. He's had a bit of a scare, but he's resting comfortably right now."

"Will you have to, you know, pump his stomach?" I asked. I wasn't sure what was involved in the procedure, but it sounded nasty.

Dr. Zach Braff, whose name tag said he was actually Dr. Evans, shook his head. "I don't think that's going to be necessary. Mr. Watson seems to be doing well, under the circumstances."

Plus he'd already regurgitated everything in his tummy, if the piles in his apartment were any indication.

I could tell that Dr. Evans was hesitant to say too much, considering we weren't family members. He kept looking at the chart he was carrying, as if it had all the answers and we should be asking it questions and not him. Finally the doctor lowered his voice and spoke in a confidential, I-probably-shouldn't-say-this tone. "Mr. Watson has consumed a large quantity of alcohol, though. In short, he's made himself very sick. We'll need to keep him overnight for observation, and—"

"Is that necessary?" Gene asked. "I mean, we can look after him."

Dr. Evans shook his head. "Sorry. It's standard procedure in cases like this."

Cases like this, meaning suicide attempts. Gene and I hadn't used the words since we'd bundled Shawn out of his apartment, but we knew exactly what we were dealing with. Somehow, though, it seemed like if we didn't actually use the phrase, we could believe it was all a horrible accident. Like people often down a few pills along with a hefty amount of Jack Daniel's around dinnertime. I inwardly thanked Dr. Evans for not stating the obvious.

The doc stayed with us for a few more minutes, assuring us that he thought Shawn wouldn't have any lasting effects from his dance with death—my phrase, not the doctor's. "We'll see how he is in the morning," he said in conclusion.

FEELING SOMEWHAT useless, like we were leaving a problem unsolved, Gene and I left the hospital. We didn't speak for most of the ride back to my place, then Gene finally asked, "What was the name of the guy that Shawn was dating?"

"No idea," I admitted.

"I didn't even know he was seeing someone."

"Neither did I."

There was another silence until we were nearly at my place. Then Gene said, "Must have been one hell of a guy, to warrant this."

"I just can't believe anyone would have such a devastating effect on Shawn. He always comes across as such a cocky guy. Like nothing can faze him."

"This did."

"Obviously." I shifted a little in the passenger seat, nibbling on my fingernail. "Makes you wonder, doesn't it?"

"About?"

"Dating. Is it worth it?"

"Well, I don't think you can go by this example."

I wasn't so sure. It seemed like an omen to me, telling me that the world was a dark and dangerous place without Jason to look out for me.

THAT NIGHT I slept fitfully.

AND THEN I was working on the Christmas tree, rearranging ornaments Jason had already placed on it.

"Something wrong with it?" he asked. He was dressed in sweatpants and an old T-shirt. One of his white socks had a hole in it and a toe poked through.

"Just… there's too much red in this area!" I put a Santa figurine on one of the boughs, near a blue lightbulb.

Jason was smiling at my nit-picking. "Should I get you a ruler? So you can make sure everything is equidistant from each other?"

In the background, Bing Crosby was hoping for a white Christmas. I plucked a gold ornament from one branch and found a better spot for it. "These things," I said, "have to be done right."

Laughing, Jason leaned over and picked up a small package from under the tree. It was wrapped in green and red paper, adorned with cartoon kids playing in the snow. He thrust the package toward me. "Merry Christmas," he said.

"It's not Christmas yet," I protested.

"This can't wait. Open it."

He seemed so eager I couldn't refuse. I tore off the paper and opened the box. It was empty. "I don't understand," I said. When I looked up, though, I was alone in the room. Jason wasn't there.

I awoke with a start and sat up in bed. It took me a few seconds to realize that I'd been dreaming. My sudden movement woke Fantine, who'd been nestled at my feet. I made a clicking sound with my tongue, and she crawled closer. I hugged her until the pain in my heart subsided a little.

"I'm not going to cry," I told Jason, even though he wasn't there. "Dammit, it's been over four years! I refuse to cry."

Fantine looked up at my face questioningly.

"I just wish," I said softly, "that I'd had the chance to say good-bye."

CHAPTER FIVE

THAT FRIDAY night we all met up at Dixon Street. Well, all of us save Shawn, who was out of the hospital but pretty uncommunicative. By phone, he'd assured Marril that he was "fine" but that he needed some time by himself. Truthfully, I was okay with putting off meeting up with Shawn again. What do you say to someone who, whether by stupidity or design, tried to off himself? The story was still sketchy, and no one knew if Shawn really wanted to shuffle off this mortal coil or if he got really drunk and then tried to take sleeping pills to actually sleep.

The story that Marril got when he went to pick Shawn up at the hospital was that it had been an accident, or at least a huge lack of judgment, and that there had only been a few pills in the bottle in the first place. This was somewhat corroborated by the doctors, who didn't find high levels of toxins in his blood.

Shawn may not have shown up at Dixon Street that night, but it seemed nearly everyone else in Indianapolis did. When I got there I had to shove my way through the crowd to get to the show bar. It took some effort to get the door there open, as the side room was so packed that people were leaning against the door and there was hardly anywhere else to stand. Finally I wedged myself in, much to the consternation of a tall guy who seemed to think he owned the space right inside the doorway.

Once inside it wasn't hard to find our table. Both Zach and Marril were in full drag, and Marril had a Dolly Parton wig perched on his head, so he rather stuck out even in that crowd. It wasn't quite ten o'clock yet, and the boys' first show was at eleven with another at one, so we wouldn't have a lot of time to socialize. Not that there was much chance of that anyway, what with the huge crowd and the music blaring.

I began to force my way over to my friends. Zach spotted me and waved a hand. I waved back, and that's when I noticed that there were four people seated at the table. Zach, Marril, Gene, and....

Donny Rodriquez. There was no mistaking that smile and that mop of hair. He saw me, and the grin grew wider. He even half rose from his seat by way of greeting.

"Hey, how's it going?"

You know how in movies and TV when someone in a bar starts talking and suddenly the music gets muted so that you can actually hear what the hell they're saying? Yeah, well, this wasn't like that. I sort of heard his words. The rest was just lip-reading. "Um… it's going," I replied. God knows if he heard me. I shot Zach a glare that Donny couldn't see, the meaning quite clear. *What the hell is he doing here?*

Marril even affected a country twang to go with his getup. "Look who joined us!"

Donny sat back down and indicated the chair next to him, which he'd been saving for me. The table the guys had snagged was a small one, not really meant for five, and I found myself sitting very close to the young Hispanic. He didn't seem to mind.

"Donny here has been searching for you," Zach said. He didn't bother to hide his wicked smirk. "He recognized us as the guys you left with the other night and asked if he could join us, and how could we refuse such a charming young man?"

Donny leaned his face toward me to make sure I could hear him. "Hey, I need to apologize. I came on a little strong Tuesday night, I think."

"You think? Ammonia doesn't come on that strong, kiddo."

Blushing, Donny said, "I'm older than I look."

On my other side was Marril, who I'm pretty sure said, "You'd have to be."

I tried to look at Donny without actually looking at him. Not easy to do. I wanted to drink in the details of his face. He was just what I needed for my painting, I decided. No one else would do. Sometime during the night I'd have to find a way to ask him if he'd be willing to pose for a session or two, and do it in such a way that he'd know it wasn't a come-on or an invitation for him to come on to me.

I think Zach caught my sidelong glances, because his eyes were twinkling. I knew him well enough to know that he was plotting something, probably some way to convince me to give Donny a try. I could hear him in my head. "What could a little fling hurt?"

Answer: It could be devastating.

Zach, dressed in black with a flowing wig, fishnets, and somewhat scary makeup, asked me what I wanted to drink. I said a rum and Coke, and Zach stopped Donny when he rose, intending to get it.

"Honey," Zach said, a gentle hand on the young man's arm, "let me go. I know the bartender, and he'll serve me quickly. You might get lost in the shuffle."

On his way to the bar, I noticed that Zach had no trouble getting through the crowd. In fact, they parted for him like he was Moses and they were the Red Sea. A tall guy like me, in good shape for an old codger if I say so myself, and I had to push and shove to get in the door. A stocky guy resembling Queen Latifah doing some horror movie, and he goes right through. Go figure.

"So, Frank," Donny said, "Zach tells me that you're an artist."

How much had the guys told him? I was a little worried. I wouldn't put it past Zach, and even Marril, to beef up my biography to make me more enticing. For all I knew, they had told Donny I was once a Navy Seal and had scaled Everest twice. "Sometimes," I admitted. "Sometimes I'm a cater waiter."

The words must not have all been clear over the music. Donny frowned. "You serve food to alligators?"

"Not a gator waiter, darling," Marril said, laughing. "A cater waiter. For a catering company."

It occurred to me, not for the first time, that clubs like Dixon Street aren't the best place to socialize. They're there for the drinking, the dancing, the drag shows, and hopefully hooking up with someone to spend the night with, depending on your needs. The music is much too loud to make conversations really viable. Since it was where Marril and Zach worked, though, we had no option.

Zach came back with my drink and another one for himself. As he sat he said something that I didn't catch, but it made Marril and Gene laugh. My suspicious nature made me think it was some crack about me and Donny. Donny showed no sign of hearing it either. He was too busy examining my face.

"So what kind of art do you do?"

"Painting, mostly," I told him.

Zach snorted. "And toilets."

Donny blinked, certain he hadn't heard right. I assured him he had. "Zach is referring to a piece I've done for an upcoming show." I quickly added, "At a very small gallery."

"The Stephenson Gallery is nothing to sneeze at," Marril said.

I let that pass. "Anyway, I do have a piece involving toilets. Nothing I'd expect to sell. It's more to get people talking. You know, come see the show where some madman had an art piece involving toilets."

"I'd like to see your stuff sometime," Donny said.

"I bet you would." This time I was sure of Marril's words.

I knew he was just teasing, trying to be funny, but I wished he'd stop with the cracks. If Donny overheard them, he might feel uncomfortable around my friends, and I still needed to reel him in to model for me. I gave Marril a glare that I hope he interpreted correctly. *Tone it down a little. Okay?*

Gene drained the rest of his glass. "Well, I'd love to stay and see the show, but I promised Kathy I'd be home early. We've got a big weekend planned."

Zach, his eyes twinkling, said to Marril, "We'd best get backstage, ourselves. Get ready for the show."

They were already ready, I knew, and I saw that they were trapping me into being on my own with Donny. I can't say I felt panicked, but I wasn't sure I had much to say to the young man. "You don't have to go yet," I said. "Surely!"

Marril winked. "Got to make sure everything is laid out for my costume change."

Zach pointed a finger at me. "And you've got to stay for the second show. I expect you to be here. I'm doing 'When You're Good To Mama' from *Chicago*. Just for you."

My mouth fell open. "I love that song."

"I know!" Zach looked at me and then Donny, as if to say I was an idiot but he loved me anyway. "Duh! Now, you two get to know each other. I expect to look out and see you nice and close to the stage!"

Not likely, what with the crowd Dixon Street hosted that night.

In moments the gang had fled, and Donny and I were alone at the table. I noticed that, even though we now had room, he didn't shift his chair, and his side was still plastered against me. I didn't want to move and appear rude, so I just sipped my drink and pretended that a young man who had the hots for me wasn't stuck to me like a barnacle.

"Your friends seem nice," Donny said.

"They are." I wanted to say something more, but no words came. I sipped some more rum and Coke.

After a very, very pregnant pause, Donny said, "So what are you working on now? Anything?"

This would be the perfect chance for me to ask him about modeling, but my vocal cords failed me. I managed to stumble a few words out. "A painting. Only a few sketches so far, but…." Wow, that rum and Coke was tasty. I had some more.

Silence. Well, except for the hundreds of patrons and the thundering music.

Donny leaned harder against me. "Do you want to dance?"

I didn't. There was no way. I'd feel conspicuous, a guy in his forties out on the dance floor with someone half his age. Impossible.

"Sure," I found myself saying.

I was really going to have to have a chat with my vocal cords when this night was over.

IT WASN'T the worst thing I've ever gone through in my life. Jason had once dragged me to a Nickelback concert. Still, I felt that as soon as we hit the dance floor out in the main room, every eye was on us, critically censuring me. The song playing was by some female singer, someone new and unknown to me, and the beat was bouncy and the words innocuous. Donny was a good dancer. The best I could hope for was to bounce around in time to the beat and hope that my flailing arms didn't smack someone in the face or blind somebody.

Donny said something that I couldn't hear. I cupped a hand over my ear to indicate that it didn't get through. He leaned in. "You… are… so… fucking… cute!"

I smiled and may have even blushed. "Right."

"No, really."

I got accidentally jabbed in the ribs by a guy I got too close to. It was just as crowded on the dance floor as in the rest of Dixon Street. I began to relax a little. Surely Donny and I wouldn't stand out with all these people around.

"I want you to model for me!" It just spilled out.

"What?" I think Donny heard me but just couldn't believe his ears.

"I want to do a portrait. Of you. You've got this energy…."

He slipped his arms around my waist and pulled me closer. "Sure," he said.

"I'm not being a creep or anything. I'm not talking nude here. In fact I'd want you in something like you wore the other night." Tonight

Donny had chosen black jeans that hugged his legs without actually strangling them and a shiny blue button-down shirt.

"Fine by me," he replied. There was a twinkle in his eyes.

"Just modeling. I want to make it clear. I don't want you to, well, get any ideas."

He grinned cheekily. "I scare you, don't I?"

"You terrify me," I said honestly.

The song ended and morphed into another. I could barely tell the difference, save that now the singer was male.

"I'm not into the whole daddy scene, if that's what's worrying you. Not looking for a sugar daddy." Donny scrunched up his face as if he was thinking hard. "In fact, I've never gone for someone…."

"Older? Ancient?"

"Older. There's just something about you. And you're absolutely nothing like my ex, which is a good thing. I don't know. I think I just… like you."

I don't know why, but I reached out and ruffled his hair. Probably not the thing to do when you're trying to convince someone that a romance is out of the question. "It's senility setting in. Don't worry. You'll get there someday."

He removed his arms from around me. "I just have one condition. For this modeling thing."

"What's that?"

He reached up and cupped my face in his hands. Donny then pulled my face toward him until our lips met.

Damn it all, if it didn't cause my heart to flutter. Just a little. Now my heart was in as much trouble as my vocal cords.

CHAPTER SIX

"YOU CAN have something else if you like. Just send it back."

We were at a restaurant. At first I thought it was a fast-food place, but there was a waiter and menus so I guess it wasn't. I had a burger and fries. Jason had spaghetti. The plate of spaghetti was huge. My hamburger was way undercooked.

"I can't get the waiter's attention," I told Jason.

Someone in the booth behind us—it was Zach!—spoke up. "Sometimes, honeychild, you have to snap your fingers to get what you want."

I snapped my fingers. No waiter appeared at my elbow. "So much for that," I grumbled.

Jason looked up from his plate, which was nearly empty now. "Waiter!" he called.

A young man in a tux came forward. It was Donny Rodriquez. "Yes, sir?"

"My friend's burger isn't cooked properly. Can you get him a new one?"

"Certainly, sir," Donny said, holding a pen poised over a pad of tickets. To me, he asked, "Is there anything else you need, sir? You can get just about anything you want, you know. It is, after all, Alice's Restaurant."

Suddenly I was aware that Arlo Guthrie, the folksinger, sat over in a corner, strumming a guitar. From the kitchen came a yell. It was Marril, who came out wearing a chef's uniform. "We're out of shrimp! Goddammit, we're out of shrimp!"

"Except shrimp," Donny added.

"I'll have some shrimp," Jason said. His spaghetti was gone.

"Certainly, sir." Donny wrote on his pad.

I WOKE up, rubbing my eyes. I knew there had been more to the dream, but it was already fading in my mind. It's a weird thing about dreams. They can be as mad as anything, but they make perfect sense while you're having them. You'd think I'd have *known* it was a dream. After all, Jason was dead, Marril wasn't a chef, and I doubt Arlo Guthrie sits around restaurants strumming his guitar. But while I was sleeping, that world seemed so real. Jason seemed so real.

I sat up in bed and took inventory. It was Saturday. I had a catering gig to do in the evening. I had to reply to an e-mail from the gallery. And—something that was escaping me. It would come. I got up and padded my way to the bathroom. Examining my face in the mirror, I wondered what the hell Donny saw in me. Okay, I wasn't bad-looking, and I didn't look my age. Does anyone think they do? But... he was so young. Why me? Did I remind him of someone he once knew? I mean, I wasn't hard on the eyes, for a guy of my age. Plus I had that little scar on my left cheek from a fight in my bad old days that made me look just a tad dangerous, although the years had faded it so that it was barely noticeable. Still....

Donny was hot. Short, true, but devastatingly handsome. That thick black hair and those dark eyes. He surely could have his choice of any guy he wanted. Why me?

I reflected on the previous night as I brushed my teeth. After the kiss, I'd quickly decided I'd had enough dancing, and we had squeezed our way back into the show bar to watch the first show. We couldn't get a table, so we had to stand at the back. Marril did "9 to 5," and Zach chose that old chestnut "I Will Survive." Both proved popular with the crowd. The other girls did pretty good as well. A lot of the crowd filtered out after the first show to go hit the dance floor, so Donny and I finally got a table. We got some drinks and sat and chatted a little.

I learned he was twenty-five—I made him show me his driver's license to prove it—and that he was an assistant manager at the Gap. He had been born in Cabo San Lucas but was now an American citizen. His parents were still in Cabo. He hadn't seen them in three years.

When I'd asked what brought him to the states, he'd replied, "A boyfriend. Thought he was the one I'd spend my life with. What can I say? I've got a thing for whities."

I'd snorted at that. It sounded weirdly racist, and yet it was honest at least.

I learned the boyfriend had helped Donny get his citizenship but had then found someone else. Donny had had a few other boyfriends but nothing serious.

"How about you?" he asked.

There was no way I could talk about Jason. Not in a bar with dance music blasting. Not with people laughing and joking around us. So I shrugged. "Oh, the usual, I guess." Lame, I know. Luckily the second show started shortly afterward, and talk had to be suspended.

Soon after that, I left. I could tell Donny wanted another kiss, but I ignored his pleading eyes. We did exchange phone numbers, though. Even that caused me some worry. Yes, if he was going to model for the painting, I needed to be able to get in touch with him. But I could also see Donny burning up the airwaves with texts and calls to me.

I really had to convince him that he and I were impossible. Too big an age difference.

Why, then, had my heart given a little leap when he'd kissed me?

Because I hadn't had a proper kiss since Jason. Simple as that.

Was I trying too hard to convince myself?

LUCKILY I was too busy most of the rest of the day to even think about Donny. One of the waiters called and said he couldn't make it, so I had to find a replacement. That took several calls and a little arranging, since I found someone who could work but didn't have transportation. I finally got him a ride with one of the cooks and made a final call to Connie to let her know disaster had been averted. Whenever I called Connie, her greeting never failed to make me smile. She called her business Connie's Catering Company, and she always overenunciated the Cs to the point where it was humorous to everyone except her.

The event went smoothly. The hosts, a middle-aged couple with, from what I could tell, loads of kids from ages six to sixteen, were giving a going-away party to one of the husband's coworkers. It must have been a really good coworker, as no expense had been spared. There was even a string quartet set up in the living room. Lots of bubbly was consumed, and everyone seemed happy. On our end, there were no mishaps. No one spilled champagne on the hostess or tripped over the family dog.

The whole affair finished by ten o'clock, and we'd packed everything up and departed. The husband was effusive in his praise, and he promised he was going to call Connie to let her know how wonderful he'd thought the service was.

I was pleased, but I also was done much earlier than I'd planned. I wasn't tired. In fact, I was still pumped. I couldn't face going home and watching TV. Nor could I face another night at Dixon Street, with the throngs of sticky, sweaty boys. What to do? I wasn't hungry. Zach was working. So was Marril. Gene had weekend plans with his family, and I had never really hung out with Shawn on his own, only with the group.

For one insane second, I contemplated calling Donny to see what he was up to. Maybe we could get a start on some sketches for the painting.

What was I thinking? What message would that be sending? Hi, I know it's late on a Saturday night and that I've told you I wasn't interested romantically in you, but do you want to come over and spend some time in my attic?

I decided to get a drink to unwind. I'd go to the Varsity Lounge, an old bar on Pennsylvania Avenue. I hadn't been there in ages. I think Jason and I had gone there once because we'd heard the food was pretty good. Food I didn't need, but I wouldn't say no to a little gin.

The place wasn't nearly the size of Dixon Street, but it had a warm and cozy atmosphere. The bar was fairly crowded, but I found a vacant stool close to the door. Once I settled at the bar and had a look around, I decided maybe the place could use a little sprucing up. Somewhere I think I'd read that the Varsity was one of the oldest gay bars in the Midwest, and it was starting to look it. Along one wall were some booths—all filled with people, most drinking from pitchers of beer. They seemed happy. There were several other tables scattered about, also taken. Still more pitchers of beer. There was a chalkboard on an easel close to the entrance, announcing a special on pitchers of beer, which explained a lot.

Music played on a jukebox, but it wasn't so thunderingly loud that you couldn't hear the person next to you. Not that the person next to me was saying anything. He looked to be around my age and was drinking a draft beer with his head down. His whole persona screamed "Don't talk to me!" I smiled at the bartender.

"Gin and tonic," I said.

While he was getting it, the grumpy draft beer guy got up, slipped on his jacket, which he'd been sitting on, and left. Almost immediately a guy approached and asked if the seat was taken. I shook my head, and he sat down. He also looked to be around my age, with nice hazel eyes and dark hair. When the bartender placed my drink before me and took my money, the guy smiled at me.

"Let me guess. You're a gin and tonic guy."

"Sometimes," I said. "Depends on my mood."

He had a nice smile. Dressed in a tight-fitting yellow shirt and snug jeans, the guy obviously worked out. Indicating one of the booths, he said, "I was over there with some friends, but they were getting a little tedious, so I thought I'd find someone else to chat with."

They didn't look tedious. In fact they kept stealing glances our way, whispering, and then laughing. I guessed they were keeping close tabs on whether or not their friend would be successful in picking me up.

If I had anything to say about it, he would be.

He offered his hand. "I'm Kelly."

"Frank Hunter."

"Come here often? What's your sign? If I said you had a beautiful body, would you hold it against me?" He chuckled. "I just thought I'd get all the lines out of the way right off the bat."

"No, Taurus, and probably."

Kelly grinned. "Honesty. I like that. So what do you do, Frank Hunter? For a living?"

"I work for a catering company, and I'm an artist."

"An artist, huh?"

Was there just a hint of condescension in his tone? I'd heard it often enough from people who didn't believe that "artist" was a legitimate way to make a living. Unless you were a Picasso, you were a dabbler who just called yourself an artist.

"Would I know any of your works?"

"If you're into toilets," I replied cryptically. Maybe I'd explain later, but only if he turned out to be nice.

He frowned briefly but let it pass. I asked him what he did. "Manager of an Athlete's Foot store," he told me. "And I do some MMA on the side. You know, mixed martial arts fighting."

"I know what MMA is," I said. "I've seen it on ESPN as I was switching channels looking for *Ellen*." I said it lightly, but inwardly I thought I'd scored over his implied crack about being an artist. I'd liked Kelly's looks when he first sat down, but one minute into the conversation and I wasn't sure about him at all. I classified him as not only the jock type but the snooty jock type. The type that looks down their noses at you if you're not a Colts fan or if you don't hit the gym religiously or if you eat the wrong foods. I started to glance down the bar to see if there were any better prospects.

"Hey," Kelly said, "I've had enough of this place. What say we head back to my place and have a little fun?"

I'd rather have my tongue pulled out by ravenous porcupines. "Sure," I said.

What the hell was wrong with the connection between my brain and my vocal cords?

CHAPTER SEVEN

WE WENT in his car so that, in his words, he "wouldn't have to worry about losing me in traffic" if I followed him. I knew seconds into the ride that this was a mistake. His driving was erratic and aggressive in equal measures, and I could only thank my stars that traffic wasn't very heavy. He hadn't *seemed* drunk when we'd been at the bar, but as soon as he got to the parking lot he began to sway a little. Halfway down Penn Avenue I began praying that a cop would stop us.

No, I told myself, *you need this. This is good. If you want to get back into a relationship after Jason, you need to hit the wading pool before you jump off the diving board into the deep end.*

And Kelly was absolutely a wading pool.

He headed up Meridian, zipping through a yellow light when he had ample time to stop. I held on to the armrest for dear life as I stole a glance at the speedometer. He was doing fifty in a thirty-five zone. In a way it was flattering. I could take it that he was anxious to get me into the sack. That or he was trying to kill us both.

I took a deep breath. *You can do this, Frank*, my inner voice said. *It's been four years and seven months. That's more than enough time to mourn. Jason would want you to do this.*

But would Jason have picked Kelly as my return to the dating world?

"You seem deep in thought," Kelly said.

"Yeah, just… thinking." Why did I agree to go in one car? I'd have to ask Kelly to return me to the Varsity when we were through, as I couldn't spend the night. Fantine would be expecting me home. True, she had a doggie door so she could let herself out if needed, but I hated to leave her for too long.

"You artistic types. Living in your heads." Kelly shook his own head in wonder.

"Yeah, we're deep."

"So what do you do for fun?"

I didn't get the feeling that he really needed to hear the answer. He was just filling in time until we got to his place and we could get jiggy. I was just a body to him. Another notch on his bedpost. What the hell was I doing? Did I really need to get laid that badly? "Oh, you know. The usual. Listen to music. Watch TV."

"Yeah? Any sports?"

I shrugged. "I do a little running. That's about it."

"You seem in good shape." He reached over and grasped my bicep. "Pretty strong."

"I eat my Wheaties." His grope of my muscle had hurt just a little, but I refused to wince. Macho man, that's me.

"Me, I'm into wrestling. You like to wrestle?"

"It hasn't come up a lot lately."

"I thought," he said, trying to sound offhand like it really didn't matter to him one way or another, "that we might wrestle for top. It could be fun."

Ah, he was one of those. Jason and I had occasionally done some bed tussling, and we'd enjoyed it, but I wasn't in the mood. Besides, from the looks of Kelly's arms, I wouldn't stand a chance. "I don't know," I said. "I thought we might, you know, talk a little. Get to know each other."

"We're talking now, aren't we?" He swerved the car back into our lane, barely avoiding crashing into a truck. "Shit, didn't see him."

"The headlights bearing down on us might have been a warning sign," I muttered.

The near collision resulted in him slowing down slightly, although he still held the wheel like the car was driving itself and he was just there to oversee the operation.

We eventually got to his place, a little house in a neighborhood I wasn't very familiar with. It seemed like we'd turned down dozens of streets and even through an alley to get there. The driveway was cracked and in dire need of repair. From what I could see, the lawn was patchy, and I'm pretty sure I saw a car fender just lying on the ground. We entered through a side door, and Kelly flicked on a light. We were in a kitchen.

I say kitchen because it had a stove and a refrigerator. It might have been a pigsty, though, because there was junk everywhere. Nearly every surface was covered with dirty plates, old pizza boxes, takeaway Chinese containers, and whatnot. At a guess I'd say the stove hadn't been used in months, because cartons and dirty pans were stacked fairly high on it. The sink overflowed with dishes.

"Pardon the mess," he said, tossing the keys onto a cluttered table. *Good luck finding those again.*

"Did the maid kill herself?" I joked.

"Just busy, you know. Who's got time to clean?"

I witnessed a cockroach scurrying across the counter. Even he was having trouble navigating around the trash. "Yeah. Hygiene is highly overrated anyway."

If Kelly took offense to my jibe, he didn't show it. Instead he turned and wrapped his arms around me and smothered me with a kiss. It wasn't a horrible kiss; I'll give him that. Maybe this wouldn't be so bad. I kissed back, and we did a little tongue wrestling. I was glad to find that my groin stirred as he pressed himself against me. *Good*, I thought, *the little bugger still knows how to get excited by something other than my own hand.*

Kelly began to unbutton my shirt without breaking off the kiss.

Out of nowhere, a vision of Donny came into my head. Maybe it was because he was a much nicer kisser than Kelly. With Donny, it was a mutual act of affection, not an act of war.

Stop thinking about Donny! I told myself. *This guy's hot, and he's much closer to your own age.*

True, his house should be condemned and he couldn't drive worth shit, but that had little to do with how a man was between the sheets.

Just have fun, my inner voice said. *Don't overthink this.*

I smiled and started to pull off his shirt. My God, it was tight. It was like peeling a grape. I got it up to his waist, and with a sly smile, he broke off the kiss to assist. Even he had trouble getting it up over his head, and for a moment it got stuck around his right shoulder, making him look a bit like a spastic tortoise having trouble coming out of his shell. Between the two of us we finally extricated him. His hair, which must have had a lot of product in it, was now sticking every which way.

"That shouldn't have been so difficult," he said with a laugh.

"It was a tight fit," I agreed.

The kiss resumed. Kelly forced me backward until I hit the wall with some force, but our lips never parted. I could see he was serious about his wrestling challenge. He was anxious to exert his dominance. Fine with me, as long as he didn't try any of his MMA moves on me. I was looking to get laid, not to be put into a rear-naked choke hold. He undid the rest of my buttons, and soon my shirt was on the floor.

We were moaning and groping and exploring. I found myself getting a little worried. It had been over four years, and my erection was already screaming for release. What if, as they say, I popped the champagne cork before the party even started? I tried to think of sad things. Not easy to do when a hot guy has you pinned against a wall. Unwanted puppies. Orphans. Bambi's mother getting shot. None of it was working. Kelly's muscular chest was overruling them all.

Kelly began to fumble with my belt buckle. "Let's hit the bedroom," he whispered.

"Okay."

Even the short hallway was cluttered, mostly with discarded shoes and clothes. We got to the bedroom without mishap, though, and immediately resumed the kissing. I didn't get much of a chance to take in the room, as he didn't turn on a light, but I got the vague impression that it was small and just as messy as the rest of the house. We'd probably have to shove some dirty laundry off the bed and maybe a beer can or two so that we'd have room to fuck. God knows how clean his sheets were.

Shower as soon as you get home, I told myself.

His hands roamed over my torso and ended up at my nipples. He pinched both of them, hard. *Two can play that game*, I thought. *Just wait until I get my hands on your balls.*

"Ready to wrestle?" he said, grinding his pelvis against mine.

What the hell. "Yeah," I said.

He stepped away so that he could slip out of his jeans. I yanked mine off as well. As I bent over to pull off my left sock, he cupped a hand over the erection still nestled in his boxers and said, "You want this, you got to fight for it."

I was poised on one leg. "Mind if I take the other sock off first?"

Kelly laughed and stepped toward me in mock menace. Just then the sound of a car pulling into the driveway could be heard, and headlights shone briefly through the broken slats of the window blinds.

"Shit!" Kelly said. "My boyfriend's home!"

I froze, my hand hooked around the top of my sock. "Huh? Boyfriend?" No mention had been made of a boyfriend, but then I should have realized. No one person could make such a mess of the house.

Kelly scooped up my jeans and my shoes and thrust them into my arms. "You've got to get out of here. Fuck! He'll kill us if he finds us like this!"

I was a little surprised at how worried Kelly seemed. "Who the hell is your boyfriend? Hulk Hogan?"

"He'll kill us," Kelly repeated as he pushed me out of the bedroom. I started to protest, as one sock was still somewhere on the bedroom floor and my shirt was somewhere in the kitchen. Still, Kelly's anxiety was contagious, and I quickly followed him out to the living room, pictures of us both being beaten to a pulp by some six-foot-seven behemoth running through my mind.

Kelly paced the floor, listening to the sounds outside. "He's coming in through the side! You'll have to go out the front!"

With my clothes bundled in my arms and wearing nothing but my boxers, one sock, and a worried look, I was bustled out the front door. Before he closed it behind me, Kelly muttered, "Sorry about this."

I stood there for a moment, wondering what to do. Should I dress there on his front porch, or would the boyfriend look out the window and see a half-naked stranger standing there?

A light rain had begun to fall, adding to my woes. I looked around desperately. There was enough light from neighboring houses and the streetlights to see fairly well. Of course that also meant that nosy boyfriend would have no trouble spotting me. There was a fairly substantive tree and some bushes across the lawn. I quickly ran for their cover, cursing at the soaking my sock was getting as I trod across the wet grass.

Once I was leaning against the far side of the tree, out of sight of the house, I began to calm down a little. At least I wasn't going to get pummeled. Just wet. The rain started falling a little harder. I leaned over, pulled off the remaining sock, and tossed it away. It was grimy and missing a partner anyway. I set my shoes on the ground and began to get back into my jeans when I looked up and realized I wasn't alone.

On the sidewalk, carrying an umbrella and walking a small dog, was a middle-aged woman who had stopped to watch the spectacle. Under the shadow of the umbrella it was hard to read her expression, but she didn't seem alarmed. More amused.

I waved at her, one leg in my jeans. "Hi."

She inclined her head. "Troubles?"

"Oh no. I'm fine, thank you."

She didn't move on. The dog stared at me. I swear he was censuring me with his eyes.

"Friend of Kelly and Michael's?" the woman asked.

I got the other leg in and pulled up my jeans. "Sort of."

She sniffed. "Well, you better get a shirt on. You'll catch your death of cold."

The woman walked on. The dog paused before following, unwilling to stop glaring at me. I could almost read its thoughts. *Slut!*

Once my shoes were on, I took stock. I was shirtless, standing in the rain in an unknown neighborhood with my car miles away. A moment of panic set in until I reached into my pocket and felt the cell phone still nestled there.

I pulled it out and checked the time. I tried Zach's number, not expecting an answer. He'd be preparing for the second show, if it hadn't already started. Surprisingly, he answered, although he didn't sound happy about being interrupted.

"This better be important," he said. "I'm having a shoe emergency. I broke a heel."

"It is," I assured him. "I'm stuck."

"Stuck? Stuck where?"

Briefly, I filled him in on the situation. I wasn't shocked when I heard him cackle.

"Oh, this is rich. Where exactly are you?"

I moved away from the tree until I could read the street sign at the corner. "I'm on Ogden Street. At Twentieth and Ogden."

"I'm just about to go on. Stay put. I'll work something out."

"I wasn't planning on going anywhere," I said, blinking rain out of my eyes.

After hanging up I sauntered down to the street corner to await my ride, whenever it would turn up. I glanced back once at the house I'd just unceremoniously left, inside of which was still my shirt and one sock.

I stood under the light and tried not to look conspicuous, like I always hung out on street corners on a Saturday night in the rain without a shirt on. "Good one," I muttered aloud. "No, really. Great job, Frank. You just turned forty-five and you've reverted back to your college days. If this wasn't an omen, I don't know what is. Dating is just not for me."

Up in the sky there was a brief flash of lightning, followed by a rumble of thunder. God apparently agreed with my assessment of the situation.

CHAPTER EIGHT

I EXPECTED a long wait, especially if Zach took the time to change back to male attire before coming out to get me. Humming a tune from *Gypsy*, I tried to ignore the fact that the storm was picking up, with ever-increasing flashes in the sky and the low growl of distant thunder. The rain felt cold against my skin, and I sent a personal mental curse back at Kelly and Michael's house, where, no doubt, they were warm and cozy and probably making love. After wrestling for top, of course.

A few cars went by. I couldn't see the drivers, but I imagined them staring in wonder at the weirdo standing in the rain with no shirt on.

After what seemed hours but was probably no more than twenty minutes, a small dark Mustang came down Twentieth Street and slowed as it approached the corner. I hoped this was my ride, although why Zach wasn't driving his LeSabre was anyone's guess. I hugged my arms around myself to try to generate some warmth as the car stopped and the driver rolled down his window.

"Need a lift?"

It was Donny Rodriquez. It had been a really long time since I'd been so happy to see a friendly, smiling face. "Yes, please," I said. I bolted around to the passenger side and flung myself in before he had time to worry about me getting his seat wet.

Once I had made it safely inside, Donny pulled away from the curb and explained, "Zach sent me. He said you were in trouble."

"Truer words were never spoken." I brushed as much of the rainwater off my chest and arms as I could and then threw my head back and closed my eyes. The car felt so nice and warm. "Thanks for coming to my rescue."

"No problem." Donny was smiling, but with a trace of worry in his face. At least that's what it looked like to me. "Anything I can do to help. Zach said he and Marril—am I getting his name right?—couldn't leave until after the show, and that Gene was busy and some guy named Shawn couldn't be reached. So he asked if I'd mind picking you up."

"It was really nice of you."

"No problem." Donny drove slowly, as the rain was now coming down so hard the wipers were having a hard time keeping up. "I think it's getting worse. So what happened to your shirt?"

Somehow I had had no problem explaining my Kelly exploit to Zach, but I was a little embarrassed telling this young man I hardly knew that I'd made a foolish mistake. "It's a long story," I said. "Suffice it to say, I shouldn't be allowed out on my own in public."

"Let me guess. You went to some guy's house and had to leave in a hurry when his boyfriend came home."

I had to laugh. "You hit the nail on the head. Are you psychic or something?"

Donny grinned. "It wasn't hard to guess. Hey, don't feel bad. We've all gone home with someone we shouldn't have at one time or another."

"Yeah, but it's one thing when you're in your twenties and you do something like this. Quite another when you're my age."

"You make it sound like you've got one foot in the grave. You're not *that* old."

I rubbed my hands in front of one of the heater vents. "Old enough to know I should have taken my own car."

"Could have been worse. He could have been a basher, or one of those Jeffrey Dahmer type dudes. You might have ended up as stew."

His accent was pronounced when he said the word stew, and it sounded funny to my ears. I decided I liked Donny's soft Hispanic inflection.

"Thanks," I said. I noticed he was heading back downtown, even though he hadn't asked where my car was. "My car's at the Varsity, by the way."

"The Varsity? Man, no one goes there anymore!"

"It was pretty packed tonight," I said. "Full of bashers and Jeffrey Dahmer types."

"You should have come out with me."

Donny tried to keep his tone casual, but I could tell he was a little disappointed that I opted for a one-night stand with some guy at the Varsity.

"We could have hit Dixon Street. Danced again and watched your friends in the show." He navigated a turn. We were now on Meridian, in familiar territory. "And I wouldn't have thrown you out without your shirt!"

I blushed, thankful the car was too dark for him to see it. "Actually, I don't really go out that often. This week's been different, with my birthday and all. Generally I'm not much of a bar guy."

Donny took his eyes off the road long enough to wink at me. "Tell you the truth, hombre, neither am I. Tuesday night I was just out with a bunch of friends from work. Been back every night since, hoping to find you."

"Yeah, about that." I turned to examine his profile while he drove, hoping my scrutiny would elicit a truthful response. "Why me?"

"Seriously?" he asked.

"Yeah, seriously. Why me?"

"Because you're good-looking." Donny thought some more and added, "At first that was really the only thing. There weren't a lot of people out that night, and I was feeling frisky, if you know what I mean. I saw you, and I thought you looked like that movie star guy."

"Robert Redford."

"Naw, that one guy. What's his name? He's on *NCIS: New Orleans*." Donny shrugged. "I don't even know who Robert Redford is."

"Philistine." I had to think, as I had never seen the show but had caught some of the promos. Wasn't Scott Bakula in that? That was a new one. I'd never been compared to him before. Could be worse.

"Anyway, that was the attraction at first. Now I just want to get to know you."

"Why, though?"

I could tell he chose his words with care. "You're interesting. And there's just something about you. It's like a puzzle, and I only have a few of the pieces. I just like solving a mystery, I guess."

"I'm no mystery," I told him. "I'm an open book."

"You might think you are, but you're not. There's like this hidden sorrow. It's there even when you smile. Like you feel guilty about smiling or being happy."

I shivered. I really needed a shirt, or maybe just not to talk about myself. "So what about you? What makes Donny Rodriquez tick?"

"Me?" His grin stretched across his face. "Oh, I'm simple. I just want to fall in love and live happily ever after."

I turned to watch the raindrops hit the passenger side window. "Doesn't happen," I said.

"You never know, hombre, until you try."

"That's the second time you've called me hombre. Are you trying to accentuate your Mexican heritage?"

That got me another wink. "I was hoping you'd like a little south-of-the-border flavor. No?"

I turned my head to look his way again and found myself smiling. "No, I think I like it."

"Hombre it is, then." He pulled into the parking lot of the Varsity, which was behind the bar. There were considerably fewer cars parked there now. I pointed mine out, and Donny slid the Mustang in next to it. "Here we are," he said. There seemed to be a trace of disappointment in his voice.

I didn't really feel like being on my own either. Maybe I still felt like a fool after being ejected from Kelly's, or maybe I just liked Donny's smile. Tentatively, I asked, "Do you work tomorrow?"

"Tomorrow? No, free all day. Why?"

My hands fidgeted a little. Why was I acting like a lovelorn teenager? "Well, if you don't have to get up early, I was going to ask if you'd be interested in coming with me to my place. To get started on some sketches." I added the last part quickly so that he wouldn't get the wrong idea.

"Sure," he said.

HE FOLLOWED me in his car. By the time we reached my house, the storm had relented and now just a steady drizzle fell. Once we were inside, Fantine had to check out the newcomer, and she quickly decided she liked him. Loved him, if her licks to his nose were anything to go by. When they finally finished the bonding session, I donned an old, comfortable shirt and gave Donny a brief tour of the place. He seemed suitably impressed, especially with my collection of framed Broadway show posters, which adorned the hall walls.

Donny pointed to one. "I saw this movie. With Leonardo DiCaprio."

The poster was for *Catch Me If You Can*. "This is for the musical version. I actually got to see this one in New York. At the Neil Simon Theatre, with Norbert Leo Butz. Have you ever seen a Broadway musical?"

He nodded. "Kevin took me to Chicago to see *Wicked*. It was really great!"

"Kevin was your boyfriend?"

Donny's smile faltered for just a second. "Yeah. The one that cheated on me."

"The fool," I said. I hadn't meant to say it out loud. To cover up, I immediately pointed out another poster. "This is my favorite. *Phantom of the Opera.* It's kitsch, I know, but I love it."

Before long we were up in the attic. We brought some sodas up with us, and Donny sipped his while he looked around. He looked through some of my artwork, some of which was up on the walls, some piled against the wall. He was quiet as he examined them, and I found his silence disturbing. He rarely seemed at a loss for words, and I worried that his reticence was because he found them lacking. Finally he pulled aside a canvas I'd done years ago, a landscape featuring an old barn. "I really like this," he said.

"Yeah?"

"I like them all, but this one is… it's hard to say. Makes me feel a little sad."

I agreed with him. "The colors, the lines. It's supposed to evoke that emotion."

He picked up the painting and moved so he could see it in better light. "It's great. Not a happy painting, though. Everything is old and rusted." He leaned the canvas back against the pile he'd extracted it from. "You paint a lot of old things. A lot of these are sad, like a life gone by and not enough people care."

"That's a pretty good observation."

"And now you want to paint me?" The cheeky grin was back.

I shrugged. "Supposedly, all artists go through periods. Maybe this is the start of a new period for me."

Donny walked across to the other wall, where I had some reviews and magazine articles about my work hanging in frames. I had objected when Jason originally put them up, feeling that it was too narcissistic. Every now and then, though, I was glad he'd done so. After getting a horrible review somewhere, it was nice to be reminded that some people liked my work.

Donny scanned a couple and then looked at me. "You didn't tell me you were famous!"

"Hardly famous."

"So someone might buy this painting of me? Pay a lot of money for it?"

"God, I hope so," I said, laughing.

He set his soda can down on the table and went to the center of the room, throwing his arms out to his sides theatrically. "Well, then, let's get moving! We can't deny some guy the chance to plunk down a wad of dough to get a painting with my mug on it!"

I laughed and picked up my sketchbook.

CHAPTER NINE

I WAS on a game show, which seemed to be a cross between *The Dating Game* and *American Gladiators*. Johnny Depp was the host, but it was Johnny Depp as Ed Wood, from the Tim Burton film. He was even in black and white.

"Okay, and who's our contestant today?" Johnny asked, white teeth gleaming.

An unseen announcer's voice came across the stage. "Johnny, we've got artist Frank Hunter!"

I sat on a stool on one part of a soundstage. A partition separated me from three other men, sitting on stools on the other side. Although I couldn't see them, I knew who they were, which sort of gave away the game. Lined up on the other side were Jason, Donny, and Zach. Zach, in full drag, smoking a cigarette and looking very bored.

Preliminaries were skipped, so I didn't get to hear Bachelor Number One, Bachelor Number Two, and Bachelor Number Three tell me something about themselves. We went right to the questions.

"Bachelor Number One, if you were an animal, what animal would you be and why?"

Jason frowned. "That is the stupidest fucking question I've ever heard. Really, you've had all this time to come up with something to ask us, and that's the best you could come up with?"

"Oh," Johnny Depp/Ed Wood said, his plastic smile never faltering, "snap! I'd say that calls for a challenge. Don't you agree, audience?"

Applause. It sounded fake to me, but I couldn't see past the lights to know if there were any people actually out in the audience or not. A platform came down from the ceiling. Two hunky stagehands came out with ladders, and they set them up on either side of the platform. Two more hunky stagehands, dressed like the others in only Speedos and combat boots, put a big, fluffy cushion beneath it.

Jason and I were handed huge weapons that resembled enormous Q-tips, and then we were summoned by Johnny Depp to approach the platform.

The ladders the stagehands had brought out hadn't seemed that big, but now, standing next to one and looking up at the numerous rungs, I began to worry. "That looks awfully high."

"That's why there's a big, fluffy cushion. To break your fall," Johnny Depp told me.

Jason and I climbed our ladders and got onto the platform. We then faced each other, brandishing our Q-tips.

"The object is to try to knock your opponent off the platform," Johnny said.

"Why?" I asked.

"Because that's how the game is played," Johnny said.

You can't argue with logic like that. Jason and I approached each other. The big, fluffy cushion looked very, very far away. Jason swung his Q-tip and hit my arm.

"Ouch!" I said, rubbing the sore area. Annoyed, I attacked with my Q-tip, bashing Jason right across the side of his head. Off the platform he went.

As he fell, he yelled out, "I love you, Frank!" I went to the edge of the platform and looked down. Jason was safe and sound in the center of the cushion, laughing.

"And now," Johnny Depp said, "it's time for Bachelor Number Three to climb up!"

Zach stayed on his stool, legs crossed. His cigarette was longer now. "I ain't getting up on that fucking thing," he said with finality.

That threw Johnny Depp for a loop, but he only missed a beat or two. "Well, then I guess it's up to Bachelor Number Two!"

Donny shrugged and walked across the stage. There was more canned applause as he gracefully mounted the rungs of the ladder and hopped onto the platform. A hunky stagehand emerged from behind a curtain and tossed a big Q-tip up, which Donny easily caught.

"The object is—" Johnny Depp began to say.

"Yeah, we get it, numbnuts." Donny twirled his Q-tip like a baton and looked across the vast expanse of the platform at me, all twinkling eyes and cheeky smile. "You ready for this?"

"Oh, yeah!"

I wasn't. Donny was a flurry, smacking me with one end of the Q-tip and then the other. The blows didn't hurt, but there were so many of them that all I could see was a big ball of white cotton swooping before my eyes before whacking me across the face. I didn't know where I was on the platform, how close I was to the edge. Too close, it soon became apparent. I started to fall. I dropped my Q-tip and flailed my arms. Just at the last moment, a hand reached out and grabbed my collar, saving me from plummeting down to the cushion. It was Shawn Watson.

"You don't want to do that," he said sadly.

I WOKE up. I must have been making some noises in my sleep, because Fantine, who was curled up next to me, was looking at me with a puzzled expression on her canine face.

"Sorry, baby," I said. "Daddy was having a weird dream."

I'm not one of those people who think dreams always mean something. Generally they're just rehashing things that went on during that day, filtered through the off-kilter lens of a dream camera. I do seem to get a lot of celebrities in my dreams, such as Johnny Depp or Arlo Guthrie. I once dreamed that Zach and I had to smuggle Kermit the Frog out of a Las Vegas hotel, which we did by dressing him up like Elvis Presley. I defy anyone to attach meaning to that dream!

It was nearly noon when I got out of bed, but then I'd been up the whole night sketching Donny. He finally left as the sun was coming up. He seemed just as fresh as always, as if going without sleep was no trouble for him. The sight that met me in the mirror when I'd brushed my teeth before hitting the hay had circles around the eyes and looked like hell. On arising, the circles had vanished, but the feeling that another three or four hours of shut-eye were needed took their place. However, I'd promised Zach that we'd have lunch and do some shopping, so I dressed and took Fantine out to the backyard to play some fetch to make up for the fact that I didn't have time for our usual run. Once she was suitably worn out, I went upstairs to the attic. I wanted to examine my sketches before Zach arrived.

They were good, just what I had envisioned. Full of life and energy. I was still going over them when Zach's voice startled me. "Shit, it looks like a bomb went off in here!"

I set my sketchbook down. "I've been working."

"Yeah. Let myself in. You obviously can't hear your doorbell up here."

"It doesn't work."

"That would explain it."

Zach walked over to where I'd posed Donny. A white tarp was thrown across the floor, and broken boxes and crates were scattered across it. I'd even brought up one of my old, battered garbage cans from the garage and arranged it so that it looked like it had been smashed by an explosion, trash spilling out of it like a cornucopia.

"I see we've gone from toilets to garbage now," Zach observed.

"Sort of." I showed him my most detailed sketch. It almost looked like Donny was a superhero, having landed on Earth amid chaos to save the day.

Zach's eyes widened. "Holy shit. That's good."

I closed the book. "He's a good subject."

"I think he might be good for the artist as well."

"Don't be silly. He's just a kid."

"Who you trying to convince, me or yourself? All I know is that you're smiling."

"I smile all the time."

"Not like this, you don't. That boy makes you happy."

Was it true? Yeah, I was attracted to Donny. Who wouldn't be? But you can look at the *Mona Lisa* without thinking you've got to take it home with you. I shook my head. "It wouldn't work out. Can we go to lunch now?"

Zach wasn't letting it go that easily. "How do you know it wouldn't work out? Because of the age difference?" He blew a raspberry. "Please. Should we call up Catherine Zeta-Jones and Michael, see what they think about it? And don't tell me that it's too soon after Jason or I'll have to put you over my knee."

The sketchbook lay on the table. I opened it and flipped over a few pages. There was Donny, energy just flowing off the paper. Damn, it was good. If I could transfer my vision onto the canvas, it might end up being the best thing I'd done in years. "It's not just the age thing. It's just...." I couldn't meet Zach's eyes. "I'm a little frightened. I don't know if I can go through all that again. Letting someone in."

Zach put a hand on my shoulder. "Of course you're scared. Who wouldn't be? It's hard to let someone into your heart. So much can go wrong. But if it goes right...." Zach smiled gently. "It's heaven. And I think you deserve a little heaven."

I nodded. "Says the guy who hasn't had a steady relationship for over a year."

He shrugged dismissively. "I never said I was an expert. Write Dear Abby, see what the fuck she says. I just know that when Donny looks at you, there's a gleam in his eyes. Right now it's just lust, but with a little tender care, that lust can turn to love."

"Let's not talk about this right now," I said, closing the book. "I'm starving."

"Oh, yeah. About that. Shawn's coming with us. We've got to pick him up on the way."

"Shawn?" I was a little surprised and, I must admit, apprehensive. I hadn't seen Shawn since his trip to the hospital, and I wasn't sure what to say to him.

"Honeychild, it took quite a lot of cajoling to get him to agree to come out. We got to show him that he's got friends who love him." Zach made a sour face. "Even if he can be a bitch every now and then."

As we walked downstairs, I made an observation. "You call me honeychild. Donny calls me hombre. You guys know you're promoting a stereotype, right?"

"I can see where the Hispanic guy saying hombre can be viewed as stereotypical, but what's wrong with me calling you honeychild?"

"Well, a black man—"

"See, that's where your logic fails." Zach gestured flamboyantly with his hands. "I ain't black. I'm just working my George Hamilton tan to the max!"

AS MOST of our shopping was going to be downtown anyway, we decided to have lunch at the Old Spaghetti Factory. Shawn hadn't said much up until the point where our waiter took our orders, and I wondered if he was going to sit there giving one-word responses to our questions indefinitely. His glum mood was contagious, and I worried that the shopping trip was going to be a bust.

I preferred a sourpuss, snarky Shawn to a maudlin one.

We were seated in one of the back corners, and there was little chance of our conversation being overheard. Not that I cared, but Shawn might. When I couldn't take the silence any longer, I toyed with my napkin and said, "So are we going to talk about the elephant in the room or not?"

"Who you calling an elephant?" Zach quipped.

Shawn, looking a little haggard and sporting at least two days' worth of stubble, smiled gently. "No, it's okay. Actually, I want to talk about it."

"Thank God," Zach put down his water glass hard enough to make it thunk against the wooden table. "I don't know if I could stand not knowing for much longer. Who was this guy you were seeing, Shawn?"

At first I thought he wasn't going to answer, but eventually he sighed. "His name was Pete. He's a loan officer at a bank."

"I hate him already," Zach said. "Go on."

"We met at a cocktail party. Seemed to hit it off." Shawn cupped his hands around his water glass, but he didn't drink. "I was going to say something to you guys, but you know how it is. There's the curse of telling your friends about a relationship that's still gelling. Tell 'em too soon and the whole thing falls apart."

Zach and I nodded, although I wasn't sure I believed in "the curse." But then I was hardly a dating guru.

"I thought things were going really well," Shawn went on. He blinked back some tears that were threatening to fall. "We actually started dating around Christmas."

"You kept a secret that long?" Zach was astounded.

"I can't keep anything from you guys for more than a day or two," I admitted.

Shawn ignored us. "I should have known there was something wrong. I mean, the sex was great, but he was so often unavailable. And I only had his cell phone number. He said he didn't have a landline at home, only used cell."

I had rid myself of the mostly unused landline years ago, as it was an expense I truly didn't need.

"And he broke dates often. I just told myself he was busy. But… dammit! The sex was fantastic! Epic! It was like he couldn't get enough of me!"

"He had a boyfriend, didn't he?" Zach asked.

Shawn shook his head. "A wife! And kids!"

I'm sure my eyes bugged out. "Holy shit!"

"Yeah." Shawn looked miserable as he remembered what must have been a horrible scene. "I ran into him and his family one night. I was taking my mother out for her birthday. We went to the Rathskeller. And there, right at the next table, was Pete and his brood! He acted like he didn't see me at first, but I was too mad to let that go. So I stood up and walked over to him. And that's when it got worse."

The waiter brought us our salads and breadsticks right then, but we quickly sent him on his way. Once he was out of earshot, Zach asked, "How could it get worse?"

"I was seeing red. Well, you know me. I must have been glaring at wifey since we had been seated, and I was only vaguely aware of his kids. I noted that there were two, a son and a daughter, but they were just there, you know? I didn't really get a good look at them. I could tell they were older. The girl was maybe fifteen, the boy college age. They didn't matter. But when I approached the table, the boy gasped, and I looked his way. Remember about six months ago, that young guy I had sex with in the parking lot at Dixon Street? The backseat of the Impala?"

"No! It wasn't!" Zach's mouth was hanging open.

Shawn nodded. "I didn't know. I mean, the kid was just a thing, you know? Just a quick fuck in the backseat of a car. But it turned out he was Pete's son!" Shawn rubbed a hand wearily across his brow. "I didn't know what to do. Pete looked at his son. The son looked at me with terror in his eyes. I'm sure he was afraid I was going to out him to Mommy and Daddy."

"What did you do?" I asked.

"What could I do? I was stunned. I just went back to my own table and told Ma we had to eat somewhere else. We got up and left. Right after I dropped off Ma I went to a liquor store. I didn't open the bottle then, though. I think I was too flabbergasted to do anything. It didn't really sink in until after I had breakfast with Gene and Marril that day. When I left them, I went home and opened that bottle, and I think I drank off and on until you guys came to rescue me."

"Holy shit," I repeated.

"The pills were nothing. I think there was only three or four in the bottle. Honestly, I wasn't trying to off myself. I just hadn't had any sleep, and my befuddled brain was saying that a couple of pills wouldn't hurt."

"Now what does our patron saint, Judy Garland, say about mixing pills and liquor?" Zach said in his best schoolmarm voice.

I leaned against his shoulder and said in a stage whisper, "I think she'd have said it was a good idea."

Zach nodded. "Probably not the best example I could have come up with."

Shawn began to eat his salad, but I wasn't done with true confessions time. "But Shawn, it's not like you to get so depressed over something like that."

He munched a little, then said, "I don't know. I was thinking that maybe this time was it. That Pete was the one I'd settle down with. Maybe I'm having a midlife crisis. But when I realized that I'd slept with not only Pete, but with Pete Junior... something snapped in me."

"Would have made for some interesting family reunions, though," Zach said.

I elbowed him in the side.

Shawn pretended not to hear. "I didn't cheat on Pete with his son. Son came first, and he was just a one-night fumble in the parking lot. I never even knew his name."

"I take it Pete gave you no clue that he was married?" I asked.

"Always look for wedding ring marks. That's my motto." Zach pulled his salad closer to him and began to dig in. With a mouth full of lettuce, he said, "You might need to give Frank pointers on bedding down with the younger generation. He's got a younger boyfriend now."

Shawn looked up with more than a little surprise in his eyes. "Really?"

"He's not my boyfriend," I insisted.

Zach shoveled more salad into his mouth. "Not yet, maybe. Give the kid a few days. He'll have you eating out of his hands."

CHAPTER TEN

"WHAT ARE we listening to?"

"Julie Andrews as Guenevere in the original production of *Camelot*," I replied.

We were taking a little break. Donny sat on the floor with Fantine's head in his lap amongst the clutter that would feature in the painting. He rubbed her ears, and she was eating it up. I sat at the table, sipping some coffee.

"Do you ever listen to anything other than Broadway scores?"

"Sure. I listen to Patti Lupone, Liza Minnelli, Barbra. People like that." I didn't mention that they also were known for musicals.

"I've never heard of any of them."

I shook my head. "Ah, youth."

Donny nodded toward the stereo. "She's got a nice voice."

"You bet your sweet ass she does." I set the coffee mug down and rubbed my eyes. We'd been at it for quite a while, and I wasn't sure how much more I had in me. Maybe I could continue after another cup of java. Maybe it would be better to call it quits for the night. For me, a clear and fully functioning brain was required for artwork. "So what kind of music do you listen to?"

I was expecting some group or performer I'd never heard of, or perhaps Lady Gaga, so I was a little shocked when Donny grinned and said, "Sinatra!"

"You're kidding?"

"And Tony Bennett. Saw him in Chicago last year. He's still got it, even though he's really old now. I think he's over eighty."

I suppose I shouldn't have been too surprised over Donny's choice of music. He seemed to like things from other eras. I'd learned he read everything he could about the *Titanic*, he was a huge *Downton Abbey* junkie, and he was fond of exploring old buildings with his friends, who were part of a ghost-hunting group calling themselves Team IGAP, Indiana Ghost and Paranormal.

"Wait, you like Sinatra, but you've never heard of Barbra Streisand?"

"Maybe I have. What has she sung?"

I sang a few lines from "People" and "The Way We Were." Donny stopped me when I got to the chorus of "Evergreen."

"Oh yeah. I've heard her. She's not bad."

"I may have to smack you."

Donny moved Fantine's head so he could stand up. Getting to his feet, he did some stretching to ease his muscles. "Ready to get back to it?"

Truth be told, I didn't even really need to have Donny there to pose for me any longer. I'd begun painting onto the canvas several days ago, and I had enough sketches—not to mention the details firmly in my mind—that his presence wasn't strictly necessary. But I liked having him there. His energy seemed to seep right into the brushwork. I was pleased with what I'd done so far.

I shook my head. "I think I'm done for the day."

"Ah, hombre! It's early yet! Look, even Fantine is ready for more action!" She was snoozing at his feet. "I don't have to work until tomorrow afternoon, and I set aside this whole evening just to pose for you." He emphasized the words "whole evening," playing at my guilt. "I got nothing else to do."

"Call up some of your friends. Go see a movie or something."

Donny bounded over to the table and leaned across the surface, getting his face close to mine. "Good idea. What do you want to see?"

"I didn't mean…."

"I know what you meant, but I've been good." He batted his long eyelashes at me. "I've come here, several nights now, whenever I've had time off from work, and posed for you. I haven't pushed for us to go out on a date—"

"You've mentioned it seven times."

"Yeah, but I haven't pushed. Just suggested. Now I'm pushing."

"Glad to see there's a difference."

"Come on! What can it do, kill you?" Donny pulled at my arm. "You know you want to. You're just afraid that you'll find out you like me a lot! Come on! One little date. What's it going to hurt?"

I'd been asking myself the same question for over a week now, and I still didn't have a good answer. I liked Donny. I really did. I loved the way his face lit up whenever he saw me. I loved his unkempt hair and his soulful eyes. I loved the way he walked, like gravity had one bitch of a time keeping him on the ground. Even when he wasn't around, I found my thoughts drifting to him. I tried to tell myself that it was just the painting and the joy of creating something, but that wasn't true.

After four years, seven months, and several weeks, someone had—metaphorically speaking—smacked me upside the head and brought me out of my self-imposed exile.

But was I ready to start dating someone considerably younger than myself? I envisioned us going out to restaurants and having waiters take my order and then look at Donny and ask what my son would like to have. And once the freshness of the sex wore off—if we ever got to that point!—what the hell would we talk about? So far the only things we had in common were *Downton Abbey* and the fact that we'd both seen *Wicked*.

I knew, though, that I couldn't keep putting him off. And deep down, I really didn't want to. I was just scared, and there was the nagging feeling that, even after all these years, somehow I was being unfaithful to Jason's memory.

"Okay," I said.

Donny's eyes widened. "Really?"

"I have conditions, though."

Donny did his best to try to look serious. "What are they?"

"First, I want to make sure you want to date me, Frank Hunter. You're not looking for a sugar daddy or trying to resolve some weird issues with your own father."

He made a what-the-fuck face. "You know me better than that, don't you? For one, when I first met you I didn't know if you had any money or not, and if I was looking for a sugar daddy, there are loads of guys out there with more cash than you. And you don't resemble my father in any way, shape, or form. For one, you're white. He's not. I'm actually kind of offended that you even needed to bring the point up."

I nodded. "I'm sorry. I hadn't really meant for that to be the first point, hadn't even meant to bring it up. And I knew the answer, but I guess I had to hear it from your own lips. Can I start again?"

"Sure."

"Okay. First, we take things very slowly."

"So what you're saying is no nookie for dessert." The cheeky grin returned.

I laughed, even though I didn't want to. "I'm trying to be serious here."

"Sorry." Donny composed his face once more. "Serious now. What's your second point?"

"If we're going to go out, date, whatever you want to call it, you've got to know what you're getting yourself into."

I could tell that puzzled him. "You sick or something?"

"No. Well, not in the sense you mean. Come with me."

I took his hand and led him downstairs. We went down the hallway, passing my bedroom and the bathroom and the room I used as my den, until we came to the closed door at the end of the hall. Fantine had followed us and now stood at our heels as we stood facing the room. Slowly, I turned the knob.

I must have opened the door with a sense of reverence, because Donny muttered, "*Ay dios mio*! What's in there? The crown jewels?"

"Sort of," I said, leading the way into the room. Donny followed me, but Fantine hovered in the doorway, as if awaiting special permission to enter. Donny's mouth opened as if he was going to say something, but no words came out. He scanned the room, and I'm not sure if he believed what he saw.

The room was the largest bedroom in the house. I rarely went in there anymore, but the room remained nicely furnished. There was a neatly made queen-size bed, several dressers, two big closets, and even a fireplace. I knew, however, that the furnishings weren't what had caught Donny's attention. He was gawking at the artwork scattered about the room.

Two walls held several framed sketches while another was devoted to photographs, all of Jason. Dominating them, though, was the portrait over the fireplace, which was also of Jason. In the painting, in my opinion one of my best, he stood by the fireplace in the living room, one hand resting on the mantelpiece. It was supposed to be a throwback to portraits done in the Victorian era, and he was even dressed in a frock coat, ruffled shirt, and cravat. When I'd painted it, Jason had laughed and asked if I was going to have him dress as Gainsborough's *Blue Boy* for the next painting I did of him. Sadly, there had been no other portraits.

Donny moved closer to one wall to take in some of the sketches. One with Jason holding a cat we'd once owned, another of Jason standing in the bathroom, foam covering his face, preparing to shave. Donny examined the one with Jason in bed, nude, reading a book. The next was of Jason out in the garden, digging in the ground.

Donny went on to the photographs. Jason sitting in the driver's seat of our old Cadillac, a crooked smile on his face. Jason with some of his friends at a party, his eyes revealing that he was more than a little plastered. Jason, dripping with sweat having just come back from a run, wearing only basketball shorts and his battered tennis shoes.

"They're all your ex," Donny said softly.

"Yeah."

Jason had been mentioned in passing several times during Donny's posing sessions, but we'd never talked about him in any detail.

"He was very handsome." Donny's eyes strayed to the portrait over the fireplace. "You've made a shrine to him. This room. It's a shrine."

"I guess it is." I sat on the edge of the bed, feeling a little out of breath. The only other person who'd been allowed to see the room was Zach, and he'd not approved of it, thinking it excessive. I couldn't argue the point with him, as I wasn't sure he was wrong. "I thought you should see it," I said to Donny.

"This was your bedroom. Yours and his."

It hadn't been posed as a question, but I answered. "Yes."

"And you don't use it anymore."

I couldn't look at him. I clicked my tongue, signaling to Fantine. She padded into the room and hopped up next to me. I stroked her neck. "No. After Jason died, I moved into the spare bedroom. I couldn't sleep in here. I moved all my work featuring him in here shortly after. The painting you're looking at, that was always here. The rest came... after."

Donny turned to look at me. I couldn't read his face. Sadness? Disappointment?

"I didn't know he died. No one ever said. I figured you two just broke up."

"He drowned," I said. "Dumb accident. I wasn't there." I concentrated on Fantine, rubbing her ears. "Open the closet. The one closest to you."

Donny moved like a somnambulist. Opening the door, he saw the clothes inside, all Jason's. Shirts hanging on hangers; shoes, especially those old canvas basketball shoes Jason loved, on the floor as if waiting for him to put them on. "You kept his clothes."

I nodded. "I couldn't throw them away. I just couldn't." Fantine looked at me, her big eyes wondering why I'd ceased stroking her. "I wanted you to see this. To see what you'd be up against. You'd be like the unnamed heroine of *Rebecca*, although I don't think Fantine here fits too well into the role of Mrs. Danvers."

I thought it unlikely that Donny got the reference, but he didn't question me. His eyes went from the portrait to the sketches and then to the photos. He seemed stunned, and I couldn't blame him. It killed me that I'd wiped the smile off his face, but he had to know.

"Did you still want to go out?" I asked quietly.

He blinked. His eyes looked watery. After a deep sigh and another gaze about the room, he said, "I don't know. I think I need to go home. Be on my own for a little while. Is that okay?"

Nodding again, I said, "Sure." My heart felt like lead. I gave Fantine another stroke about the ears. I wanted to say that I was sorry. I wanted to say that I wished I hadn't had to show Donny the room. I wanted to say that I understood. No words came to me, though, and I knew that if they did I couldn't hold back the tears. "I'll show you out."

I wasn't sure I could, though. Wasn't sure my legs would hold me up. Luckily Donny shook his head.

"I can see myself out," he said. He paused in the doorway. "I'll call you, okay?"

"Sure," I said. I was sure he wouldn't.

Donny seemed reluctant to leave. "You going to be okay?" God, his eyes seemed so huge.

"Yeah, I'm sure."

It was a lie, of course. Donny knew it, but there wasn't anything he could do or say to change things. He forced a smile and said, "See ya."

And then he was gone. I listened to him as he walked down the hall. I heard his footsteps on the stairs and as they made their way to the front door. I heard the door open and shut.

"And that's that," I said to Fantine. She blinked at me. "Probably for the best."

Something in my heart told me that was another lie.

CHAPTER ELEVEN

I WAS drinking a soda. I couldn't trust myself with alcohol. I might never stop.

The yearning to have something to numb my senses, though, nearly overpowered me. I closed my eyes as I drank, trying to imagine it was gin. It didn't work.

"I can't believe you showed him that room," Zach said. His tone was conciliatory, but I felt a rebuke just the same.

"What choice did I have? He had to know."

We were at one of Zach's favorite restaurants, a Thai place near Fountain Square. The food was fine, but we really came for the desserts. Today, though, I toyed with my food, uninterested in eating. Zach sipped a white zinfandel and gobbled his panang curry. He then helped himself to some of my cashew chicken, seeing that I wasn't going to finish it.

I marveled at his ability to chow down on copious amounts of food when we were supposed to meet Gene after dinner and go bowling. Me, I'd feel bloated, like I should be rolling down the alley to knock over some pins instead of the ball. Zach must have read my mind, because he said, his mouth still half-full of chicken, "I digest quickly."

"Shall we have the waiter inform the kitchen to have another chicken handy, just in case?"

Frowning, Zach sipped his wine and said, "You're trying to change the subject. You've got an obsession, and it's not healthy."

"I know that."

"You're not doing anything about it. It's been nearly five years."

"Four years, seven months, and—"

"Yeah, twenty-some days. Yada, yada, yada. Whatever. Way too long to grieve. Sorry, but that's the truth. When you showed me that room, I couldn't believe my eyes. Didn't say anything at the time, which was my mistake." Zach set his fork down and looked me straight in the eye. "Maybe you should seek professional help."

"I should have done that years ago. Now I'd feel stupid. Hey, shrink, I can't get over my dead boyfriend. How long has he been gone? Oh, four years, seven months—"

Zach reached across the table and took my hand in both of his. "You've got to let go."

"Don't you think I know that? I dream about him, almost every night."

"Honeychild, Jason wouldn't want to see you like this. You've got to know that."

"I do! And I thought…."

"What?"

It was hard to admit. If I voiced it aloud, that would make it all the more real, more true. "I thought Donny had broken through, opened up some part of my brain that I thought was dead. Rattled my cage." I pulled my hand away. "I think about him all the time. That silly grin of his. Those dark eyes. The way his hair dips over one eye."

"That's good!" Zach exclaimed.

"He's twenty years younger than me. When I was entering college, he wasn't even born yet."

Zach snorted. "So who the fuck cares? If the heart desires…."

I tossed my napkin down on my now-empty plate, not that I'd helped much with the task. "It doesn't matter now. I'm pretty sure I scared him away."

With a slight shake of his head, Zach said, "I think it would take a hell of a lot more than the Jason room to scare off that boy. He sees you as a challenge."

"He's young and hot. He can have anyone he wants. Donny's not going to waste time going after an old fossil like me, not now."

"You might be surprised. And you're hardly an old fossil."

The waiter interrupted just then, asking if we were ready for dessert. Normally that would make my mouth water in anticipation, but I knew it would taste like cardboard to me, the mood I was in. I waved a dismissive hand the waiter's way. Zach looked shocked but didn't argue. He asked for the bill.

When we were alone again, Zach once again grasped my hand. "You gotta listen to your old Auntie Schubert. This Donny, he's good for you. It's gonna take someone with a lot of spunk and chutzpah to get you back into the land of the living, and he's got it in spades."

"I'm in the land of the living."

"Most of you is. Your heart isn't."

I closed my eyes. "It doesn't matter. I won't see Donny again."

"I don't think he's the type to give up that easily," Zach insisted.

"He walked out when he saw the room."

"Of course he did! That would overwhelm anyone! You mark my words, though, that boy will be back. He's got the hots for you."

I'm sure I looked as glum as I felt. "Yeah. He just wants a conquest. Someone to fuck. Once that's over, he's on to the next. That's why I showed him the room. I had to know he was serious, that he was in for the long haul. Maybe it would have worked out, maybe it wouldn't. Now we'll never know."

The waiter came with the bill. Zach insisted on taking it. As he handed the waiter his credit card, Zach said mysteriously, "We will. Auntie Schubert says so." Zach watched the waiter walk away. "Nice butt."

"I hadn't noticed."

"Yes, you did."

"Yeah, I did. Look, why don't you drop me off? I don't really feel like bowling. You and Gene can—"

"No. No way. You're going. I'm not going to let you sit at home watching old reruns of *Golden Girls* and feeling sorry for yourself."

"Neither of us can bowl."

"Never stopped us before. Come on. You're going." Zach waved his hands over the table, as if there was an invisible crystal ball in the center. "Auntie Schubert sees a strike in your future."

As we got up to leave, I asked, "What's with all the Auntie Schubert crap all of a sudden?"

Zach shrugged. "I'm an aging drag queen. I've been thinking of adding a new persona to the act. You know, instead of coming out and lip-synching to some old Whitney Houston song, I'll sit on a stool as Auntie Schubert and give advice to the lovelorn. Help out all those young gaylings with my years and years of experience."

"But you've never had a relationship that's lasted more than half a year!"

"Yes," Zach agreed. "But I've had so many! So who better to advise the youth of today! Come on! It's time to knock some pins over—or try to—and have some fun!"

Fun seemed out of the question, but I went along anyway.

I SHOULD have known something was up. You'd think that after as many years of friendship as I'd shared with Zach I'd pick up on his signals, those poker tells that should warn me when something is up. During dinner, when we'd been discussing Donny, there had been a gleam in Zach's eye, like he knew something I didn't. I had just put it down to his new all-knowing persona of Auntie Schubert, but when we arrived at the bowling alley I was in for a surprise. Once Zach and I had gotten our rental shoes and selected our bowling balls—Gene had his own ball and shoes, actually being a fairly decent bowler—we picked a lane and sat down on the bench to change our footwear. It took me several minutes to realize there was a familiar face playing in the lane next to ours. As I tied my shoes, I noticed a short guy with tight, tight jeans and a cute little bubble butt making his approach to the lane. It wasn't until he'd sent the ball barreling down the alley and turned around that I realized it was Donny Rodriquez. He beamed when he saw me.

"I was wondering when you'd get here!" he exclaimed, running over to me. I stood, wondering if I was seeing things, but when he threw his arms around me and planted a big wet kiss on my mouth I knew it was indeed Donny. Still nonplussed, I glanced at Zach, who shrugged.

"I may have told him we'd be here tonight."

I was happy as hell he had, but still confused. "How did—"

"I got his number the night you got stranded in the rain. Just in case he couldn't find you. So I called him. Sue me."

"Hey, Donny," someone yelled, "you got a strike. It's your go again."

Donny still had his arms around me. He looked over, and for the first time I realized he was there with several friends and that they were waiting for him. He released me with the familiar cheeky grin on his face. "Be right back."

I noticed he was wearing the white T-shirt with the black pattern on it, the one I was using in the painting. That couldn't be coincidence. I realized I was grinning like an idiot, watching as he retrieved his bowling ball and prepared for another approach. Forcing the smile from my face, I turned to see both Gene and Zach smirking at me.

"What?" I asked.

Gene shook his head and said, "Nothing," with the air of someone who really means "Something."

Zach tried to look innocent. "I didn't notice nothing," he said. He watched as Donny sent the ball down the alley and got another strike. "Just if that boy fucks as good as he bowls...."

Donny didn't even see all the pins scatter. As soon as he released the ball, he turned to beam at me again. "I didn't know you bowled."

"He doesn't." Gene snickered under his breath.

"I'm not very good," I said, which was an understatement. Generally my goal was to break one hundred, which happened more and more frequently but still wasn't guaranteed.

"And I just come for the pizza," Zach added.

While Gene worked at setting up the electric scoreboard and Zach and I made sure our shoelaces were tight, I surreptitiously took in Donny's companions. There were three of them, two young women and a tall, skinny young man. The women were laughing and nudging each other at every opportunity, making me wonder if they were a couple. One was slim and had dark hair and Asian eyes. The other was shorter and a little on the muscular side, with pale white skin and frizzy red hair. The young man was blond and good-looking in that boy-next-door way. When he bowled he looked awkward, but the ball seemed to respond to his unorthodox approach, although he wasn't nearly as good as Donny. They were probably all around Donny's age.

Once we were settled, Donny came over and took me by the elbow. "Come and meet my friends," he said.

Immediately feeling self-conscious—what would these youngsters think about me, did they know about Donny's interest in me, etc.—I obediently allowed Donny to drag me across the platform.

The young ladies, Joy and Cora respectively, met my introduction with a knowing gleam in their eyes. Joy especially took pains to look me over, as if to check that I was worthy of their friend. I hoped by her smile that I passed muster.

"So Donny tells us you're this famous artist."

I smiled. "Had you heard of me before?" When she shook her head, I said, "I can't be all that famous, then."

"Don't mind her," Cora said. "The only artist she knows is the guy that painted the Campbell's soup can."

"Warhol," I supplied.

"That's the guy."

The guy's name was Phil, and he put a little extra pressure into his handshake and didn't look nearly as pleased to meet me as Cora and Joy had.

"Nice to meet you," he said, not sounding like it was.

The bowling recommenced, and it was a good thing that our alleys were next to each other, because Donny flitted from one to the other like an exuberant puppy. He gave a few pointers to Gene about how to get a hook on his ball, and after Zach got two gutter balls in a row, Donny took him through his approach step by step. Even after this, Zach got another "puddle"—Donny's term for gutter balls—so Donny walked Zach through it all over again in slow motion, moving Zach's arms and body to show him the correct position. On Zach's next turn, he knocked over six pins, and everyone in the place looked over when he let out a scream of victory.

Joy got makeup tips from Zach, Phil and Gene discussed brands of beer, and every chance he got, Donny sat next to me, leaning against my side.

I sat down after getting my first spare of the night, and Donny quickly plopped down next to me. As he leaned his head against my shoulder, I said, "I'm surprised to see you here tonight."

"You mean because of my disappearing act the other night?"

"Yeah."

Donny looked up at me. "I was a little thrown at first, I admit. But I thought about it, and I'm glad you showed me."

"I thought it would scare you away." Hell, it scared me.

He shook his head without lifting it from my shoulder. "We all have our demons," he said darkly.

"Even you?" I asked.

Donny was saved from answering, as it was his turn to bowl. I took the opportunity to head to the snack bar for a soda. While I stood at the counter, waiting to be served, Phil came up beside me. He seemed to be watching the young man behind the counter as he worked, but I could tell there was something on his mind. Not once the whole evening had he looked me in the eye.

"So how long have you been friends with Donny?" I asked as a conversation starter.

"Known him for ages," Phil replied. There was ice in his manner. "I helped him study for his citizenship test."

I tried to remember if Donny had ever mentioned Phil by name. He often talked about people in his ghost-hunting group, but was Phil one of them? It seemed to me that Phil had once spent an evening at some abandoned hospital with Donny and several others, waiting in the dark for some sign from the beyond. Donny often told so many stories in an evening, while he posed and I worked, that it was hard to keep them all straight. Still, I needed to get Phil on my side, if he was Donny's friend. "Are you in that group that Donny's in?" I couldn't recall their name. "Indiana Ghost and…. Guys."

"Paranormal." Phil obviously didn't find my mangling of the name humorous. "Yeah, I started the group."

The kid behind the counter finally got bored with flirting with several girls who were giggling off to the side and came to get my order. I asked for a soda and looked at Phil. He nodded, so I made it two. The kid, who had been smiling broadly at the girls, couldn't be bothered to so much as grunt at us. Customer service was not, apparently, a high priority for him. He got our drinks and took my money without a word.

"Thank you," I said as he moved on down the counter so he could be closer to the girls. Suddenly the smile returned. I guess Phil and I just weren't his type.

"It's like this," Phil said, as if the words had been bottled up inside him. "Donny is a special guy."

"You don't have to tell me. I've noticed."

Phil eyed me carefully, I guess to judge my sincerity. "His last boyfriend treated him like shit."

I frowned. "He's never said anything. I knew they broke up, but—"

"He was very controlling. A real verbal abuse situation. Was always telling Donny he was stupid."

I'd found Donny to be anything but stupid. In fact he seemed to be quite an achiever. "I didn't know that" was all I could think of to say.

"Since then, Donny's not been able to connect with guys his own age. I think he sees too much of Kevin in them."

I'd not heard much about this Kevin, but nothing had been said of him that endeared him to me. Quite the opposite. "So you think that Donny's interest in me—"

"You're so not Kevin."

I wondered if Phil was ever going to let me finish a sentence. I did appreciate, though, his looking out for his friend. I faced him, hoping my face conveyed the strength of my conviction. "Look, Phil, Donny and I aren't—"

"Oh, I know. He's told me nothing has happened between you two. But I know how persuasive that little fucker can be."

I waited to make sure Phil had said his piece. When he seemed to be waiting for my reply, I spoke, hoping I'd be allowed to get it all out. "If Donny and I ever get to the point where we change our relationship status on Facebook, you can be sure that I'll treat him with love and respect. Always." I took a sip of my drink. Too much ice. I glared at the little bastard behind the counter. Not that he noticed.

We returned to the bowling, although my mind was hardly on the game. So Donny had an ex-boyfriend that he needed to forget and I had one that I couldn't. It made a sort of sense.

It was my turn. I was so inside my own head that I was hardly even cognizant of throwing the ball down the alley. I got a strike. Donny let out a whoop and threw himself into my arms. I looked at him, all eyes and hair and youthful exuberance. Also without thinking, I found myself kissing him.

It was the first kiss initiated by me. I think it surprised him as much as it did me. It certainly surprised several people bowling in other lanes. The girls the guy had been flirting with applauded, and some other people joined in. Donny looked around, blushing. He was slightly embarrassed, but he looked ecstatically happy.

"Well," I heard Zach say, "it may be time to have the decorators in to change a bedroom."

Chapter Twelve

I WENT home that night with a sense of depression hanging over me. I should have felt wonderful, but soon after I'd kissed Donny good night, regret hit and hit hard.

When I'd kissed Donny, I was bursting with happiness. I felt like I could fly. Like all highs, though, this one came with a low, and once I was alone I thought about Jason. Somehow I felt like I was cheating on him. Stupid, I know, but knowing something is dumb doesn't always alter reality.

I needed some professional help. I knew my obsession wasn't healthy. And I knew that Jason, if he could, would tell me to get on with my life. He wouldn't want me to end my days pining for him.

What was I waiting for, a sign from God?

It was late, but I knew sleep would elude me, so I put on an old shirt and went up to the attic. I worked on the painting for a while but found that looking at Donny on canvas was only making me more melancholy, so I picked up my sketchbook. I did a charcoal study of Fantine and then went on to just making some random doodles. After that I sifted through some mail that had been piling up. When that was through I played six games of solitaire on my laptop. I lost all of them.

I got up and went downstairs. Fantine trotted along beside me. It had been my intention to go to bed and read until sleep eventually took over, but my legs seemed to have an idea of their own, because I bypassed my room and went on down the hall to the closed door of the master bedroom. Slowly, I twisted the knob and pushed the door open.

For just a second I thought that I might see Jason, sitting on the edge of the bed, waiting for me. Either in the flesh or as a ghost, it didn't matter. I just needed to see him. All that met me, however, was a darkened room.

I walked in. Fantine followed, looking up at me questioningly. I had no answers. There was just enough moonlight coming in from the windows to see the shapes of the furniture but no details. I sat on the bed and patted the mattress to encourage Fantine to join me. She hesitated, knowing that bed was generally off-limits, but then happily hopped up and curled up beside me.

I gazed over at the portrait above the fireplace. I couldn't make out the details, but I knew them by heart anyway. "Hey, Jason," I said aloud.

No answer. Not that I expected one. I didn't believe in ghosts. Donny did, or at least I assumed he did, belonging to a ghost-hunting group. To my mind, though, if spirits truly existed, surely Jason would have contacted me by now and given me solace.

It felt good, though, to talk to Jason's portrait. "There's this guy. The one that was here the other day. Donny. He's a lot younger than me, but I think I really like him. I think that maybe we'd be good together. It's just that...." Words were failing me. The feelings were there, but expressing them was hard. "I need to know that you... are okay with...."

I looked down at Fantine, who was staring up at me. "They say dogs may have the ability to see things humans can't. Any ghosts here, baby? In the room?"

Fantine wagged her tail.

Yeah, there were ghosts there. Of one sort or another.

THE PAINTING of Donny was almost complete, and that was making me somewhat sad as well. Some part of me worried that after it was done, I wouldn't see him again. He'd vanish into the ether, as if he'd never really been there at all. Maybe that was why I was dragging out completing it. I daubed my brush into some red paint and added some color to the explosion happening behind the figure in the painting. I tried to sound offhand. "What are you doing this weekend?"

Donny blinked. "Nothing. Well, I work Sunday, but I can trade with Julie if need be. Why?"

I shrugged, trying to convey that his response wasn't really important to me. "I just thought we might take in a show. Go up to Chicago. Have you heard of *The Book of Mormon*?"

"Um, it's got something to do with the Latter Day Saints, doesn't it?" He made a sour face. "Religion really isn't my thing."

Smiling, I said, "I meant the musical. It was written by the guys that did *South Park*. I thought you might like it."

"Fuck yeah!" His eyes, already so big, seemed to grow in size.

In actuality I'd had the tickets for months, intending to go with Zach. We'd seen the show already, having gone on its first run in the Windy City, but wanted to go again. However, one of the drag queens Zach worked with was retiring and her final show was going to be that night, and I knew he really wanted to stay in town to support his friend, especially as we'd already seen *Mormon*. He'd breathed a sigh of relief when I said he didn't have to go.

"I was thinking of asking Donny," I told Zach when the subject came up earlier that day.

"That's perfect!" Zach gushed. "About time you two had a proper date. You've been stringing that poor kid along for weeks now!"

"I have not," I protested, knowing Zach was right.

Before Donny came over, I spent some time jotting down a list of pros and cons of dating him.

Cons:

The age difference.

You have an enormous amount of emotional baggage, i.e., you can't let go of Jason.

You don't have much in common with each other. He thought *Les Miserables* was some kind of French pastry.

You don't have time to date. You have to finish setting up for the art show at the gallery, and for some reason the catering gig has picked up tremendously.

If you did go out with him, it wouldn't last. Two months, tops. And all you'd have to show for it was two very broken hearts.

His friend Phil hates you.

You'd have to endure thousands and thousands of cradle-robbing jokes from friends who think they're being cute.

Going home for Thanksgiving, and bringing him? Just think of your parents' reaction! By Christmas, Ma and Pa would be battling each other to see which one got to stick their head in the oven first.

PROS:

He makes you laugh.

Your heart feels lighter whenever he's around.

I DECIDED the pros outweighed the cons.

"WE'LL HAVE to stay the night at a hotel. There's no way I'm driving back that late at night."

"Cool with me," he replied, a twinkle in his eye.

"I booked a double. Two beds."

"Yeah, we'll need somewhere to toss our bags."

I concentrated on the painting. "Seriously, I can't promise anything. I can't...." Why was it that words so often failed me when Donny was in the room?

He walked over to me. He was dressed as he had been that first night I'd seen him, with the too-tight jeans and the white-and-black patterned shirt. Gently he reached out and touched my chin, guiding my face so I was looking into his eyes.

"Hey, I'm just kidding. Really, it's cool."

"No, it really isn't. I want to, really I do." I knew I was blushing. "I'm just afraid that... I don't want...." I sighed and laughed mirthlessly. "I like you, Donny. I really do."

"I know that."

"I just don't want... things to get in the way. I have to be sure."

"It's okay." The grin returned. "But this is a date, right? An official date?"

"Very official. I'll have a notary stamp our theater tickets."

He kept his fingers on my chin and leaned in for a kiss. Our lips touched, and I swear I could feel electricity in the air around us. I think he meant for it just to be a quick peck, but it turned into more as our tongues intertwined and we held each other tightly. My heart was beating fast when he finally stepped away. Was that a tear in his eye? He immediately turned away from me, so I couldn't be sure.

"Hey," he said, attempting a light tone, "we'll have fun. I haven't been in Chicago in ages."

I didn't want things to get in the way, I'd said. Who was I kidding? I had Jason still to deal with, and he had the memory of Kevin. I wanted to say more, to assure him things would be all right. We just had to take it slow, know that we were doing the right thing. Who knows, maybe we'd conquer each other's inner demons.

I was too scared to put my thoughts into words, though, so I simply picked my brush back up and pretended to work again.

Donny looked at the easel. "When can I see it?"

"Soon," I said. I was sure he'd like what I'd done, but what if he didn't? I wasn't sure my fragile ego could take that.

Fantine was resting on the floor, and Donny hunched down to pet her. Speaking to me but looking at the dog, Donny said, "I think there's something you should know."

"What's that?"

There was a long pause as he scratched Fantine's ears. Finally he said, "I'm falling in love with you."

I couldn't see his face, but there were tears in the words. Goddamn the kid, he certainly knew how to make me feel wonderful and horrible in the same instant. I wanted so badly to be able to say that I loved him back, but I couldn't. Not yet. I had to say something in return, though, so I muttered, "Thank you."

Thank you! The young man says the hardest words one guy can say to another, and all you say in return is thank you! What an ass!

At least tell him how special he is!

I set my brush aside with a sigh. No, there was a barrier between us. A memory, yes, but one I was unable or unwilling to release.

Say it! Just say it! You're special to me, Donny! Surely Jason wouldn't object to that! You know he wouldn't! Just let go and allow yourself to love someone else!

"I'm really tired," I said. "I think we should call it quits for tonight."

Donny nodded, still keeping his face concealed from me. Fantine was certainly enjoying the extra attention, though.

Time seemed to stand still. Eventually Donny rose and looked at the clock above the doorway. "Guess I should be going."

Tell him to stay. "Yeah, okay," I said.

He turned to me. His eyes were dry now, but there were streaks down his cheeks. I felt like a heel. "Saturday, though, right? We're still going to that show?"

"You bet."

After he'd gone, I wandered the house aimlessly for what seemed like hours but must have only been a few minutes. I ended up, predictably, in the master bedroom. I turned on the lights and went over to the fireplace and stared up at the portrait.

"Let me go," I said to it. "For God's sake let me go."

Chapter Thirteen

"Can I have my cell phone back?"

Marril sniffed. "You certainly may not!"

Somehow Zach had, through the weird sixth sense friends sometimes share, known I was about to phone Donny to cancel our weekend plans, and he and Marril showed up at my house to intervene. It was Friday night and I knew they would have to leave at some point to get ready for their show, but they showed no sign of budging.

They'd burst in just after I'd finished dinner and started dialing. Before I'd punched the last number, though, Marril plucked the phone from my hand and shoved it into his pants. Not, mind you, into the *pocket* of his trousers. Oh no! Marril dropped the phone down into his underwear.

Maybe I didn't really want it back after all.

We were in the kitchen. Zach was busy with the coffeemaker, brewing a pot. He eyed me suspiciously. "You were just about to call him, weren't you?"

There didn't seem much point in denying it. "Maybe," I said. "You don't know me."

"I know you're taking that young man to Chicago. You're definitely not canceling the night before."

"How do you know? Maybe I was calling to remind him to pack an extra pair of underwear."

"Honeychild, at lunch today you were moping. You didn't say much, but I knew you were feeling guilty about going. So here we are, and just in the nick of time, from the looks of it."

"I was calling my grandmother, if you must know."

Zach was getting three mugs out of the cabinet and paused, uncertain. "Really? I— wait, your grandmother is dead."

"The other one. People have two, generally speaking."

"Swear to the great goddess Barbra that you were calling your granny and not Donny." Marril was less trusting than Zach.

He had me there. I accepted a mug from Zach and added several spoonfuls of sugar before sitting down at the table across from Marril. "I can't do that," I admitted.

"What," Zach asked, "is so wrong about taking someone to a show in Chicago? Why do you have to do this to yourself?"

"If I knew the answer to that question, I wouldn't need you guys."

"Well, you're going," Marril replied, taking a sip of his unsweetened coffee. He fluttered his eyelashes in appreciation of its boldness, or maybe he just needed the caffeine jolt.

"I... can't," I said lamely.

Zach arched an eyebrow. "And why can't you?"

"A catering gig came up. I have to work."

"So you get someone to cover for you."

Marril snorted. "He's lying! Can't you tell when he's fibbing? He always narrows his eyes when he tells a whopper."

I felt a little affronted. "I do not."

Marril rolled his eyes heavenward. "And he wonders why he loses whenever we play poker."

I sighed. "Okay. I don't have to work. I wasn't calling my grandmother—both of whom are dead, by the way—and I wasn't wanting to tell him about underw—"

I stopped there, as a chirping came from Marril's crotch. He looked down and then at me. "I think it's for you."

"Well, I'm not fishing it out of there!" I protested.

Gingerly he reached into his pants and after some rustling around came up with my phone, which he attempted to hand over to me. I glared at him, and he wiped the phone off with his shirt. "I assure you it's perfectly clean down there. I haven't had a good case of crabs in months!"

"I feel so assured," I said, taking the still-ringing phone from him. My ringtone was from *Phantom of the Opera*, and I managed to answer before the next crescendo. "Hello."

"Hey!" It was Donny. "Didn't catch you at a bad time, did I?"

"Nope. Just took me a while to answer because my phone was down Marril's pants. What's up?"

"Who is it?" Zach mouthed.

"My dead grandmother," I told him.

"Huh?" Donny asked.

"Nothing," I said into the phone.

"So I just wanted to check to see if there was anything special I should bring tomorrow. Should I pack us a lunch? It's a long drive up to Chicago, and I thought—"

"Yeah, about tomorrow. I'm afraid—"

Zach snatched the phone out of my hand so fast I couldn't react. He shot me a killing look and then said into the phone, "Hello, Donny. Honey, this is Zach." He moved away from me fairly nimbly for a stocky guy, out of the reach of my grasping arms. "Yes, Frank can't talk on the phone right now. He's… choking on a banana."

"I am not!" I screamed.

"Well, it looked like a banana," Zach quipped. "Anyway, he wanted me to tell you to come over to his place early tomorrow so you guys have plenty of time to get there. Around nine." Zach looked at me for confirmation, as if it was my idea.

I couldn't hear what Donny said, of course, but I saw Zach's face soften as he listened.

Finally he said, "Well, yeah. To be honest, he's fucking petrified." After more words from Donny, Zach continued. "Well, aren't you just the sweetest thing! Are all people your age this fucking nice? 'Cause if they are, I maybe need to expand my horizons and start dating the younger set. You take care now, and Frank will see you in the morning. No, you don't have to pack a lunch. There's this lovely little diner in Merrillville that you've just *got* to try!" He listened some more. "Okay, honey, see you soon." He terminated the call and turned defiantly to me.

"What did he say?" I asked. "What was that about me being petrified?"

"Fucking petrified was the term I used, and he realized that you were about to give him the bum's rush. He asked me if you were nervous about going with him, so I told him the truth."

"And?"

Zach smiled. "He said that you didn't have to be nervous, that nothing would happen if you didn't want it to, and that he understood. Really, I think the kid's too fucking good for you. If you dump him, mind if I take a shot?"

I ignored him and took a too big sip of coffee, scalding my mouth. Once the sputtering had subsided, I said, "Don't you two stooges have some place to go? Isn't Dixon Street missing two of its drag queens?"

"And as soon as we go, you'll be on the phone to Donny with some excuse or another," Marril said.

"No, I won't," I said, and I meant it. My panic attack had gone, thanks to drag's answer to Abbott and Costello.

"I think he's sincere," Marril said, examining my face. "The eyes aren't narrowing."

"Maybe we should bring him with us, just in case," Zach replied.

"Guys, I'm right here. Stop talking about me like I am some little kid."

"When you start acting like an adult, we will." Zach downed the rest of his coffee, only twitching a little as it burned down his throat. "We'd best be going. No calling, or you'll have to answer to Auntie Schubert!"

"God knows we don't want that."

Marril seemed less sure of me. "Why don't you come with us anyway? Be good for you to get out, have a few drinks and a few laughs. See our show—"

"I've seen your show about a million times!"

"And doesn't it just improve with every viewing?"

The truth was that I was a little weary after an afternoon spent first at the Stephenson Gallery and then catering a law office party. "I'm probably going to hit the hay early tonight. After all," I added, glaring at Zach, "Donny will be here *early* tomorrow."

Zach waved a hand, dismissing my gripe. "Nine is hardly early."

"And when do you ever get up before eleven?"

"Honeychild, I work my butt off until two in the morning, in heels no less! I deserve my beauty rest!"

Marril pushed aside his coffee mug. "Come on, darling. We'd best be going. Those songs ain't going to lip-synch themselves."

Fantine and I showed them to the door. When they'd finally gone I looked down at the dog. "They mean well," I said.

Fantine didn't answer, but she looked like she agreed. We trotted back to the kitchen, and I started washing up the coffee mugs. It wasn't until I was done that I realized I couldn't recall what had become of my cell phone. I looked around for it, but it was nowhere to be found. The last I'd seen of it, Zach had it in his mitts.

He'd taken it with him! Aloud I said, "Those bastards don't trust me!"

Not that I'd given them much reason to.

CHAPTER FOURTEEN

I SPENT an ungodly amount of time getting ready for the trip.

After trying on several different looks, I decided on a pair of crisp black jeans and a bright blue button-down shirt. I felt this looked too "old man" and not hip enough, so I added a pair of Nike running shoes to the ensemble. Not too dressy, not too casual. I was just tying the laces when my doorbell rang.

When I opened the door, my jaw dropped. It wasn't just that Donny was overdressed. He was overdressed but looked *gorgeous*, wearing a dark blue suit with a scarlet tie over a new-looking white shirt. On his feet were shiny black oxfords. He was grinning from ear to ear, and his raised his left leg to show off his shoes. "I had to borrow these," he said. "They're actually Phil's. I'm swimming in them, so if I lose a shoe sometime during the day, that's why. You gotta do what you gotta do to look good, though." He blinked at me. "Aren't you ready yet? I thought from what Zach said you wanted to get an early start."

I ran a hand down my shirt. "Actually, this was what I was going to wear."

Donny looked crestfallen. "Shit! Is the suit too much? You said the tickets were for the dress circle, so I figured…." He plucked at his coat buttons, as if uncertain if he should take it off or not.

"No, you're fine," I assured him. "Dress circle really just means the first section just above the orchestra seats. I think originally people used to actually dress up for those seats, but nowadays—" I stopped. He looked so sad and cute. "Tell you what. Give me a minute, and I can change real quick."

Brightening, Donny said, "That's cool. Actually, I left my overnight bag in my car. I'll run and get it while you change." He turned and started off at a trot down the walk, pausing when his right shoe nearly came off. He glanced back, awkwardly hopping on one foot while he adjusted the quarrelsome oxford. "See what I mean?"

I laughed as I bounded upstairs to change.

WE'D REMOVED our jackets for the drive so they wouldn't get sweaty, laying them out on the backseat next to our overnight bags. After a stop at a gas station, we hit Interstate 65 to Chicago and made fairly good time. I had a CD in. Sarah Brightman was singing "Wishing You Were Somehow Here Again" from *Phantom*. Donny was uncharacteristically quiet, but I figured he was simply enjoying the music until he muttered, "Sorry about the suit."

"No, the suit's fine. You look fantastic in it, by the way."

He beamed. "Yeah, I don't look bad, do I? Clean up pretty good for a guy from Cabo."

"You seem as American as I do, frankly. Just a touch of accent."

"I am just as American as you. Got a certificate and everything."

"That's true."

"I bet I know more American history than you do. Can you name the first five American presidents?"

I thought a moment. "Well, Washington, of course. And then… Jefferson? And there were the Adams guys. John and John Quincy."

"Washington, Adams, Jefferson, Madison, and Monroe." Donny rattled them off, adding, "John Quincy was sixth."

I could see Donny was proud of his citizenship. "I probably wouldn't be able to pass the test. I doubt most Americans could."

Donny shrugged. "Maybe not. You've got to prove yourself, though, if you're a foreigner and want to be an American." He smoothed out his tie, which I could tell was still bothering him. "I put this on for you, you know."

I smiled. "And I put on what I was wearing for you. I didn't want to look like an old fuddy-duddy."

"Touché!" The grin found its way back onto Donny's face. He nodded at the CD player. "Is this from the show we're seeing?"

"No, this is *The Phantom of the Opera*. I've got *The Book of Mormon*, but I thought we'd wait until the trip back to listen to it. I didn't want to ruin any surprises for you."

"As if!" Donny unwrapped a chocolate bar he'd bought at the gas station, careful not to touch the chocolate itself. "Don't want to get it all over me," he said.

We drove along, listening to the rest of *Phantom*. He finished his snack and looked around for a place to deposit the wrapper.

"Shove it in the glove box," I told him. "We'll clean it out later."

It was a nice, clear day for driving, and the traffic wasn't bad. I felt relaxed, and at one point I allowed my right hand to drop to my side, confident that the left could handle the wheel on its own. After several moments, Donny reached over and put his hand on mine. His hand was nice and warm.

"That okay?" he said, staring straight out the window.

"Yeah, that's okay," I told him.

I hated it when, in order to pass a slow-moving truck, I had to move my hand from under his and put both hands on the wheel.

CHECK-IN AT the hotel wasn't until three o'clock, so we found a parking garage close by and locked our bags in the trunk. Donning our suit jackets, we got into the elevator and made our way down to street level. Donny looked like he was about to burst with excitement.

"We've got time to kill," I said. "What do you want to do?"

"I don't know." It didn't sound like it really mattered to him. Whatever it was, he was bound and determined to love it.

"We can do some shopping. Check out Macy's. Maybe stroll down to Millennium Park and get someone to take our picture in front of the Bean."

He looked at me as if I'd lost my marbles. "The what?"

"It's a sculpture, actually called Cloud Gate, but everyone calls it the Bean. You've surely seen pictures of it."

"I'm guessing it's shaped like a bean." He straightened his tie. "People are going to think we just came from a wedding."

"They probably will."

We were closest to Macy's, so we went there first. Donny's feet barely touched the pavement as he walked, he was so excited. He marveled at how huge the downtown Macy's was, insisting we hit every floor. Down in the basement, he decided to buy some candy for the drive home and spent quite a few minutes determining just what to get. As he pondered, he stood in front of the counter, a finger against his lip, obviously torn between several choices. I wished I had my sketchbook with me. He was, at that moment, Youth Eternal.

"Get whatever you like," I said.

He decided on some truffles. As the salesgirl wrapped up his purchase, Donny turned to me with such a grin on his face I had to ask if he had something on his mind.

"This is just so cool," he said. His accent, I noticed, was more pronounced when he was excited. "I didn't really get to see much of Chicago when I was here before." He accepted his bag of goodies from the salesgirl with such gusto that all three of us ended up laughing.

We were close enough to check-in time that I suggested we could retrieve our bags and head for the hotel. Outside on the street, I started to hail a cab, but Donny stopped me.

"I want to walk. Don't want to miss anything!"

He took in everything he could, the buildings, the people, even the homeless unfortunates huddled in the entryways. He gawked at the marquee of the Oriental Theatre, commented on the hotels and restaurants we passed, and cooed at the pigeons. Myself, I just enjoyed seeing life through a new pair of eyes.

As we wandered down Randolph Street, he said, "So who's watching Fantine this weekend?"

"She's staying with Uncle Gene. His kids will wear her out enough that she won't miss me too much."

"What are your Saturdays usually like?" It was a casual question, but I felt the answer was important to Donny.

"I usually have catering gigs. Why?"

"Can you get out of one if needed?"

"Sure." Connie's Catering had always been a fallback job for me, just in case sales from my artwork dried up. I could easily get one of the other guys to cover for me. "What did you have in mind?"

He shrugged. "IGAP—that's our ghost-hunting group, remember?— is doing an investigation soon. I thought you might like to come along."

He was trying to make it sound unimportant to him, as if he didn't really care if I came or not, but he wasn't doing a very good job of it.

"I don't believe in ghosts. Not in that sense," I said.

"Doesn't matter. In fact, it can be a good thing to have a skeptic along. Keeps the rest of us from getting spooked by our own shadows."

"I'd love to come." Actually, it sounded awful. I envisioned spending hours upon hours in some cold, clammy building hearing nothing but the wind whistling through the cracks and crevices. Plus, I was sure Phil would be there, and I'd have to endure his disapproving glares. On the other hand, I'd be seeing Donny doing something he enjoyed. We'd be on his turf, not mine.

"Excellent! We're going to this old farmhouse, just outside of town. It's supposed to have a lot of activity."

"From mice and bats, no doubt." I hoped I didn't sound too condescending.

Donny didn't seem bothered by the remark. "And before we go, you can come to dinner at my place."

"Sounds fine."

"You can meet my aunt Rhonda. I live with her. I have since, well, since I broke up with Kevin. She's really cool. I've told her all about you."

"Oh dear."

He smiled so broadly I wondered that he didn't damage his face muscles. "In a good way. She's dying to meet you." He paused in front of a restaurant window. "Wow, look at this! All that old wood, it almost looks like something out of Sherlock Holmes, like it belongs in another time. We should eat here later."

I wasn't sure. "This was one of Jason's favorite places to…."

Donny looked at up me. "It's okay to mention him, you know. He existed. He was a fact, just like Kevin was. They're going to crop up every now and then."

"Yes, but—"

"But nothing. We can't pretend they weren't part of our lives."

We moved away from the window and continued down the street, but I noticed we weren't walking quite as fast as before.

Uncertain if it was the best thing to say, I nonetheless said, "Your friend Phil was telling me that Kevin wasn't always very nice to you."

"That's putting it mildly. He was pretty controlling. Don't get me wrong. He helped me a lot. I don't think I would have become a citizen if he hadn't pushed me. But… yeah, he wasn't always nice."

"Why did you stay with him?"

Donny thought about that a moment. "Hard to say. At the beginning, he was great. He really was. The nasty stuff came later. The trouble is, if someone continually tells you you're stupid, after a while you begin to believe it. Then you can't leave them, because you're convinced you'd never survive without them."

"I'd say you were anything but stupid."

"Aw, thanks!" Donny dismissed the compliment verbally, but his face told a different story. "Now, are we close to the hotel? These shoes are killing me!"

Chapter Fifteen

WE STEPPED up to the reservations desk together, but Donny was the one who answered when the desk clerk asked if she could help us. "Reservation for two. Name is Hunter."

She checked her computer screen. "Ah, yes, Mr. Hunter. Everything is taken care of. You're in room 712."

After checking my ID, she handed both of us a key card. Donny accepted his and asked with a cheeky grin, "Are the beds comfy?"

She got the inference and tried to hide a smile. "I think you'll find them very satisfactory."

"How about the walls? Thick? 'Cause we don't want to—"

"Thank you," I told the clerk, pulling Donny away by his elbow. "Come on, you."

"Just showing common courtesy, hombre."

We got into the elevator. Luckily we were the only passengers. "No, you were showing off," I said with a smile of my own. "She probably thinks you're my paid escort for the night."

Donny pulled at his jacket. "Dressed like this? Naw, she thinks we're two dudes spending a night in Chicago."

"Uh-huh."

"Who are going to be bumping uglies before the sun comes back up."

We reached our floor. As the doors opened, I said, "I can't promise—"

"I know! I know! Geesh, can't a guy have a little wishful thinking?"

The room was small, containing two beds, a desk, a chair, and a small table, and not much else. Donny threw his bag on the closest bed and then threw himself on the other, one shoe falling completely off as he landed with a bounce. I set my suitcase next to his and went over to the window. Opening the blinds, I grimaced. The glass was so grimy that it was hard to see outside, not that the view was spectacular. I closed the blinds again. "So much for the outside," I said.

Donny patted the bed. "View's pretty good over here."

I shook my head. "You don't give up, do you?"

He kicked off his other shoe and sat up, sliding his legs under him and almost looking like a puppy begging. "Not when the prize is worth getting."

I frowned. "Wait. Am I the prize, or are you?"

"Maybe we both are." He scooted on his knees until he got to the edge of the bed and was within reach of me. He grabbed hold of the end of my tie and pulled me to him. His lips parted, making it obvious that he wanted a kiss.

I obliged. A little kiss wouldn't hurt.

Except it wasn't a little kiss. I closed my eyes and enjoyed the contact. I wanted him, and I knew he wanted me. So why was I hesitating?

Well, we all know the answer to that question. Luckily, sometimes the brain is overruled by the groin, and my genitalia was screaming. I sat on the bed, our lips never losing contact, and held Donny close to me. I took in his scent, his energy, his very being. I'd been afraid that Jason would keep coming into my mind, but other than a fleeting thought that maybe, just for a few moments, my past would release me, he didn't. Donny wasn't Jason. For one thing, he kissed me like he was clutching on to a lifeline. Lust was certainly a factor, but I felt there was something else. Desperation to be loved, perhaps.

It wasn't the time for thinking, though. Donny pulled us both back onto the bed, our legs dangling over. The kiss ended with a funny-sounding squeak that we both ignored. He looked into my eyes. "We got time before dinner, don't we?" His voice was husky, his accent thicker.

"Who needs dinner?" I asked.

I went in to kiss him again, but he placed a finger against my chin. "Don't want to rumple our suits, do we?" He slid off the bed, and I thought for a moment that he was putting the kibosh on any further lovemaking, but he slowly removed his suit jacket and carefully placed it on the other bed.

I sat up and took mine off. I tossed it, and it landed on top of his.

Donny loosened his tie with the most serious look I'd ever seen on his face. "We don't have to do this, if you don't want to."

"Oh no. I do." I unlaced my shoes and kicked them off.

Donny's tie came off with a flourish. "Took me seven times to tie that stupid thing."

He began to unbutton his shirt, but I stood and took his hands in mine. "I want to undress you," I said. "If that's all right."

"Oh, yeah. Long as I get the pleasure in return."

Realization dawned on me. "Shit! I didn't bring any condoms." Hell, I hadn't had need of them in years. "Maybe we should…."

With a twinkle in his eyes, Donny picked up his overnight bag and unzipped it. Rummaging through the contents, he said, "Condoms. Lube. Dammit, I forgot the whip and handcuffs!"

"I'm sure we can make do," I said. I had to force my voice to come out sounding at least seminormal. Was I shaking? Why the hell was I shaking?

Donny's radar was working well. He glanced over at me. "You're nervous, aren't you?"

"No," I lied.

"It's okay. So am I." He moved close and grabbed hold of the knot of my tie. "I think this is going to work best if we turn off our brains for the next hour or so."

"Hour? You're optimistic. It's been over four years. I'll be lucky if I last a minute." I looked into his eyes, so black and lovely. His smooth, flawless skin. That gorgeous, so-black hair. A minute was probably optimistic.

He smiled, loosening my tie. "The first time, maybe."

The tie slid from around my collar, and I had a sudden pang of panic. "Maybe this isn't such—"

Donny placed a finger on my lips and shushed me. "Brain off, remember? No thinking. No worrying. No second-guessing. No promises. And most importantly, no regrets. Just *amor*."

I breathed out slowly. "I'll try."

"Do or do not. There is no try," Donny replied in a fairly decent Yoda impression. In response to the surprise in my face, he said, "What? I've seen *The Empire Strikes Back*."

The slow striptease continued. He took off my shirt. I took off his. He unbuckled my belt. I reciprocated. In between there was a lot of kissing and groping. Donny must have sneaked a mint earlier because his kisses tasted slightly of cinnamon.

We stood, entwined, until we were naked. For a shorter guy, Donny had a fairly impressive erection. Actually, he had at least an inch on me. Little bastard. He was pressed up against me, his face upturned to meet mine. We swayed a little until we both, by unspoken mutual consent, knew it was time to fall back onto the bed.

Donny lay on top of me, kissing my mouth, my chin, my neck. He moaned a little. "I've waited so long for this," he whispered.

It was on my tongue to say something self-deprecating, like "Really?" He was right, though. This wasn't the time for thinking. If I thought about what I was doing, I'd stop. And I didn't want to stop. Just think with the dick, I told myself. God knows it's made enough decisions in my lifetime.

Donny was writhing around, and I felt like I was about to explode. He nibbled on my neck, making my toes curl. It was like he automatically knew what drove me crazy. "We'd better," I said huskily, "start doing something, or I'm going to shoot before we even get to the good stuff."

"It's all good stuff, Frank," he said with a grin. He reached over to the nightstand, where he'd placed the bottle of lube and the condoms. With a quick rip of his teeth he had the condom out of the package. He sat up, straddling my torso. Without taking his eyes off mine he reached back and began to slide the thin rubber sheath over my very erect—and very sensitive—dick.

"Ah!" I said, almost expecting to shoot just from Donny's touch. Luckily, I didn't.

Not at that moment, anyway.

He applied the lube generously and poised himself, ready to take me in. He smiled. "I think you're still supposed to breathe."

"I don't think I can," I whispered.

Slowly, gently, Donny guided me inside him. He paused as he allowed time for his muscles to relax, and then he began to ride me.

It was, it must be said, a short ride.

I counted. Four strokes, and I exploded.

I knew it was coming and tried to hold it off, but it was like an ant holding off a rhino. I cried out, loud enough that I was sure we were going to get a call from the hotel management threatening to toss us out if we didn't hold it down. I closed my eyes, slightly embarrassed over my premature ejaculation, but also because it felt so wonderful. Donny felt like part of me, like he belonged.

I opened my eyes, an apology on my lips, to see Donny stroking his own cock furiously. In seconds, long, thick ropes of goo shot onto my abdomen. He bucked as his body shuddered, his eyes closed, his face angelic and lustful in equal measures. He was both altar boy and thief, beauty and beast. I wondered if I could ever get tired of looking into his eyes.

My heart sounded loud to my own ears. After an eternity of about twenty seconds, Donny opened his eyes and grinned. He slowly raised his rump off my deflating cock and stretched out, lying on top of me again with a contented sigh.

"Sorry about that," I said.

He chuckled. "You weren't kidding about the minute. I doubt if we're going to get into the *Guinness Book of World Records* with that."

"Not in a good way," I agreed.

He nestled against me, and I stroked his hair.

"That was nice," he said.

"Short, but nice."

He held me tight and sighed. "*Te amo*, Frank Hunter."

"I don't speak Spanish, but I'm pretty sure I know what that means." Say it back, you fool.

I couldn't, though. Saying it would be too much, be too honest. I wasn't ready for that. Donny seemed to understand, because he said, "I know," in a way that made me think that maybe he knew what was in my mind. Suddenly he raised his head, a wicked grin across his face.

"So, ready for another go?"

I laughed. "I just turned forty-five! I'm old! Remember?"

Donny ran a hand down my cheek. "Not anymore, you're not."

Ten minutes later, we made love again. Maybe he was right. Maybe I was young again.

CHAPTER SIXTEEN

IT WAS Shawn's birthday, and the gang was having a little celebration at his place. Not only were we excited to honor our friend's forty-first, but we also were to meet his new beau, making it a special occasion indeed.

I brought Donny and a bottle of peppermint schnapps, Shawn's favorite. When we arrived, Zach and Marril were there but the mysterious new beau of Shawn's wasn't. Gene would be by later, after he tucked his kids in for the night.

Shawn met us at the door, looking slightly nervous. "Hey," he said, kissing my cheek and then Donny's, "you guys made it."

"Wouldn't miss it for the world," I said. I was, truthfully, anxious to meet this Bob guy. After the fiasco that was Shawn's last romance, I was a little worried that perhaps he was jumping into a new relationship too quickly and would end up getting hurt even worse.

We were ushered in, and Marril and Zach greeted us with hugs and kisses. I noted that before Donny began to hang out with us, we were rarely effusive in our greetings. Was it wrong of me to think they gave me a quick peck and squeeze just so they had an excuse to do the same with Donny? Ah, young blood. The effect you have on the middle-aged. We hate you, we love you, and we want you, but we're pissed as hell that we're no longer you.

Zach in particular seemed to linger over the salutation of the young man. After a sloppy kiss on Donny's cheek, Zach held him out at arm's length. "My, my! Aren't you a sight for old, sore eyes! Frank, honey, you've got to feed this boy more. He's so thin. He can't weigh much more than a twig!"

I was slightly annoyed at Zach's assumption that Donny and I were now a couple. In one sense we were, I suppose. We hadn't discussed our relationship, but after the weekend in Chicago, we'd spent more and more time together, both in bed and out. I'd even passed on a night of catering just so I could sit on the couch with Donny as he introduced me to *Game of Thrones*.

I could not, however, express to Donny how I felt about him. Nor could I ignore the nagging guilt I felt that I was somehow being untrue to Jason's memory.

My reasoning went something like this: If you don't tell him you love him, it's just a "thing" and is somehow not all that important and doesn't encroach upon your feelings for Jason or his memory. Bollocks, I know, but emotions often are.

As Shawn accepted the bottle of Rumple Minze from me, I asked, "So when do we get to meet this paragon you've been telling us about?"

"He should be here any minute now. I think you guys will like him. He's…." Words seemed to fail Shawn for once. "Well, you'll see."

There were snacks and nibbles set on the dining room table, as well as one of Marril or Zach's gaudy hats from a long-ago drag show. The hat was turned over, and several slips of paper had been dropped inside. Next to the hat were pencils and pads of paper.

"What's this?" Donny asked.

"It's danger. That's what this is." I picked up one of the pads. "It's a game we play. We call it You're Screwed. Basically we write down challenges on a slip of paper and put them in the hat. They can be pretty much anything, just as long as they're physically possible. Something like 'Hop around on one foot and sing "The Star Spangled Banner."' If you choose not to take the challenge or can't complete it, you have to take a shot. Some challenges are easy, some aren't. It generally means that we all end up extremely drunk and passed out on the floor." I jotted down a challenge and slipped it into the hat. "We haven't played it for years. I'm not sure we should now."

Smiling, Donny grabbed a pad and began writing. "I don't know. Could be fun. Sort of like a drunken Truth or Dare." He paused. "It can be anything, right?"

I had a sudden vision of him jotting down that I had to say "I love you" or something of the sort. "Well, you don't know who's going to get your suggestion, so it has to be something everyone has at least an option of doing."

"And if you succeed in your challenge, what happens?"

"You don't have to drink. Silly, isn't it?"

Donny dropped his slip of paper into the hat. "And they say my generation is frivolous."

We had time to write a few more suggestions for the game before there was a knock at the door.

"That'll be Bob," Shawn said, obviously nervous.

He went to the door and came back with his arm around a tall blond guy. "Everyone, this is Bob. Bob, these are the guys."

We tried not to gawk, but it wasn't easy. I'm sure we were all stunned, and as Shawn introduced each of us in turn we shook hands and pretended that nothing was amiss. Inwardly, though, I was busting a gut, laughing. Bob Whatever-his-last-name-was could have been Shawn's brother, they looked so much alike. Same height. Same eyes. Hell, they even had the same hair.

"Frank, it's nice to finally meet you," he said when it was my turn. The man had a strong handshake.

"Likewise," I said. "We've heard so much about you."

Actually, other than his name, we hadn't. But one always lies in these situations. Bob and Shawn couldn't have been seeing each other for more than a week. Shawn was famous for his whirlwind romances. The fires burned bright but often quickly smoldered.

As soon as we could reasonably excuse ourselves, Zach and I went into the kitchen so we could release the laughter that had built up within us. Luckily Shawn was busy explaining the rules of You're Screwed to Bob, so they hardly noticed our absence.

Alone in the kitchen, Zach held on to my arms as if I might have to keep him upright. "Oh my God!" he chortled. "Oh, honeychild, I don't know if I can behave myself tonight! You see it, don't you?"

"See it? A blind man would have spotted it! They're almost twins!"

"I wonder if Bob's father used to be Shawn's mother's milkman."

We tittered like little kids, feeding on each other's laughter, until tears were falling down our cheeks. Just when we thought we had ourselves under control, Donny came into the kitchen to get a drink. As he opened the refrigerator, he noticed that our shoulders were still shaking from repressing our mirth. "What are you two up to, holed up in here?"

"Nothing," Zach said through gritted teeth. I was afraid to speak, sure that any vocal utterance would once again lead to laughing.

Donny popped open a soda can. "Hey, have you guys noticed that Bob looks a hell of a lot like Shawn?"

We lost it.

THE THING about You're Screwed is that if you want to stay sober enough to drive home, you've got to make a complete ass of yourself. Of course, if you end up taking enough shots, you also tend to make a complete ass of yourself, so it's a lose/lose situation. Unless, of course, you're like Zach and Marril, who *like* to make asses of themselves.

Gene had finally sent Marril a text saying he wouldn't be able to make it, so it was just the six of us playing, which was a shame as I'd have loved to see Gene try to accomplish one of my challenges, had he been so unlucky as to draw one.

"If you accept the challenge," Donny asked just before play commenced, "who's to say you completed it successfully? The person who wrote the challenge, or is it by mutual consent of the rest of the players?"

"It's by vote," Shawn said as he poured out a few shots from the bottle I'd brought in readiness for anyone who forfeited.

Donny wrinkled his nose. "I *hate* schnapps!"

"Then you'd better hope you're up to the challenges," Zach told him. He put a reassuring arm around the young man's shoulders. "Don't worry, honey. If you come even close, you get *my* vote."

Looking at me with a slightly worried look, Donny said, "Well, one of us should stay sober. We've got to drive home."

"Maybe you will, and maybe you won't." Shawn waggled his eyebrows suggestively.

"If you draw one of your own challenges," I told Donny, "you get a pass that round."

"How many rounds are there?"

"Depends," Marril said, picking up the hat, "on how many slips there are. We go through them all." He looked inside. "I'd say we're definitely screwed tonight." He sifted through the slips, mixing them up, and then held the hat in front of Shawn. "Birthday boy goes first."

Shawn picked out a slip and read it aloud. "Name five people who have played Catwoman."

Donny blinked. "That's easy!"

"I wish you'd have picked this one, then," Shawn said. He pursed his lips as he thought. "Let's see. Halle Berry, of course. And Michelle Pfeiffer. Eartha Kitt. And… um…."

"Oh, come on!" Donny obviously couldn't believe anyone would have difficulty with the question.

"Don't fluster me, kid. Julie… what was her name? Newmar! Julie Newmar! And…." Shawn's face went blank.

"That's only four," Marril pointed out.

"Yeah, I can count." Shawn frowned. "There was a third one that was in the old TV show, wasn't there? What was her name?" He shook his head and picked up one of the shot glasses. "Oh, well."

Donny was beside himself. "Anne freaking Hathaway! You know, *The Dark Knight Rises*?"

"Oh yeah. Didn't see that one," Shawn said after downing his shot.

"And Lee Meriwether was the other one from the TV show," Zach said. "Also, the one with the best hair."

"And after birthday boy, we go in alphabetical order." Marril shook the hat. "Which would be Bob."

Shawn's date looked uncomfortable and cleared his throat. "Actually, my name is officially Robert."

Marril grinned. "In that case, Donny."

Donny read his slip out loud, looking at the words as if they were a death sentence. "Strip to the waist, stand on the table, and sing 'I Want Your Sex' by George Michael, but do it as Laura Petrie from *The Dick Van Dyke Show*." The slip of paper fell from his fingers to the floor. "Who the hell is Laura Petrie?"

I felt bad, as I'd written that particular challenge. "She was played by Mary Tyler Moore." Surely he knew who Mary Tyler Moore was. "On the show, she was always saying 'Oh, Rob!' in a sort of wail." I demonstrated for him.

"Hey, that's cheating!" Shawn shouted. "You can't give him hints!"

"He's probably never seen the show!" I protested.

"I don't even know the song." Donny looked like a sad puppy as he picked up a shot glass. "Well, here goes." He threw his head back and drank. He coughed several times as the alcohol hit his stomach.

Zach smiled as he patted Donny's back. "And so it begins. Welcome to the group, young one."

Donny didn't look pleased to be officially accepted as one of us.

"OH, ROB," Donny sang in a drunken wail, "I want your sex!" He still didn't have the tune quite right, but he was too inebriated to care. He paused in his singing to observe, "Sure. *Now* I can do it!"

We were at my house, and I slowly guided him up the stairs to my bedroom. "You didn't have to play, you know. It's *our* stupid game. No one would have thought any less of you if you hadn't participated."

"No," he insisted. "Rules is rules. Gotta play. Don't matter if it isn't fair to those that weren't born in the 1970s." He spat out the last words with venom. He glared at me with mock severity. "Mean old fuckers."

Donny certainly had reason to be disgruntled. His next challenge had been to sing the theme from *Gilligan's Island* while doing a liturgical dance. It had gone downhill for him after that, and by the time we left he could barely stand. Perversely, the challenges I got had all been easy. Name fifteen songs by Stephen Sondheim. Enact a scene from *Whatever Happened to Baby Jane?* playing both parts. I had only downed two shots the whole night.

At the halfway point of the staircase, Donny suddenly stopped and leaned heavily against me, looking up at my face. "I love you, Frank." His eyes were glassy, but there was a smile on his lips.

"I know you do," I replied. Immediately I wanted to hit myself. I had a perfect opportunity to say how I felt, as it was unlikely that Donny would remember much in the morning. It was like getting a free pass, and I let it slip through my fingers. "Come on, let's get you into bed."

We resumed our slow climb. He rested his head against my arm. "I've only ever said that to one other person, that I loved them. Not counting family. Do you know who that was?"

"I'd imagine Kevin."

You'd have thought I came up with the name by magic. "That's right! And do you know what he did? He treated me like crap."

"I know." I really didn't, not in detail, but it seemed like I should say something in commiseration.

We'd reached the top of the stairs. Donny stopped again, swaying uncertainly. "And I loved him. I really did. He did a lot for me. Made sure I passed my citizenship test. Taught me how to drive!" He turned to me. "Did you know that?"

"No, I didn't."

Donny grabbed hold of the balustrade to steady himself. "But I was like his property. Wasn't allowed out without him. Couldn't have friends of my own. And he'd say really mean things to me."

He shifted his weight, and I thought he might stumble back down the stairs, but he righted himself at the last moment.

"Do you think I'm stupid? He was always saying I was stupid."

"You're definitely not stupid. You're incredibly smart, in fact."

Donny's face scrunched in disappointment. "I wasn't smart tonight. Didn't know the lyrics to fucking *Gilligan's Island*."

"I'd hardly say that showed stupidity. Quite the opposite."

Tears came into his eyes. "Please tell me you'll never call me stupid. I don't think I could bear that."

I put my arm around his waist. "I can promise you that will never happen."

"Good." Donny sniffed loudly. "'Cause if you did, I might just have to kick you in the balls, and I wouldn't like that."

I laughed softly and held him tightly. "I wouldn't like that either."

I eventually guided him into my bedroom. He managed to throw himself onto the mattress with a loud groan, landing on his stomach. He rolled over and remained in the center of the mattress, arms and legs spread out so that he resembled a drunken version of da Vinci's *Vitruvian Man* or someone who had attempted to make a snow angel and gave up midangel.

I thought he was unconscious, so I moved a wastebasket next to the bed in case he awoke and couldn't make it to the restroom in time to vomit. I sat down on the edge of the bed and moved a tuft of his long dark hair out of his face. His eyes opened. The tears he'd been fighting back began to stream down his cheeks.

"I think I deserve to be loved, don't you?" he asked, his voice cracking so much it was hard to understand the words.

"Yes," I said. "Yes, you do."

He put his head on my lap, and I stroked his cheek, wiping away the tears, until he fell asleep. When I was sure he was out, I gently moved his head until it rested on a pillow. There was a little wet spot on my pants where his head had been, either tears or drool. Maybe both. I brushed his hair back into place and thought about what I should do. To get into bed with him, I'd have to shift him, as he was pretty much dead center of the mattress. I figured he'd sleep for hours at least, and I didn't want to disturb him. As carefully as I could, I removed his shoes and got a blanket out of the closet to cover him. Then I kissed his forehead and bade him good night.

I'd have to sleep in the master bedroom tonight. I hadn't slept there in over four years.

I wasn't sure I'd have a restful night in any case.

CHAPTER SEVENTEEN

I DREAMED.

I was on a beach that seemed to stretch into eternity. The beach was deserted, save for one solitary figure off in the distance. He was too far away to make out any features, but I knew instinctively that it was Jason. I called out to him, but the crash of the waves drowned out my voice.

I began to run. I was wearing a pair of jeans but was barefoot, and my feet were kicking up clouds of sand as I hurried after Jason. I yelled as loud as I could, but he kept walking away.

Above me, a sea bird squawked. An albatross? Oh, that would have to mean something! I didn't have time to ponder the implications, however. The figure was getting farther away, even though he was ambling and I was running like the wind. No matter what I did, I couldn't bridge the gap between us.

Finally I ran out of breath. I hunched over, my hands on my knees, panting. The figure suddenly turned and waved at me.

And then he vanished.

"Don't go, Jason," I whispered. "I have so much to tell you."

The bird was now a crow, or perhaps a raven. It landed on the sand several yards in front of me, eying me critically.

"Nevermore," it said. So it must have been a raven.

I became aware that someone stood behind me. I could see their shadow mixing with my own. I turned, expecting it to be Jason, who had magically transported himself back down the beach. Instead it was Vincent Price, wearing long black robes and a red turban.

"You think you see, but you don't," dream Vincent Price intoned. "You think you know, but you are as a newborn babe."

"Where's Jason?" I implored. "I need desperately to speak to him."

Price looked pained as he put his fingertips to his temples. "Pray speak quietly. Every sound is exquisite agony to my ears."

I frowned but lowered my tone. "Sorry."

"It's all right," Price told me. "You'd think after being dead for so many years I'd be used to this sort of thing."

"That's right. You're dead." I'd forgotten the actor had passed away. I looked down the beach to the spot where Jason had disappeared. "Jason is dead too."

"We're all dead here." Price gestured theatrically. Even in a dream, he was a bit of a hammy actor. He pointed at me. "Even you."

"I'm not dead."

"You live as the dead. But you have one chance at redemption."

Strangely—as if disappearing people and Vincent Price weren't strange enough—the folds of Price's robes shifted and a tiny face appeared. It was the Count from *Sesame Street*. "One!" he shouted. "Ah-ha-ha!"

Price shoved the Muppet back into the inner recesses of his robe. "You have one chance at life," he continued as if the interruption hadn't occurred. "But first, you must make amends."

"I've tried!" I cried out. "But Jason's dead! I can't tell him how sorry I am!"

"Make amends or you are doomed!" Vincent said. He then began turning in circles, the sand swirling about him, until he was engulfed in a tornado of dust and sand. The tornado vanished quickly, taking Price and the Count with it.

DONNY WAS obviously hungover, and he sat at the breakfast table like a rag doll. Every now and then he'd put a hand up to his head as if willing it not to explode.

"How do you like your bacon? Crispy?" I asked.

"Ouch! Yeah, but you don't have to shout about it!" Donny protested, reminding me of Vincent Price in my dream. Did Vincent represent Donny in the dream, or was it just another celebrity guest appearance in my subconscious? One can overinterpret dreams. Sometimes they're just, as Scrooge suggested, an underdone potato.

"Sorry," I said softly. I brought the skillet over to the table and used a spatula to scoop several strips of bacon onto Donny's plate next to his eggs. "Eat up. Do you have to work today?"

"Yeah, but not until two. What time is it now?"

"Just about ten."

Donny groaned and threw his head down onto the table. His hair just narrowly missed getting into his Frosted Flakes. "I'm doomed," he said, his voice muffled by the close contact with the wood. "I'll never make it by then."

"Get some food in you," I suggested. "That might help." Donny was doomed due to alcohol excess. I was doomed, according to dream Vincent Price, because I hadn't made amends. A lot of dooming going around.

Donny's head rose as if controlled by a puppet master. Taking a deep breath and squaring his shoulders, Donny picked up a spoon and dipped it into his cereal bowl. And then he froze, as if that was all the movement he had in him. "Frank, would you do me a favor and kill me? I feel like death anyway. I might as well complete the process."

I set down the skillet and ruffled his already messed-up hair. "You poor thing."

"Did I do anything stupid last night?" Donny didn't wait for a reply. "Or worse, did I vomit on anyone? I didn't, did I? Please tell me I didn't."

"You didn't, and if it helps, you weren't even the drunkest. Zach ended up passed out on the couch, and Shawn was nearly incoherent by the time we left."

Donny ate a little, chewing slowly as if his teeth hurt. "I was surprised when I woke up and you weren't there with me."

"You were taking up a lot of room. I slept in the old bedroom."

Donny raised his eyebrows. "The Jason room? Really? How did you sleep?"

"Not well." I sat down opposite him and started in on my own breakfast. "I woke up several times, thinking there was someone in the room with me."

"Maybe there was. I got up to puke at one point and might have got the room wrong. Check in the corner later to make sure there isn't a pile of sick on the carpet."

I smiled. "No, I'd have known if it was you. It was just nerves. That and the house settling."

"Any dreams?"

I nodded, my mouth full of eggs.

"Who was the celebrity in this one?" Donny was, by now, well aware of my odd dreams.

"Vincent Price."

"Old horror actor? The guy that was in *Edward Scissorhands*?"

"That's the one."

Donny stuffed some Frosted Flakes into his mouth. "And I thought I dreamed weird shit."

I pushed my plate away from me, the food only half eaten. I hadn't enjoyed sleeping in the old bedroom at all, but I had learned a few things about myself. One was that I had to let someone know about the last time I saw Jason alive, and Donny was the person I wanted to tell. I looked at my plate. Anything to avoid Donny's eyes. "I need to tell you something. Something I've never told anyone, not even Zach."

Donny set his spoon down. "Okay."

"Just before Jason left on his trip, we had this big fight. I mean, a real nasty blowout. I said a lot of things I regret." Tears came to my eyes. I let them fall. "I told him that he really needed to think about our relationship before he got back. That I wasn't sure if he really loved me." The weeping increased in intensity. I heard Donny scoot his chair back and the ticking of the clock on the wall. The room seemed so still. "I was just mad that he was always going away, you know? That he didn't have a normal job, something regular. He traveled for work, and he traveled to see his folks. It seemed he was always on the road. I just wanted him to be here, with me. Always. That's really what I was mad about. I didn't really mean...."

Donny got up and came around the table to throw his arms around me. "Hey," he said, his hangover seemingly forgotten so he could console me. "It's okay. You know he knows you weren't really mad. People say things they don't mean all the time. Jason knew that."

"I never got to tell him I was sorry," I said between racking sobs.

"You did," Donny said. "You've told him time and time again. He's heard you. Trust me, he has."

I've never wanted to believe someone more in my entire life.

"SHOPPING FOR men's clothes," Marril whined, "is so dull. Can we hit Nordstrom's now? Or, better yet, Victoria's Secret?"

"I'm not going into Victoria's Secret with you," Gene said emphatically. "Not after last time."

I had to ask. "What happened last time?"

We were in Gap Kids so that Gene could find a pair of jeans for his son. He sifted through the choices, knowing that his young offspring was a choosy little dude. "He kept holding things up and modeling them, asking what I thought. The salesgirls thought we were a couple."

"You should be so lucky," Marril cooed. "Besides, you spend more time with me than you do with wifey."

It was true. We'd all noticed that, for the last year or so, Gene had spent less and less time at home. In the last couple of weeks it had reached the point where we were sure he was making up excuses not to go home. All of us had heard countless stories of the fights, but we knew he was reluctant to leave home for good because of the kids.

Gene found a pair of pale blue carpenter jeans. "I think he'll like these."

"Great." Marril seemed exasperated. "Buy them. Then Nordstrom. And lunch at Johnny Rockets."

"You just want to eat there because of the cute guy working the counter." Gene hesitated, fingering another pair of jeans and weighing the merits of both. "You don't even like the food."

"I like it as long as I can look at him while I'm eating," Marril insisted.

Zach was over at another display, going through some shirts as if interested in buying one. Considering he had no kids to buy for, I could only conclude that his shopping instinct was so finely honed he couldn't help himself. He called over to me, "Hey, is this the Gap Donny works at?"

I straightened the stack of jeans Gene had gone through. "I believe so. He's off today, though."

"You should have asked him along, then."

My body language must have set off alarms, because Zach seemed worried.

"You two didn't have your first fight, did you?"

"No, no fight." I didn't dare look up. If Zach got a good look into my eyes, he'd know for certain that something was up. "What kind of fries do they have at this Johnny Rockets? Any good? I hate thin, stringy fries. All fry and no potato."

"I don't know," Zach said slowly. "We'll ask for a sample before we order. What's up with you and Donny?"

"Nothing." Technically true. I'd just been avoiding him for the better part of the week. After the night spent in what was now called the Jason room, I needed to reevaluate my life and decide just where Donny fit in. I was enraptured with him, perhaps even loved him, but

I wasn't sure I was ready to put him through any further heartache. And I was sure dating me wouldn't be easy for him or me.

But damn, that young man was good in bed. The night we'd spent in Chicago after the show had been magical. Donny was—what was the best way to put it?—athletic in his sexual prowess. When he'd finished with me, I'd felt drained both physically and emotionally. But happy.

The real world, however, kept getting in the way.

I'd finished his painting, and the showing at the gallery was just around the corner. I hadn't shown the picture to Donny yet, telling him I wanted to save the moment for the show. I'd also made a promise to myself that by the showing, I had to make up my mind to either dive into a Donny-and-Frank relationship with everything I had or make a clean break of it. I couldn't continue to string him—or myself—along for much longer.

Zach sauntered over to me, his eyebrow raised and radiating "Mom" vibes. "Nothing, you say," he said.

"He's been busy, I've been busy."

"Honeychild, you fuck this up, and you and I are going to have to have a serious talk."

"There's nothing to fuck up."

"Uh-huh." Zach didn't sound convinced. "You were doing so well. You were glowing like a brand-new bride with a bun in the oven. Now you're looking all glum and gloomy again. Auntie Schubert doesn't like what she sees."

"I'm fine," I said. Inwardly I sighed.

Zach fixed me with a stare for a full fifteen seconds. He then nodded at Gene and Marril. "You two go on. I want to talk with Frank. We'll meet you in Nordstrom."

Marril clapped his hands excitedly. "Yay, Nordstrom! Finally, a decent place to shop!"

He and Gene moved off toward the cash registers while I straightened shirt displays that didn't need straightening. I was aware I was receiving the brunt of Zach's patented Exasperated Stare, but I did my best to ignore it. In an offhand manner, I tried to deflect the lecture I was about to receive. "So why didn't Shawn come with us on our little shopping trip? Too busy with Bob, I suppose. Bob could have come along. We're not that scary."

It didn't work.

"For that matter, Donny could have come with us."

"He's working today."

"You just said today was his day off."

Time for Lie Number Two. "I think he's doing something with his aunt today. She needed some help around the house. They're really close, you know. She really helped him out after that mess with Kevin."

"Or maybe," Zach said slowly, "he's at home, wondering why his boyfriend is suddenly being distant with him."

"I'm not his boyfriend."

"You should be."

I left the shirts alone. You can only be just so straight. "I don't even know what that means."

"It means he loves you. I know he does. Besides, he's told me he does. And you love him. You haven't said it, not to me and I'm sure not to him, but I can see it in your eyes." Zach tilted his head in thought. "Now, there's the age difference. That could be part of the problem. But I'm guessing that's not it. I'm thinking that the problem is your obsession—and I'm not using the word lightly—with your late lover."

This time the sigh was audible. "Maybe."

"There's no maybe about it." Zach sidled up next to me and wrapped an arm around my shoulders. "Thing is, if you give up on Donny, you're going to have the same problem with the next man in your life. Until you let go of Jason, you're never going to be truly happy with someone else." He reached into his pocket and pulled out a card. Handing it to me, he said, "I think you should call her."

I looked at the name on the card. "A shrink?"

"Shrink is such a derogatory term for her profession. I prefer to think of her as a mental voodoo priestess."

What the hell. I'd thought about seeking professional help so many times in the last few years, why not take the plunge? I flicked the card with my fingers. "I'll think about it."

Zach looked to the heavens. "Hallelujah! Progress at last!" He began to lead me toward the exit. Despite the fact that we could be overheard by several clerks and shoppers, he asked loudly, "So, tell me, what's Donny like in bed? I'm betting that young 'un is a firecracker!"

I blushed but smiled. "He's good."

"Good? Honey, I bet he makes your toes curl just looking at him, lying there all naked and waiting for you...."

I'm betting Gap Kids had had few conversations quite as explicit as that one that day.

CHAPTER EIGHTEEN

"Do I lie down on the couch?" I asked.

Dr. Eleanor Brokaw smiled at me. "Not unless you feel like it. The main thing is for you to be as comfortable as possible. Why don't you sit here and we can chat. Get to know each other."

I settled into the armchair she indicated. It was comfortable enough, but I noticed the one she sat in was a little bigger and seemed more cushioned. A subtle indication that she was in charge of this session, or did she just like the green chair as opposed to the red one?

Dr. Brokaw was slightly older than myself, at a guess, and wore a smart black-and-white suit with a gold brooch over her heart. A handsome woman and one of taste, if her office furniture was anything to go by. I was facing the window and had a nice view of the downtown skyline.

She sat with her legs crossed, a notepad and pen ready on the arm of her chair. She didn't look like she was about to jot down notes about my problems as yet.

"I should tell you straight off that I've got one of your sketches. Bought it—let's see, when was it?—about ten years ago now. It's in a place of honor in the foyer of my home."

"That's very nice," I said, meaning it. "Thank you. I guess, then, that I can skip the bit where I tell you about what I do."

"We can skip it, but we may come back to it later. We may skip a lot of things and come back to them. First, tell me why you've come to see me and what you hope we can accomplish here."

"Ah," I said, suddenly embarrassed. I twiddled my thumbs. "That's a tough one."

"If it wasn't, I don't suppose we'd be sitting here like this."

"I suppose not." I took a deep breath and let it out. "Something tells me that I should have come to you several years ago."

"Let's not worry about that. You're here now."

I realized I was still twiddling my thumbs and began to make little circles with my finger on the armrest instead. I laughed mirthlessly. "I suppose you've heard just about everything in here."

"Just about."

Boy, talk about noncommittal. On the other hand, she was coming across as very nonjudgmental, which should have put my fears to rest. It didn't.

I frowned. "I really don't know how to just come out and say it."

Dr. Brokaw shrugged. "Then don't. Let's try something else. Why don't you tell me five things that make you happy. Really, really happy."

"Okay. Well, my work. Painting, especially. My friends. Zach, especially. He's a drag queen." I paused, expecting her to raise her eyebrows or at least make a notation in her little book. She did neither. "Fantine, my dog. Broadway musicals. *Les Miserables*, especially."

"I gathered that from your dog's name."

Score points for Dr. Brokaw. I pursed my lips, thinking of number five. "And... Donny."

Dr. Brokaw leaned forward. Maybe something in my body language or tone of voice gave me away. "Tell me about Donny," she said.

I smiled. "He's... something. Special. So full of life. He's funny. He could charm the diamonds off a rattlesnake. He's also twenty years younger than me."

"Is that a problem?"

"I thought at first it might be. Now I'm not so sure."

I took her through everything. Meeting Donny in the restroom at Dixon Street. Asking him to model for me. The painting. Kevin. The weekend in Chicago. I kept waiting for some sign of disapproval from Dr. Brokaw but received none. Her face remained impassive.

"He sounds wonderful," she said when I'd finished. "Your friends like him. His friends, with one exception, like you. I sense there's a barrier, though. Something that's stopping you from committing to this relationship. Is there?"

Oh, she was good. I swallowed. "Jason."

"Tell me about Jason."

It was the first time she picked up her pen and began to take notes.

"THANKS FOR doing this," I said. "Usually, if I'm going to be gone all night, Zach checks in on Fantine, but he's working."

"My pleasure," Shawn said. He was sitting on the couch, scratching Fantine behind the ears. She was loving it. "It's me that should be thanking you. This sketch is phenomenal. Bob's going to flip when he sees it."

Sometime during Shawn's birthday party, Zach and I had managed to take a picture of Shawn and his new boyfriend standing side by side, and I'd used that image to make a pen-and-ink drawing of the two of them. Shawn stopped petting Fantine to pick up the sketch from the coffee table to examine it anew.

"Maybe I should get a frame for it and present it to him on a special occasion."

I thought that with Shawn's track record of burn-and-die relationships he shouldn't wait too long, but I kept my big trap shut on the matter.

Shawn smiled as he looked at the sketch. "He reminds me of someone, but I can't put my finger on it."

"Hmm. I can't say he reminds me of anyone." I couldn't say it, because if I did I might laugh.

"Anyway," Shawn said, laying the drawing down to resume his attentions to Fantine's ears, "I don't mind hanging around here tonight. There's a movie I want to watch on cable, and Bob's away visiting his folks. Might as well be here with your dog as anywhere." He looked down at Fantine. "We'll have a good time, won't we?"

Fantine wagged her tail.

"Help yourself to whatever, of course," I said. "There's plenty of food, and I bought you a six-pack of beer." I hated beer myself.

"What's the big occasion tonight, if I may ask?"

"No big occasion."

That seemed to puzzle Shawn. "But you said you're planning on staying out all night."

"I said I *might* stay out all night. I'm being spontaneous. Sort of a homework assignment."

It hadn't really been an assignment, more a suggestion from Dr. Brokaw after several sessions, but I'd thought it a good one. I was going to remove myself from all traces of my past life for a few hours. No old, comfortable house. No paintings and photographs of Jason to remind me of what used to be. No going to the bar to hang out with Zach. One night of new experiences, with no net to catch me if I should fall.

I had to show Shawn how to use the remote control to the television—which, in his defense, really was tricky—and kissed Fantine good-bye. Out in the car, I even tuned in a local radio station rather than listening to a Broadway score. By the time I pulled out of the driveway, though, I'd turned the radio off. Some guy was wailing about his baby, baby, baby, and I instantly wanted to kill him, kill him, kill him.

"Surely there's a good station somewhere." I tried again, twisting the dial with one hand while I steered with the other. Country. Country. Talk radio. More country. Oh, classic rock. I listened to Crosby, Stills & Nash singing about Judy Collins. Much better. I even sang along. Well, on the "do-do-do-do-do-*doo*" bits. That was all I knew by heart.

I headed north, feeling good already. A light rain had fallen earlier, giving the roads a dark sheen. There was a lot of traffic, but no one cut me off or turned in front of me without using their signals, and the music kept things worry-free. The sight of me warbling and occasionally using the steering wheel as a drum set might have gotten me a few bemused looks from other drivers, but fuck 'em. Like they'd never done it.

I pulled into the parking lot of the mall and eventually found a spot not too far away from the Sears entrance. Once inside, I didn't linger too long in the department store. It didn't hold any fascination for me. Instead I made a beeline for the Gap.

Donny was there, wearing a headset and looking fairly busy. He moved about rapidly, answering questions from customers and checking on employees. Strangely, I got a feeling of pride, watching him so much in charge. I waited until he seemed to have a free moment and then sneaked up behind him.

"Excuse me, sir. I was hoping to get a little assistance."

"Yes, sir, what can I…." He turned, and his face broke into a huge grin. "I thought I recognized that voice. What are you doing here?"

"Are you saying I'm too old to shop at the Gap?"

"Heck, I'm too old to shop here."

He hovered, and it seemed to me that he wanted to kiss me but was too aware of customers and coworkers around him.

"Well, if I'm not going to buy any clothes, maybe we could do something when you get off work. Or do you have plans?"

"I do," he said. "I can cancel them, though. What did you have in mind?"

I shrugged. "I don't really care. You decide."

A gleam came to his eye. "Really? Anything I want?"

"Within reason."

"When have you ever known me to be reasonable?"

A customer came up at that moment, and Donny excused himself to help her with her question. I waited, enjoying watching him at work. He seemed so confident, so poised. He was in his element. But then, I wondered, when wasn't he? Donny was a chameleon, adapting to his circumstances.

Finished with his customer, Donny returned. "I don't get off until late, though. It'll probably be eleven thirty before I'm free."

I shrugged. "That's okay." I tried not to show my disappointment. What was I going to do with myself for four hours? "There's that pub down the road. Smitty's. Why don't we meet there about midnight?"

Donny grinned. "It's a date." He was about to say more, but someone must have said something in his headset because he put a hand to the side of his head to hear better. He listened for a moment, then said into the little microphone, "Be right there." To me he said, "Gotta go. Sorry. See you later, though."

On an impulse, he sprang forward and kissed me briefly on the lips. The action brought a slight blush to both our cheeks, and he quickly turned to attend to whatever Gap crisis was going on. Our little kiss didn't go unnoticed. Several customers and at least one coworker were staring at me. The coworker, a young girl who might have still been in high school, was having trouble hiding her pleased smile. One customer, though, an older woman with thick glasses and a disapproving glare, humphed at me.

"You're just jealous that you can't have him," I told the old bitch.

She sniffed and stalked out of the store.

I REALLY didn't want to spend hours in a pub, but I couldn't think of anything else to do. I checked out the movie theater, but there was nothing I wanted to see. I kept a sketchbook and a selection of pencils in the car, though, so I brought them in with me to prevent being bored out of my skull by the time Donny got off work.

I wasn't familiar with Smitty's Pub, but I found it suitably dark and pleasing. There were two televisions, both showing a boxing match. Nearly every table was taken, but I found a small spot back near the restrooms and settled in. A busty waitress approached and asked if I needed a menu.

"I'd just like a gin and tonic," I told her. She turned but stopped when I added, "And maybe some french fries. They're not the thin kind, are they?"

She assured me they weren't and started to leave again.

"And maybe a hamburger." I hadn't realized I was hungry.

The waitress brought out her pad and jotted down my order. "How do you want your burger?"

"Medium. Thank you."

She hesitated, perhaps afraid I wasn't really through with my requests. "Salad?" she suggested. "We've got a really nice house dressing."

"That sounds good." So much for just a gin and tonic.

I was halfway through my meal, which I ate while watching the boxing match. It was a brutal bout, and both fighters had bloodied faces by the end of the fourth round. I wasn't really interested and didn't know either fighter from Adam, but there was little else to hold my attention.

"Well, if it isn't Frank fucking Hunter!"

I turned to find Gene Ross standing over me, swaying a little. He had apparently been sitting at the bar and was on his way to the restroom when he'd spotted me. "Gene," I said, genuinely surprised, "what are you doing here?"

There are roughly a million people in the Indianapolis area, if you count suburbs like Carmel and Avon, and my list of friends and acquaintances wasn't large, so the idea of bumping into someone I knew at a bar I didn't frequent hadn't occurred to me. I certainly didn't expect to see a very drunk Gene Ross. And drunk he was, down to the slurred speech and the glassy eyes.

The restroom trip forgotten, he pulled out the other chair at my table and plopped down on it. "I'm just out having a few," he said.

"Just a few?"

"Depends on your definition." He looked about him, obviously confused. "Where's my drink?"

"Probably back at the bar, where you left it. You're not driving, I hope."

"I'm good," he insisted. "I drive better when I'm drunk than when I'm sober. Really, it's no problem."

I'd heard that one before. "Maybe I should drive you home."

Gene shook his head. "Can't go home," he muttered. "Me and the wife are fighting."

They seemed to always be fighting. "What is it this time?"

More head shaking. "Doesn't matter." He looked down at the table, and I thought for a moment he was going to burst into tears. "I love my kids. I really do. But Kathy... we never should have married."

I placed my hand on his, hoping I was providing some sort of comfort. "What seems to be the problem between you two? I mean, if you want to...."

He shrugged. "It's okay. Actually, I want to talk about it. We just don't... get along. Never have. Never will."

Well, presumably there must have been *some* time when they did, otherwise they wouldn't have married and produced three kids. There didn't seem to be any point in reminding Gene of this, though, so I stayed mum.

"You know I'm bisexual, right?" Gene said a little too loudly.

I hadn't. "Sure," I said. "Yeah. Bisexual. We all knew that."

He blinked and examined the table in front of him, perhaps wondering once again where his drink was. He shrugged again, dismissing his missing beverage. "Do you think Marril likes me?" he asked.

"I... I guess I haven't really given it much thought. You guys have always been close friends."

"Yes, but...." Gene leaned forward over the tiny table until our noses were almost touching. "Do you think he likes me, likes me?"

"I don't know." Wow. Just wow. I never saw this coming. "Are you saying that you've got a thing for Marril?"

Gene sat back glumly. "I just wish I knew how he felt about me."

Hokey smokes, was I hearing right? It made sense, though. Gene and Marril had always been close. And Gene, a straight guy spending so much time at drag shows. I should have seen this coming, but it hit me like a bolt out of the blue. Was I blind? Now little things seemed to make sense. Gene sitting just a little too close to Marril during our get-togethers. How attentive to Marril Gene had always been, making sure he was happy.

I was sure I hadn't been the only one who hadn't seen this development coming, or Zach or one of the others would surely have brought it up by now. I was the first to know. Gene had a thing for Marril. Like I said, wow.

"You need to let him know how you feel," I said gently.

"What if he doesn't feel that way about me? I'd fuck up a friendship and a marriage in one fell swoop."

"I'm sure your friendship with Marril will endure, no matter what." The marriage, however, was rocky and perhaps a foregone conclusion. The immediate problem, though, was keeping Gene from getting behind the wheel. "Come on. We'd better get you home."

"Can't go home. Kathy threw me out."

No wonder the poor sod was drunk off his ass. I got up and took him by the elbow. "You can stay at my place, then. Shawn's there, looking after Fantine."

I helped Gene get unsteadily to his feet. He grinned lopsidedly. "What, no Bob tonight? The doppelganger busy or something?"

So Zach and I hadn't been the only ones to notice. "Come on. Let's get you out of here." I could easily get Gene to my place and be back well before Donny would show up.

We made our way slowly to the door. The waitress, a worried look on her face, came rushing up. "Sir, you forgot your book and pencils."

They were still on the table with my half-eaten food. I also hadn't paid my bill. I handed her some money, way more than was necessary, and asked her if she'd watch after my belongings. "I'll be back later," I told her.

My monetary obligations taken care of, I continued to lead Gene to the door.

"Why can't love be easy?" he asked just as we got outside.

Ah, if only I knew.

CHAPTER NINETEEN

"WHERE ARE we going?" I asked.

Donny and I were in his car, a somewhat battered old Mustang that could use some exhaust work. The radio didn't work, nor did the heater. Luckily it wasn't a cool night. I had my window down just an inch or two.

He frowned. We were on I-70, just out of the downtown area. I asked my question because he seemed to be heading to my place, which he confirmed.

"I don't want to go there," I told him. "Let's go to your place. I've never been there."

Donny snorted. "There's a reason for that."

It occurred to me that I knew little to nothing about his home life, other than he lived with his aunt. "Well, we can't go to my house. Shawn is there, taking care of Fantine and a very drunk Gene."

"Huh?"

I explained the situation to Donny. "Besides, I really want to know about you, how you live."

He flashed me a questioning look. "You know I live with my aunt, right?"

"Yes. It's been mentioned." Donny was effusive in his praise for her, but he seemed reluctant to show me his place. Well, crumb. Maybe we could check into a hotel. I really didn't want to go home, not after all the trouble I'd taken to ensure I could enjoy a night away.

As I pondered hotel possibilities, Donny said, "I guess we can go to my place. Aunt Rhonda is working late tonight, so we'll have the place to ourselves."

"You're sure?"

"Yeah. It's fine. Just don't expect my room to be really clean. That's the one place I allow myself to be lazy."

Donny had to exit the highway and turn around, as Aunt Rhonda's house was on the east side of the city, near Washington Square. The neighborhood wasn't a bad one, just a little run-down. The porch of Aunt Rhonda's house sagged a little, and the driveway was in bad need of repaving, but inside it was quaint and nicely furnished. Donny seemed a little nervous showing me around, as if afraid I'd pass judgment on his living conditions. He smiled, pleased, when I complimented his aunt's tastes.

"She works pretty hard," he said with a touch of pride. "I guess I get that from her."

We watched a little TV after I nixed his suggestion of playing video games. "I'm no good at them," I told him. I had to insist that I was unteachable as well.

The show ended, and Donny picked up the remote control. "Do you want to watch something else, or we could play some cards, or...."

"You haven't shown me your bedroom."

That got me a sly smile. "I show you my bedroom and you're not getting out of it anytime soon. Just so you know."

"Okay," I said.

We were seated together on the couch, and he leaned away from me to examine my face carefully, checking to see if I was kidding him. "Really?"

"Yeah. I'd like to see it."

He was right; it was a little messy. It wasn't a large room, and most of the floor was littered with soiled laundry. As we entered, Donny picked up several pairs of socks and underwear and stashed them in the closet. "Well," he said, "this is it."

The bed was unmade, and an entertainment center dominated one wall. The shelves were crammed with video games and books, some of which had fallen onto the floor. I had to check out the books. Harry Potter, some Stephen King, and a lot of science fiction. Some of the paperbacks, especially the Stephen Kings, looked like they'd been read several times.

Donny saw my interest and said, "My favorite is still *The Shining*. That one really creeps me out."

"Me too," I admitted.

When he thought I wasn't looking, he snapped up some socks off the floor and deposited them in a drawer of an overflowing desk. When I turned around, he grinned.

"So... what to do, what to do? Hmm...."

I put my arms around him, already feeling the lust rising within me. "Shut up and kiss me," I said.

It started off as a sweet kiss but soon became more passionate, until I thought we might damage each other. Before long our clothes joined the others dotting the carpet and we fell onto the bed, entwined in each other's arms. There was a little jostling on top of the sheets, and I could tell from Donny's erection that he was as excited as I was. We kissed and fondled for what seemed ages until I couldn't take it any longer. I maneuvered him onto his back and began kissing his mouth, then his chin. I slowly made my way down to his groin.

"Dios mio!" he muttered as I slowly slid my lips around the head of his cock.

I didn't speak Spanish, but I had an idea of the meaning nonetheless.

I did my best to take him all in. It wasn't easy. Goodness knows I was out of practice, and Donny was more well-endowed than Jason or any of my previous boyfriends. He didn't seem to mind my attentions, though, and his squirming drove me crazy. Soon I was giving him head like a pro until he gently pushed my face off his genitals.

"You almost made me come," he whispered.

"That was kind of the idea."

"Yeah, but I want to come inside you."

I batted my eyes at him. "Oh, you do, do you?"

"Yeah." His voice was husky. "Please?"

I hesitated. "It's been—"

"Yeah, I know. Years. Decades, even. I'll be gentle. Promise."

Well, at least he hadn't gone on to include eons and epochs. "Okay, but I hope you have plenty of lube."

He did, of course. And he was gentle. At first, anyway.

Soon he was ramming his dick into me so hard that I was afraid the bed might collapse. We were certainly giving the springs a workout, and the headboard kept time with every thrust. Bang, bang, bang, against the wall. Donny reached a fever pitch, plowing into me with increasing force. There was a sheen of sweat on his lovely face, and even his hair was damp.

"I'm gonna come," he said between clenched teeth.

I had been waiting for him to tell me that. It only took a few strokes of my own dick to bring me to climax. I shook with pleasure as the milky semen shot onto my belly. Donny smiled as he saw me come, but the smile quickly vanished as his body quivered.

"Oh, shit!" he called out, "I'm gonna… ah! Ah! Ah!"

Sometimes you don't have to say actual words.

It felt good, though, I must say, Donny coming inside of me. I felt so close to him, so alive.

It was time. I opened my mouth, ready to tell him how I felt about him. I wanted to do it before he slid his cock out of me, while we were still joined. Before I got the words out, though, there was a knock at his bedroom door.

"Donny?" a voice asked. "You okay in there?"

"I'm fine, Aunt Rhonda!" Donny quickly pulled out of me and yanked the condom off. It joined the dirty laundry on the floor. "Don't come in—"

Too late. The door opened. "It sounds like you're having a fight in h—"

Donny cried out and yanked up as much of his sheet as he could and tried to cover us up. "Jesus Christ, Aunt Rhonda, we're fucking in here!"

Donny tried to shield me by holding part of the sheet over my naked body, but the bed wasn't large and there wasn't a lot of room. To avoid getting hit in the face by his arm, I leaned back. Unfortunately I was too close to the edge of the bed and ended up falling off, giving Aunt Rhonda a wonderful view of my naked ass. I was too busy falling to see her reaction, but I heard the gasp and something about Jesus before the door rapidly closed. We heard her moving quickly down the hall, but I couldn't tell if she was laughing or crying. Maybe both.

Donny sighed and reached down an arm to help me up. "That was Aunt Rhonda," he said.

"So I gathered."

We sat side by side on the edge of the bed. Donny still had the sheet covering his genitals. We were silent for several moments. Then Donny said, "I think you made an impression on her."

"I'm sure I did."

"In her defense, it probably did sound like we were trashing the place in here." He ran a hand over the top of the headboard. "I think we may have even made an indentation into the wall."

"Sorry about that."

He leaned his head against my shoulder. "I'm not," he said softly.

GETTING UP in the morning was an odd experience. Aunt Rhonda had breakfast ready for us when we finally crept out of Donny's room. I had hoped to avoid actually meeting her, but she wasn't about to waste the opportunity to get a better look at me.

Donny, no doubt sensing that Aunt Rhonda wanted some alone time with me, said he was going to take a quick shower. Once he was out of sight, Rhonda invited me to sit down at the kitchen table, which I did. She was a thin woman, with skin slightly darker than Donny's but with the same dark eyes and hair. Her age was hard to gauge, but at a guess I'd say she was around thirty-five. She eyed me critically over the rims of black-framed glasses as she finished setting down glasses of orange juice near each plate.

"You look younger than I thought you would," she said.

"Thank you," I said. Under my breath I muttered, "I think."

"Donny says you're in your midforties."

"Forty-five exactly."

Rhonda nearly smiled but caught it in time. She wasn't ready to let me off the hook yet.

"He's very fond of you. You know that, don't you?"

"I do."

She nodded and sat down opposite me, still fixing me with her stare. "You know that if you hurt him, I'm going to hurt you, right?"

"I have no intention of hurting him," I replied honestly.

She nodded again, and her face softened slightly. "He talks about you all the time. Says you're a big shot artist, really famous."

"He might have exaggerated just a tad."

"If Donny likes you, I like you." I was even rewarded with the thinnest of smiles.

"Thanks. That means a lot to me. Donny is—"

She wasn't finished. "Nice butt, by the way."

"Um... thanks." It almost came out as a question.

Donny arrived, his hair damp and his face shining. He gave me a peck on the cheek before sitting down himself. "So what have you two been talking about?" he asked.

Rhonda sipped her orange juice. "You. About what a little shit you are."

"Oh, that," he said, shoveling scrambled eggs into his mouth. "But you love me, though. Pass me the ketchup, will you?"

She practically threw the bottle at him before returning her attention to me. "So tell me about yourself, Frank Hunter."

"What do you want to know?"

Everything, it seemed. She gave me the third degree, which I didn't mind. She just wanted to know as much as she could about the man her nephew was seeing. By the time we'd finished breakfast, I think Aunt Rhonda had grown to like me. I certainly liked her.

"So what are you two planning to do today?" she asked when I'd finished with my biography.

"I have no plans," I said, looking at Donny to see if he had any ideas.

He was swallowing some orange juice, washing down the eggs and hash browns, and couldn't speak for a moment. He waved a hand in the air to indicate he had something definite in mind and would reveal it just as soon as the juice was down his throat.

"You free all day?" he asked me once his vocal cords were unimpaired.

"Yep."

Donny grinned. "Then tonight, we're going ghost hunting."

I blinked. I had managed to get out of the last ghost hunt due to an emergency catering assignment. I'd promised Donny I'd accompany him on the next one, but I hadn't figured on it coming up for months.

Rhonda crossed herself and said, "I hope you don't find anything. Messing with the dead is just asking for trouble. But you seem to like it, so who am I to judge."

Donny's eyes were sparkling as he beamed at me. "You don't mind staying up all night in some drafty old house, do you?"

"Not at all," I replied.

"It's the same house we were at the last time. This will be a follow-up investigation. Wait until you see this place! It's so cool. Out in the middle of nowhere, and it just *looks* haunted. We'll have a blast!"

"I'm sure we will," I said.

Hopefully with more conviction than I felt.

CHAPTER TWENTY

MOST RECENT dream (that I can remember):

I'm at my show at the Stephenson Gallery. The walls are filled with my photographs and paintings, and on the floor, spaced out so people can move around, are some of my sculptures, including *Life Is Shit*. The place is crowded with people, all dressed to the nines and drinking champagne. The room is bigger than the actual Stephenson Gallery because dreams work that way, but no one seems put out by the dimensional anomaly. Several famous people are in attendance, such as the Dowager Countess from *Downton Abbey*. She doesn't seem at all amused by the toilets. Joan Baez is in a corner, strumming her guitar and singing something in Spanish.

I'm with Donny, who looks beautiful in his tux. I'm also with Jason, who looks handsome as well, even though his pants are held up by his favorite Rasta belt and his feet are shod in black canvas sneakers. They both look proud of me and my accomplishments.

Zach is wearing a red gown and has a huge blonde Dolly Parton wig perched on top of his head. He's had a little too much to drink and is flirting with the waiters, who are all from Connie's Catering. There's a cake on a table, but strangely it's a wedding cake. The figures on top are two men, both of whom resemble Shawn Watson. Or perhaps Bob. Or both. Marril, dressed as the Mad Hatter from *Wonderland*, is serving cake to the guests.

Gene comes up, looking very cute in his formal clothes. He holds an empty plate up to Marril, but the drag queen shakes his head.

"None for you," he tells a disappointed Gene, who goes away with tears in his eyes.

"Nice party," Jason says. He's on my left. Donny's on my right. We're standing under the painting of Donny, and people are taking pictures of us. Jason's moving his upper body slightly in time to Joan's music.

I listen for a moment. It's very pretty, but of course I can't understand a word of it. It's dream Spanish anyway, undoubtedly having little to do with actual Spanish.

"What's she singing about?" I ask Donny.

Donny's smiling for the photographers. "She's singing about what a colossal ass you are."

AND DURING a recent visit with Dr. Brokaw:

"Donny believes in ghosts. He belongs to one of those ghost-hunting groups, which really is comprised of his friends, and they go out and spend a night at spooky, drafty old places and get frightened by their own shadows. It all seems a little silly, to be truthful. I mean, if there were ghosts, why doesn't everyone see them? And why aren't there ghost kitties, and ghost cows, and ghost squirrels? Why don't we hear ghostly moos coming from the fields in the dead of night?" I shrugged. "I don't believe in ghosts."

Dr. Brokaw didn't say anything, but she smiled thinly.

"What?" I asked.

"Don't you find that interesting?" she asked me.

"Which bit?"

"Your statement that you don't believe in ghosts when you're certainly haunted by one."

DONNY AND I were in a tiny little bedroom in a farmhouse a few miles outside of Lafayette. The owner, a guy named Max, had bought the place three years ago. According to him, strange things started happening the day he moved in, such as phantom footsteps and voices coming from rooms that were supposed to be empty. Things escalated from there, and he'd finally called in a couple of local ghost-hunting groups to see if they could capture "evidence" that his house was, indeed, haunted. IGAP was the fourth group he'd had in and the only one that had been invited back.

The room was nearly bare, save for a very old chest of drawers. The only light came from a candle Donny had set on top of the chest, although we were both armed with flashlights. We were sitting on the floor, our backs against the wall and our shoulders touching. The floor was slightly dusty. A small digital voice recorder was in front of us to capture any voices we couldn't hear.

A psychic had told Max that this particular bedroom was haunted by a boy named Vince, who'd died around 1910. The house itself, according to Max's research, had been built just before the Civil War, although it had been added to over the years and was now much larger than the original structure. It was now June, and the temperatures had been steadily high all week, but the room seemed chilly and downright spooky, even to an unbeliever like me.

"Vince," Donny said softly, "are you here in the room with us?"

I listened, sure that if there was a response I'd pee myself or maybe scream. Probably both. All I heard was the wind outside.

"Why would Vince talk into a digital recorder?" I asked, trying not to sound priggish. "I mean, it's not like they had devices like that in 1910."

Still in hushed tones, Donny answered, "I don't think it has anything to do with the recorder, per se. It's just that it picks up frequencies that adult ears can't hear. They've done experiments where dogs or children have heard voices and adults with them heard nothing, and then they've played the tapes and the voices were there, saying just what the kids heard. Maybe we just lose that ability as we get older."

I grunted. Sounded reasonable. "Have you ever actually seen a ghost?"

"Not yet. I've seen shadow people, black figures with no details. Just an outline, like." Donny seemed wistful. "But I will someday. Maybe tonight. This place feels very active."

We'd been "investigating" for several hours now, and nothing unexplainable had happened yet. A door had seemingly opened on its own, but there was a cat on the premises, and I was pretty sure that a quick feline had been the culprit and we were all just too slow in reacting to catch him in the act.

We were quiet for several minutes. Then Donny said, "Vince, if you want to say anything, now is your chance. We want to hear your story."

"You do," I muttered under my breath. Donny jabbed me in the ribs.

"That whisper was Frank being a butt," Donny announced to the recorder. To me, he explained, "Whenever someone says something low or whispery you've got to tag it so that when they review the tape later, they don't think it's an EVP."

Donny had already informed me that an EVP, or Electronic Voice Phenomena, was when a voice showed up on tape that wasn't heard at the time. Earlier in the evening, when we'd first arrived and were settling in, Max had played some EVPs previous teams had caught. The sound was muddy, which may have just been the speakers on his laptop, but one was startlingly clear. An investigator could clearly be heard asking if Vince was in the room. A whispering voice, which apparently wasn't heard at the time, replied, "I'm here. Where are you?" It sent chills down my spine, but I remained skeptical. After all, I hadn't been there at the time. How did I know if someone else in the room hadn't just whispered the words?

"Why don't you try asking some questions?" Donny suggested.

Ah, what to ask a ghost? I thought a moment. A demonstration would be nice. "Vince, if you're here, how about blowing out that candle?"

We watched. The candle guttered somewhat but didn't go out. A breeze could easily have caused the movement of the flame. The house was extremely drafty.

"Vince, do you have any message for us? Anything you'd like to say?" I felt a little silly, talking to the air.

The air didn't reply.

Donny asked a few more questions, then picked the recorder up off the floor and switched it off. "You're bored to tears, aren't you?"

"No," I replied honestly. "It's kind of interesting. Besides, I just enjoy sitting here with you. And I like Joy and Cora."

Donny smiled, a little sadly. "I notice you didn't say Phil."

"Phil doesn't like me."

"He's just protective of me. He wants to make sure you're not going to break my heart."

Phil had a point. I wasn't sure I could make that promise myself. I just knew I was trying my best. "Take it one step at a time," Dr. Brokaw had told me.

"When do I get to see my painting?" Donny asked, not for the first time.

"At the showing."

"So what are you working on now?"

"Something. You'll see." It was, in fact, another portrait of Donny.

Donny frowned. "Can you be more vague? Does it have anything to do with all those photos you took of me?"

It did, but I wasn't about to let the cat out of the bag. Not yet. So I lied. "Nope."

"Well, I—"

He stopped, because at that moment the candle was extinguished.

The flame just went out, as if someone had blown on it. The room was plunged into darkness, and I felt tingles run up and down my spine. I barely felt able to breathe.

"What the fuck?" I muttered.

It was like Donny and I were frozen in place. Neither of us dared to move a muscle. There had been no movement in the room, and we had heard no one moving about in the hall. There was no logical reason I could think of for the candle going out.

But out it was.

Slowly, Donny got to his feet. He walked softly over to the chest and ran a hand around the candle, feeling for a breeze. "That was weird," he concluded.

My heart was beating fast, and goose pimples rose on my arms. Weird was hardly an adequate enough word.

LATER THAT night, we switched partners. Joy and Donny went off to check out the basement, and Cora manned the "command desk," a table with a laptop showing images from the cameras they'd set up earlier, which left me to investigate the old barn with my buddy Phil.

Oh, joy.

I'd brought a light jacket and slipped it on before Phil and I headed out into the quiet night. The temperature had dipped somewhat as the sun had gone down, and the night had brought a breeze with it. It would be tragic but apt if, on a ghost hunt, I caught my death of cold. Phil, it seemed to me, was inwardly sneering at the old dude bundling up for a trip outdoors. He remained in his worn T-shirt and jeans, the brave young soul. Equipped with flashlights, recorders, EMF detectors, and God knows what else, Phil held the back door open for me, and we stepped out into the night.

It was cloudy and the moon only made rare appearances, and the air felt like rain wouldn't be out of the question later. I zipped up my jacket and made sure my flashlight worked before following Donny's friend along the path leading to the barn.

The house was old but had been renovated over the years—Max was continuing the work—but the barn, especially seeing it looming over us in the night, looked like it was about to fall apart. The red paint had faded, and there were gaps in the wooden boards where the wind could whistle through. Max had warned us earlier to be careful if we went up in the loft, as the floor wasn't in good condition and we stood the chance of falling through. I decided that going up in the loft was out of the question.

The big doors were standing open, and Phil turned on his flashlight and stood at the entrance, shining the light inside. There wasn't much to see. Some rusting old farm implements and a tractor that didn't look like it had moved since President Truman's days. Maybe it was just the decrepit nature of the rotting structure, or maybe there really was something paranormal about the place, but I got the distinct feeling that someone or something didn't want us to enter. I shivered and pulled my jacket tight across my chest.

Phil turned off his flashlight. "Donny tells me you two had quite an experience earlier."

"Yeah. The candle."

Phil eyed me carefully. "What did you think about that?"

I knew he was expecting me to scoff at the investigation, the candle incident, and ghosts in general, but if so, he was in for a surprise. "I'm honestly not sure what to think. There's no logical explanation for that candle going out. It was a small room, but even if Donny and I had huffed and puffed from where we were sitting we wouldn't have affected the flame one bit, and no one else was around."

"Donny says just a few moments before, you asked Vince to blow out the candle."

The shivers made a return engagement down my spine just thinking about it. "That's true."

"So what do you conclude?"

"I don't know. Maybe there's something to all this. The house is drafty, but it would take a good puff to have blown out that candle. I can't explain it."

Phil nodded, satisfied with my answer. He looked into the darkness of the barn. "Supposedly, a farmhand was killed in here years ago. Kicked in the head by a horse."

I liked that he had added the *supposedly* and told him so.

He chuckled and said, "Well, I believe in the paranormal, but I don't believe every story I'm told. Often when you do some research you find that it's just an urban legend, a story."

He led the way inside the barn. I flicked on my flashlight. A lot of hay, grime, dirt, and rotting boards was mostly what I saw. What I felt was harder to describe. A sense of foreboding mixed with an odd thrill, like when you've reached the top of a particularly high roller coaster and you know that, any second now, you're going to plummet. The hairs on the back of my neck were bristling, and I had the uncanny feeling that Phil and I weren't alone. I tried to tell myself that my feelings were compromised. I had heard the stories, heard that the barn was haunted, so my brain reacted and now I *felt* like spirits surrounded me.

"I think I'm spooking myself," I told Phil.

Phil turned his light beam on me, momentarily blinding me. I sensed more than saw his smile. "Easy to do. Especially in a place like this."

He did some readings with his instruments, but if he was finding anything interesting he didn't share it with me. He held what he'd told me was an EMF meter before him and slowly moved around the barn. I kept close, just because I didn't fancy being left on my own.

Still taking readings, Phil said, "Donny really likes you."

I didn't really want to discuss my relationship with him, especially as, in my mind, what with Dr. Brokaw and Jason and everything, it was a work in progress and even I didn't know exactly where I stood with Donny. So I muttered, "I've noticed. I really like him too."

Phil frowned, but I wasn't sure if it was because of what I was saying or the readings on his device.

"And you've handled yourself pretty well tonight, I must say. You've been skeptical but respectful. You haven't scoffed at everything we've done."

I played my flashlight beam into a corner. Had I heard some rustling? Were there rats out here, or a cat or something? There didn't seem to be anything there. Maybe it was the ghost of the guy that got kicked in the head. "I'm not sure how much of a skeptic I am anymore," I said.

Phil chuckled at that. "You're okay, Frank."

"Thanks. You're okay too, Phil."

"For an old dude, I mean," he said with a smile. He noticed my attention to the corner. "Did you see something?"

"Heard something. Not sure what."

We watched the spot for several moments. Nothing happened. Phil went back to checking EMF levels.

"So," he asked, "if you saw an actual apparition, a real ghost, what would you do?"

"You mean after all the blood drained from my face and my hair turned gray?"

"Yeah."

"I don't know. I think I'd be too shocked to do anything except stare at it."

Phil nodded. "If you could contact someone on the other side, ask them anything, what would you ask?"

I didn't have to think too hard about that one. "I'd ask if I was forgiven."

CHAPTER TWENTY-ONE

I DIDN'T get much sleep that night—mainly because it was nearly dawn by the time I crawled into bed—but I did have a dream.

We were in a haunted house. Not the farmhouse we'd investigated but a genuine old Victorian mansion with rotting furniture and cobwebs covering nearly everything, straight out of *Scooby-Doo*. There was a table in the dining room that had been cleaned off, though, and a board game was in progress. On one side of me was Phil, and on the other was Jason, both of them holding cards. Sitting opposite me was Elton John, who was rolling the dice.

"Seven," he said and then moved his marker. "Okay. I'm in the study. And I think it was Miss Scarlet in the study with the lead pipe."

"I'm Miss Scarlet," Jason protested.

"I know," Elton said.

Something scratched at the window. Everyone ignored it except me.

"I think someone is trying to get in," I said.

"It's just a ghost." Phil showed Elton a card from his hand, putting an end to the musician's guess.

"No, there's a face there. Can't you see it?"

"I don't see anyone," Jason said without looking up from his cards.

"I swear there's someone there, wanting to come in out of the storm."

A flash of lightning lit up the sky outside and illuminated the figure for just a moment. It was Donny.

"Isn't anyone going to let him in?" I asked. I looked at my hand. I seemed to be holding quite a lot of cards, more than were needed for a game of Clue. I put the cards face up on the table. "Gin," I announced.

Elton John smiled sadly at me. "You really need to get a clue," he said.

"WHAT HAPPENED then?" Dr. Brokaw asked.

We were in her office. She sat in the big, comfy chair, was wearing a tan outfit, and had her glasses on a chain around her neck. She wasn't taking many notes. I was in the less comfy chair, but I felt relaxed. I enjoyed the parts of the sessions when I could just tell her stories about what had gone on during the week. Less fun were the parts where she tried to get me to analyze my feelings.

"Well, we ended up the evening gathered around the dining room table, sharing our experiences. Joy, Cora, Phil, Donny, and myself. Max, the owner, had fallen asleep upstairs. The gals were excited because they caught a strange mist with their camera. We downloaded their pictures to the laptop so we could see them better."

"And?"

I shrugged. "There was certainly mist in one of the pics taken in the living room. Could have been Cora's cold breath showing up, though. It did get awfully chilly that night."

"Inside? Cold enough for someone's breath to show up? In June?"

"You sound like you believe in the paranormal."

"I don't dismiss it. I like to keep an open mind."

I was a little surprised but also pleased. It validated, at least in some way, my own changing feelings about Donny's hobby.

"Anyway," I said, "the picture was pretty interesting. On its own, it wouldn't have swayed me one way or the other, but… well, what with everything else that went on that night—the candle in particular—I'm not sure what I believe anymore."

"Sometimes a little indecision is a good thing," Dr. Brokaw said. "So did you do your homework assignment?"

"Yep." I picked up my sketchbook off the floor, where it had been leaning against my chair. There was a coffee table with a glass top between me and the doc, and I took out the five pages in question and placed them facing her on the table.

She examined them one by one. "And these are the five things most important to you? The most precious?"

I nodded. The drawings were simple because the doc hadn't wanted me to agonize and overthink my choices, and I'd waited until that morning to make the sketches. One was of Donny, although now that I was looking at it again I had gotten his eyes slightly too big and he uncannily resembled one of those big-eyed figurines. Another was of an easel, with a painting half-finished on it to represent my love of art. The next was Zach, although I drew him in drag, and if one didn't know better they'd think I'd sketched a big black woman. Fantine was the fourth image, curled up next to her favorite toy, and the last was

Jason. I'd made him a little hazy to show that it was his memory that was important to me.

"These are very good," Dr. Brokaw said.

"I did them in about a half an hour," I admitted.

"Really? I'm impressed. I myself have trouble making convincing stick figures." She sat back and fixed me with a stern look. "Now I'd like for you to put them in order. The one that makes you the happiest on this end, and then go in descending order."

I stared at her. "I can't do that."

"Sure you can. Don't overthink it. It's not diminishing the importance of the other drawings if they're not number one. Just put them in order of what brings you the most happiness."

Still I hesitated. "I'm not sure I want to."

"Of course you don't. I want you to do it just the same."

I did as she said, although the temptation to put them in the order that Dr. Brokaw would want to see was in the back of my mind. I did my best, though, to just move the pictures in descending order without analyzing too much. Donny. Fantine. Zach. Art. Jason.

Dr. Brokaw smiled gently. "I'm a little surprised but very pleased."

"You thought I'd put Jason's picture first."

She shook her head. "No, but I didn't think it would come last. I predicted second."

"It was kind of hard to place it last."

"I bet it was."

"Please God, if you ever run into Zach, don't tell him that I put the dog before him."

Chuckling, Dr. Brokaw said, "I won't. So Donny takes the prize, not art or your best friend. What do you think that says?"

I narrowed my eyes at her. "I thought you said I shouldn't overthink things."

"That was just to get them in order. Now we overthink."

"You're a tricky bitch sometimes."

She smiled. "It's my job."

I picked up the Donny drawing and looked at it. "I think that before I met Donny I was dying. I was stuck in a rut, and nothing—or so I thought—could get me out. It took someone with Donny's verve and tenacity to get me to wake up and see that life wasn't over for me. Before him I was just going through the motions."

"So in a way this drawing symbolizes not only Donny, but a reawakening."

"Yeah. Fantine is my treasure, so I put her second. She never judges. She just loves me. Zach loves me too, but he judges." I pursed my lips. "I still feel a little bad that I put the dog before him."

"I won't tell. I promise. Art comes after all those?"

"Without them, art wouldn't mean anything."

"And Jason?"

I picked up his drawing. "God knows he's still important to me, but—" I struggled to find the right words. "—maybe not like he was. I don't think I'm as obsessed with him as I used to be."

Dr. Brokaw was quiet for a moment. Then she took in a deep breath and slowly let it out, a habit she had whenever she was about to ask me to do something she knew I wouldn't like.

"If Jason were here, right here in this room right now, what would you say to him?"

"I don't know." I bit my lip in thought.

"I think you know very well. You've brooded over this for four years. You just don't want to say it aloud. Do it. Say Jason is sitting over there in that empty chair. Look him in the eyes and say what you've waited four years to say."

I turned to the chair in question, feeling slightly silly but also extremely vulnerable. "Hey there," I said. I sighed deeply and then continued. "I really miss you, but I guess you know that."

"He misses you too," Dr. Brokaw said. "Keep going."

"And I'm really sorry we had a fight before you left. I never got to tell you how sorry I was for the things I said."

"Jason, I'm sure, said some things he didn't mean as well. We're human. We say things to hurt our loved ones that we don't really mean. I'm sure Jason forgives you."

I was beginning to get emotional, and my voice cracked as I said, "Does he?"

"Of course he does."

I tried to choke back the tears. "I just wish I knew for sure."

Dr. Brokaw signaled for me to turn back to face her, which I did with a lowered head. I hated to cry in front of her, although she must have seen millions of tears fall in her office.

"What sort of person was Jason?"

The question took me by surprise, and I looked up. Damn the tears. "What? What do you mean?"

"It's a simple enough question. What kind of person was he? Manipulative bastard? Mean to dogs and children?"

"No, he was...." I felt my anger rising until I realized she was baiting me. "Yeah, I get it. Of course he would have forgiven me."

Dr. Brokaw leaned forward. "You've known that for four years. See, that's not really the problem."

"Then what is?"

She didn't answer right away. She sat back and played with her pen, hovering it over her notebook without actually having the nib make contact with the paper. "Tell me about him," she said after the silence had dragged on for nearly half a minute.

I pictured him. In my mind's eye I saw him wearing his favorite jeans, the pair that had a hole in the left knee. A beanie cap was on his head, only a tuft of his dark hair peeking out. There were dark circles under his eyes, as he often had trouble sleeping. "He was a good person on the whole. He worried too much and was always trying to push himself too far and too fast. I think he was afraid that he wasn't living up to his potential. But he loved people. Everyone brought their problems to Jason."

"Did you?"

I chuckled at the thought. "No, I think I was the one person that didn't. Jason brought his problems to me. He was everyone else's oracle, but I was his. He had a lot of friends, unlike me. And God, he could talk. Sometimes he'd be on the phone for hours with a friend that was having a bad day. But he'd talk them through it. I think everyone felt better after talking with Jason."

"He sounds like a paragon."

"Oh, he had his faults. He drank too much. I think deep down he was very hurt that his parents never accepted his being gay. He rarely talked to them, and when he did it was short and not so sweet. He'd be moody for days after that. And he was vain. I've never met anyone who was so concerned with keeping their looks. He was always asking me if he could pass for someone in their early twenties. I lied and told him yes. Well, maybe from a distance he could. Up close, though, his eyes gave him away. The young don't have that much sorrow in their eyes."

"Why sorrow?"

"Like I said, he was a worrier. He fretted over everything. Meals had to be events. Parties had to go just right. Christmas had to be old-fashioned and cheery. And he had to make my birthdays huge occasions. He was always trying to arrange a surprise party for me, but of course, when you have a surprise party every year the surprise is sort of ruined."

Dr. Brokaw nodded. "He sounds nice. I think I would have liked him."

I wiped the tears off my cheeks. "Yeah. He was a great guy."

"So we've established that he would have forgiven you. Why is there still a problem?" When a full minute had gone by and I hadn't said anything, the doc continued. "Maybe there's someone else you need to forgive."

"You mean myself."

"Bingo."

CHAPTER TWENTY-TWO

"IS THIS thing working? You know me and technology. Can you hear me? I'm bad with these things."

Zach was hosting a Southern Comfort night at Dixon Street's drag bar. He was dressed as a very nontypical Southern belle, all orange ruffles and black trim, with an enormous bustle and a hat that looked like small planes could use it as a runway. He tapped the microphone, resulting in feedback that made the entire audience wince.

He smiled. "I guess that answers my question. So how are we tonight? Are we good?"

He received a hundred answers, most of them in the affirmative. Phil sat on my right, sipping a cocktail. The previous drinks he'd downed had broken down his reserve, and he loudly announced that he was good. Donny's chair and mine were jutted against each other, making a little love seat. He was leaning against me, and I had my arms around him. He smiled at his friend's outburst.

On the other side of the table were Cora and Joy. At the end were Shawn and Bob. The table we'd claimed was really only meant for four people, but we confiscated a few extra chairs and made do. Shawn and Bob were only nominally at our table, having to reach out and stretch to get their drinks if they wanted them, but they didn't seem to mind being half in the aisle. They held hands, each dressed for the evening as a Southern gentleman, complete with frock coats and sporting drawn-on Rhett Butler mustaches. They uncannily resembled the wedding-cake grooms from my dream.

"Okay, show of hands," Zach said to the crowd. "How many *feygeles* do we have tonight?"

This was met with laughter, cheers, and quite a few raised hands.

"Good," Zach continued. "I didn't have to translate."

A woman near the stage shouted something at him that I couldn't quite catch. Neither, apparently, could Zach, but he looked at her with a mock angry glare.

"Calm down, sister. The lesbians will get their turn."

Donny shifted slightly. I kissed the top of his head, and he settled down. I smiled, as it reminded me of Fantine, who also was calmed by my kisses. Maybe I had a thing for puppies. Best not to worry about it too much. Dr. Brokaw wouldn't approve. "Sometimes," she'd told me once, "you have to go with your heart and not your head. The head's not always right."

"Okay, now how many lesbians?"

A good show of hands and more laughter. It helps when your audience is liberally laced with alcohol.

"Good," Zach said, nodding. "Now, how many transsexuals?" No hands. "Oh dear. Now we'll be criticized for not being all-inclusive. How many straighties?"

Several women raised their hands, and one table near us had several guys who were indulging their girlfriends by attending a drag show. They seemed to be having a good time and getting into the spirit of the thing. One guy was huge, well over six feet tall and broad-shouldered. His arm rarely left his girlfriend's waist, just to show any onlookers that he definitely wasn't in the market for a change. Still, he was grinning like a happy ape, so good for him.

Zach fixed his gaze on him. "Honey, put your hand down. We knew you were straight. You've got it tattooed on your forehead. I hope you like getting teased, darling, because you're going to get a lot of it tonight. Not from *moi*, of course. I'm a lady and would never stoop so low. However, I can't vouch for the rest of the girls in the show." He looked off to the wings, as if he could see the rest of the drag queens. "They're evil bitches."

"It's weird," Donny said, his voice barely audible over the crowd noise. "Seeing Zach in drag and Zach in real life. It's like they're two different people."

"In a way, they are," I replied. "Hetty Suxual is a character Zach created. Hetty is a part of Zach, but they're separate as well. We're all like that, in a way. We have many personas. I'm sure I'm not the same now as I am when I'm creating. Different mind-set."

"I dunno," Donny said. "I think I'm pretty much me all the time."

"Oh no, darling. You are legion."

Donny twisted his head to look up at me. "You called me darling."

"Yeah."

"Does that mean—?"

I stopped him with a playful smack on his arm. "Don't ruin the moment."

He grinned and returned his attention to the stage.

Zach was still getting the audience warmed up for the show. "Now I know you are sitting there all hot and ready, wanting to see us lovely ladies strutting our stuff, but I've got a few announcements first."

Someone in the crowd let out a good-natured groan.

"I know, it's a drag, isn't it?"

Now several people groaned.

"Anywho, I know my many fans will be dismayed to learn that I won't be performing on this wonderful stage next Saturday. Now, don't panic. I'll be back the week after. But next Saturday a very dear friend of mine is having a very special occasion. Some of you may be familiar with my friend, Frank Hunter, or maybe you know his artwork. Well, the Stephenson Gallery is having a showing of his work beginning next week, and though I loathe to break your hearts, I must attend to support him. The management of the bar will kill me for saying this, but I hope a lot of you will come out as well. You can always come back here afterward to get drunk and dance and sweat and take your shirts off and—"

Zach stopped to take a fan out from where he'd had it secreted in his bustle. Snapping the fan open, he waved it rapidly in front of his face. "Lawdy, I done got myself all worked up now. Where was I? Oh, yes. Frank's show. Come out and see it. You might even get some culture, looking at all them fine works of art."

There was a smattering of applause from the crowd, and Shawn leaned forward so that he could pat my back.

"I'd have Frank stand up and take a bow, but I can see he's got his lap full right now," Zach said with a mischievous smirk.

It seemed like everyone in the room turned to stare at us, and I blushed. I'm pretty sure Donny did as well. Out of the corner of my eye I caught Joy and Cora lifting their glasses to toast me.

Luckily Zach took the proverbial spotlight off me right away. "So anyway, most of the girls are going to be at the Stephenson Gallery next week, so no drag show. Instead, Dixon Street will be hosting ChiBoyz, a group of go-go boys from Chicago who'll be strutting their booties and taking off layers of clothing just for you."

This announcement was met with cheers and wolf whistles. I smiled thinly, noting that strippers got a much bigger hand than art did.

"So enough of the chat! Let's get the show rolling! Ladies, gentlemen, and those of you who have yet to make up your mind, let's give a big welcome to Madame LaFarge!"

The drag show commenced, and I must say the girls did a good job keeping up the theme of the South. We were treated to a Scarlett O'Hara belting out Helen Reddy's "I Am Woman" and a Dolly lookalike singing the songwriter's version of "I Will Always Love You." The crowd ate it up, and lots of dollar bills left the hands of the patrons and were gathered up by the ladies on stage. The big, muscle-bound straight guy tipped at least three of the performers and even slow danced a little with Dolly, much to his girlfriend's joy and amazement.

After the show concluded, the crowd thinned a little as people sought out the dance floor in the other room, which enabled us to put another table next to ours so that we weren't quite as cramped and Shawn and Bob could actually *be* at the table.

"Are you getting nervous with your show coming up?" Cora asked.

"Not really," I lied. "I've had shows before. The scariness has sort of worn off." This one, though, had an importance that loomed in my brain and made my heart, if I thought about it too much, beat a samba tune.

Donny was no longer in my lap but still sitting very close. He put a hand on mine and squeezed it a little. "I can't wait to see it. I've never been to an art show before."

"It's mostly people standing around chatting, nibbling on food, and drinking champagne. And me, running around, schmoozing people."

"He's a good schmoozer," Shawn added.

"And hopefully selling a few paintings."

"And maybe some toilets." Shawn was on his third drink, and it was beginning to show. I hoped Bob was driving.

"The toilet piece is just a conversation starter," I said for what seemed the thousandth time. "I don't expect to sell it. In fact, there won't even be a price set for it." To deflect further chat about the art show, I pointed at Donny's nearly empty glass. "Do you need another drink?"

"Yeah, but I can get it." He started to rise.

I pushed him gently back into his seat. "My treat. I need to stretch my legs, anyway."

Donny pursed his lips, inviting me to kiss him, so I did.

"Love you, Frank," he said with a cheeky grin.

Without thinking, I said, "I love you too, Jaso...."

I cut off the name, but it was too late.

The first time I told Donny I loved him and I got the name wrong. I wished I could turn back time, as Cher had sung hundreds of times out on the dance floor, or that the Earth would open and swallow me up. It seemed like everyone in the room froze and everything went silent. Everyone was certainly stunned at our table. The rest was just in my mind.

Donny, poor Donny, was pale. The hurt in his eyes made me wish I was dead.

"What the… oh, fuck," he said, getting unsteadily to his feet.

"Donny, I didn't mean…."

I was talking to his back. He was pushing his way through the crowd, dodging tables and people on his way to the door. I followed as quickly as I could. In fact I'm pretty sure that, as I rose, my chair fell over backward. I didn't care. I just had to stop Donny and apologize.

Just how I was going to do that I wasn't sure.

He was at the door and out into the main part of the bar in no time, without so much as a glance back at me. I was vaguely aware of having to push my way past several drunk college-aged boys, and I must have caused one of them to spill part of his drink down the front of his shirt.

"Hey!"

I ignored him but couldn't ignore the hand grasping my shoulder. I tried to shrug him off, but he had too good a grip on me.

"You owe me a drink, buster," he yelled at me.

I didn't have time for him. My brain wasn't functioning properly. I was just in pursuit mode. So I hauled off and punched the guy in the face.

I wasn't even aware that I'd done it until I felt the pain shoot through my hand as it made contact with his nose. Blood gushed from his nostrils immediately, running over his lips and down his chin. One of his buddies tried to clutch at me, but I ducked out of his reach and continued on to the door, shoving aside anyone unfortunate enough to get in my way.

I had one goal. Stop Donny.

I caught sight of him, heading quickly for the main exit. Fortunately for me there was a path in between me and him, and I was able to move faster. "Donny, wait!"

He ignored me. I couldn't blame him. He pushed at the door leading outside.

"Donny, come on! It's raining outside! Let's talk about this!"

People may have been staring. I can't be sure. I felt eyes on me, but I didn't care. I followed Donny out into the street.

When we'd arrived at the bar, it had been raining. Now it was a downpour. Donny seemed oblivious to the storm and walked rapidly down the sidewalk, his hands in his pockets.

"Donny! Let's talk!" I shouted. "You're getting soaking wet!" He'd ridden with me as well. Where did he think he was going? "Please!" My feet were splashing in puddles as I chased after him.

"Leave me alone!"

He sounded as if he meant it.

CHAPTER TWENTY-THREE

BEHIND ME, I heard someone shout, "Come on back, Frank! Let him go! He just needs time to himself!"

I think it was Shawn's voice, but I barely paid attention to him. It might have been true that all Donny needed was space, but he was wandering down the street in a tsunami, soaked to the skin. I could see him by the light of the street lamps, hair matted down and his clothing sodden. Mine were as well, of course, but I couldn't care less.

I had splashed in so much rainwater that even my socks were soaked. Donny was approaching the corner and paused to wait for the light to change. He was no longer moving fast, more like an automaton now, walking because his brain knew no other course. At the last moment he realized I was catching up to him and he turned. I think he intended to head down the cross street, but the fight seemed to have gone from him and he merely shuffled over to the nearest building, a brick warehouse, and stood facing the wall. He leaned his head forward so that his forehead was against the bricks.

I came to a stop and immediately tried to put my arms around him. He suddenly came to life, fighting me off.

"Leave me the fuck alone!"

We struggled a little, and I tried to hug him. He retaliated by punching me about the arms and shoulders. I knew he was crying, although it was hard to tell just what were tears and what was rain. His agonized face, though, told me everything.

Finally he ran out of steam and stopped hitting me and instead sank against my chest, his shoulders heaving from emotion.

"You fucking son of a bitch," he wailed.

"I know," I said. "I am. I'm so sorry."

He pushed me away with more strength than I thought he possessed. "Leave me alone," he pleaded. Then he turned around again, facing the wall.

I stood behind him and encircled him with my arms. This time he didn't fight me.

"Donny, I love you. I'm so sorry. I didn't mean...." Words were inadequate.

He shook his head. "It's not just that. I know you didn't mean it. But I'm just a fucking Jason replacement. I knew that, or I should have as soon as I saw that fucking room, that Jason shrine. You'll never be able to let him go, and I'll always just be the one that came after Jason."

"That's not true," I said. I turned him around, but he refused to meet my eyes. Where we were standing, we were not only getting pelted by the rain but also by the water running off the roof of the building. Not that we could get any wetter. "Look, what I said was incxcusable. I know that. And I'm not asking you to forgive what I said. It was callous and thoughtless of me. Believe me, if I could take it back, I would."

He shook his head but said nothing. He leaned back against the bricks and slowly slid down until he was sitting on the pavement, still shaking his head. "It doesn't matter," he muttered. "Nothing does."

I got down on my knees next to him. "It does. You do. You matter so much to me." I held his face in my hands. "Before you came along, I think I was dead. I'd buried myself along with Jason. Then you burst into my life and made me realize"—if he didn't look me in the eyes soon, I thought I'd die—"that I was still capable of loving someone. And that someone is you. And you're not a Jason substitute. I think part of the reason I love you so much is that you're *not* Jason. You're so different from him, and I love that difference. I'm not saying that I won't always love him, because we both know that's a lie."

Donny actually forced a smile. It wasn't much of one, but it was a start.

"And I know I've obsessed over him, but I'm working on that. And I think I'm ready to let him go. In a good way. He'll still be part of me, but it won't touch what you and I have. It will be something separate but something from the past. I want you to be my future."

His big brown eyes found mine. "I wish I could believe you," he said softly.

"You can. Come on. Let's get out of the rain and talk about this."

He showed no sign of moving. "I do love you," he said, rain and tears dripping off his chin.

"And I love you." Slowly, I got him to his feet. "What I said—I don't know. I think I was thinking about the gallery showing, and Jason was usually a part of them in the past. My brain misfired. It won't happen again."

He was standing now, but only just. It was like his legs had lost the ability to hold him erect. I was content, however, to have him lean against me.

"Give me a week to prove it to you. Be my guest at the showing. If, after that, you still have doubts about my feelings, we'll call it quits. You won't see me anymore. But I promise you that I can convince you I'm sincere."

Donny closed his eyes to blink away the tears or the rain or both. "I know you'll try," he said. "I'm just not sure you can change."

"Give me the chance."

He opened his eyes. There was a trace of the old Donny twinkle in them, telling me I had won my reprieve. "Don't let me down," he said.

"I won't. One week. You'll see."

He punched my arm, playfully this time. "You can be such an ass."

"Tell me about it."

"I couldn't take—" Words seemed to have failed him this time. He shook his head with a sad smile. "—another relationship like I had with Kevin. I can't do that again. I can't be made to feel inadequate or that I'm second best. I have to be the one you're thinking of, Frank, not Jason. And I'll give you time, but I can't give you ages to make up your mind. As the great Stevie Nicks says, stop dragging my heart around."

I chuckled at that. "I thought you only listened to Sinatra."

"Hey, I have myriad tastes, unlike some people I could mention."

"Meaning?"

"Oh, nothing, Mr. If-it's-not-from-a-Broadway-show-I-don't-know-it."

I took his hand in mine. "Shall we head back to the bar?"

He nodded and looked up at the night sky. "I think it's raining," he said jokingly.

"I hadn't noticed," I replied.

CHAPTER TWENTY-FOUR

"WELL," ZACH said philosophically, "it was going to happen sooner or later. At least it didn't happen during sex."

"It shouldn't have happened at all," I grumbled. "Honestly, you let your mind wander for a second and it picks up something from your past. Stupid mind."

Zach craned his head to see if the line was moving at all. "How long do you think we'll have to wait?"

We were at a Barnes and Noble, standing in line to get an autographed copy of *Seeing the Other Side* by Danielle Porter. The famous TV psychic was in town to tout her new book, and I thought I'd make a special gift of it to Donny. I just hadn't counted on Danielle's popularity. The line had formed over an hour ago and snaked through most of the store.

"On the other hand," Zach said, returning to the previous topic, "at least you finally told him that you loved him."

"Yeah, but does it count if you use the wrong name?"

"You've got a point there." Zach smiled. "You guys looked like drowned rats when you got back inside."

"Thanks for finding us some towels."

"Well, you were leaving puddles wherever you walked."

"Sorry about that."

"You've really got to stop apologizing. After a while it just gets annoying. Oh, I think the line is moving. Finally."

We got to shuffle forward two steps and that was it. At this pace I'd miss my gallery showing, which was still days away. "What is she doing, reading the whole book to everyone who buys one?"

The way the line twisted and turned, we couldn't even see the table where Danielle Porter was supposedly scrawling her signature in copies of her book. For all we knew, Porter hadn't even showed and some Barnes and Noble employee was seated at the table pretending to be her. I had only seen the psychic once or twice while changing channels, so a reasonable doppelganger would likely fool me.

Whatever. As long as I got a signed copy for Donny.

"Is Donny still a little on the cool side, as far as you're concerned?"

I shook my head. "I wouldn't say cool. He's… cautious. I don't think he believes I can put the past behind me."

"Yeah, odd, that," Zach said as we got to move another few inches forward. "You've certainly never given him any reason to doubt you can move on from Jason."

"Shut up. I can do it."

Zach raised an eyebrow at me. "And the Jason room?"

I looked down at my shoes. "I never said it would be easy. Give me time."

"Honeychild, I think everyone's given you time. Four and a half years is beyond giving you time. Is Dr. Brokaw helping at all?"

"She's fantastic. Thanks for suggesting her."

"It was that or watch you fuck up your relationship with Donny, and frankly I didn't want to have to pick up the pieces from that."

We were stationed in the fiction section. I plucked a copy Sylvia Plath's *The Bell Jar* off the shelf and leafed through it.

"Oh, God, don't even consider buying that," Zach groaned. "You don't need angst. You're topped up with angst. You need happy. Maybe we'll go by the humor section on the way out. You can pick up something there. A Dave Barry or something."

I returned the Plath to the shelf. "Fine. Does Stephen King have a new one out? Donny likes Stephen King."

"Stephen King *always* has a new one out," Zach replied. "And I don't think Donny is wanting a lot of presents from you to make up for your faux pas. He just wants you."

"Yeah, but I need all the points I can get."

We could now see Danielle sitting at a table stacked high with copies of her book. She was a tall, full-figured woman with a lined face and blonde hair that obviously came from a bottle. She seemed pleasant enough, smiling at everyone who passed through the line and even pausing for photographs. No wonder the wait was so long.

Eventually we got up to the table. Just in time, as Zach had begun to complain about how much his feet hurt. The woman in front of me in line walked away with her signed copy of *Seeing the Other Side*, and I stepped up and took a copy off the top of one of the stacks. Handing it to the author, I asked, "Could you sign this for Donny?"

Danielle Porter favored me with a smile that quickly died on her lips. She took the book from my hands but kept her eyes on me, her brow furrowed. "Oh, you poor dear."

"Sorry?"

"He's telling me that you've been torturing yourself. Mentally, not physically."

I'd often heard the phrase "my blood ran cold" before, but I'm not sure I had ever fully appreciated the meaning. Suddenly the room, which had been stuffy from the presence of hundreds of human beings, seemed downright cold to me, an icebox. I swallowed with difficulty.

You've seen these psychics before, I told myself. They talk in generalities and make vague predictions. She just picked up on my body language, that's all.

I couldn't shake the feeling of icicles on my spine, though.

"Who?" I asked. I meant for the sentence to be longer, but that was the only word I could get out. "What are you talking about?"

The psychic's frown deepened. "Jacob? Jason? I think his name is Jason, but it's hard to hear. There are so many voices in this room, both from the living and the dead. You did know a Jason, didn't you?"

Next to me, Zach gasped and put his hands over his mouth. "Oh, lordy, lordy," he muttered.

"Yes, I did. My lover was Jason."

There were dozens of people within earshot, both customers waiting to snap up a copy of Danielle's book and employees of the bookstore helping to keep the line moving. For me, though, there was just me and Danielle Porter.

She nodded. "He says he loves you, and that of course he forgives you. And that he's happy for you."

I felt like I could faint. I held on to the table, just in case. "I... thank you." I was going to say something else, but what could I say that would convey my feelings adequately?

Danielle seemed to change in a flash, and she opened the book and got her pen ready. "For Donny, you said?"

"That's right," I said in a low voice.

She scribbled in the book and handed it to me. As I took it, she put her hand over mine. "Bless you, honey," she said. She winked at Zach. "Or should I say 'honeychild'?"

"Oh," Zach muttered, "she's good."

I walked away from the table as if in a trance, only vaguely aware that Zach was following me. It seemed that several people were staring at me, but I couldn't have cared less. I got far enough away from the crowd and stood near the entrance to the cafe to catch my breath. I wiped a hand across my cheek and realized I was crying.

Zach put a hand on my shoulder. "You okay?"

"I'm not sure," I said. I stopped moving so suddenly that I nearly tripped over my own feet. I held a hand up and tried to gauge how badly I was shaking. On a scale of one to ten, I put it at Katharine Hepburn in *On Golden Pond*. I turned to look at Zach. "Did you put her up to that?"

"How would I do that?" Zach seemed as shocked as I was. "E-mail her and tell her to look for a tall, blond-haired dude and give him a message from beyond? Frank, she didn't even ask your name. It was like Jason was right there, talking to her. How could she have known, otherwise? That was freaky."

I had the book that Danielle had signed tucked under my arm. With trembling fingers, I opened it to read what she'd written. It was just a fairly standard autograph. To Donny—with love from Danielle Porter. No clues there. "I've got to sit down," I said.

Rather than lead me over to one of the cafe tables, Zach grabbed a chair and brought it over to me. Maybe he thought I'd never manage walking the seven steps it would have taken to get there. He was probably right. I sank into the chair, realizing that Zach was talking and probably had been all along.

"Must be real. I mean, I've never put much stock in psychics and stuff like that, but this woman is amazing. She must be like that kid in that movie, the one with Bruce Willis. You know. 'I see dead people.' They must be chattering away at her all the time. Can you imagine? Hell, now I want to get back into line and get a book for myself. She must be—"

"Zach!"

He stopped. "Yeah?"

"You're rambling."

"Sorry."

He went and got another chair and brought it over to where I was and sat down next to me. We were taking up most of the aisle, right by the local history section. No one seemed disturbed, though. Nearly everyone was either still in line for the signing or at the registers buying their books. The cafe wasn't particularly busy.

I took some deep breaths, trying to wrap my head around Danielle's words. "Do you think that I've really heard from Jason? That she really had a message from him?"

Zach shook his head slowly. "I can't think of any other explanation. It was too spot-on to be a guess." He got up quickly. "I'm getting back into line. I want to hear what she's got for me."

He dragged his chair back to its original place and told me to sit tight, that he'd be back soon. I nodded. I didn't feel like going anywhere.

I sat staring into space for I don't know how long. After a while I began to feel conspicuous, sitting in the aisle, so I moved the chair back to the cafe and sat there for a while. Business was picking up for the baristas, and the tables around me were filling up. Some of them were people who'd been through the line for Danielle, as they were excitedly leafing through copies of her book. I tried to hear if any of them had had an experience like mine, but if so they were keeping mum.

Eventually Zach returned, toting a copy of *Seeing the Other Side*. He seemed puzzled as he sat down at the table with me.

"Did she say anything to you?" I asked.

He frowned. "She just thanked me for getting her book and said she hoped I enjoyed it." He flicked the tome open to a random page. "Gotta admit, I'm a little disappointed. At the very least she could have told me I'd meet a tall, dark stranger and we'd be married within a year."

I wasn't paying much attention to what he was saying. "Take me home," I said.

"You okay? You're still a little pale. Of course, you're always pale, but right now you'd be giving Casper the ghost a run for his money. Mind you, you've got a right to be—"

I sighed so loudly he ceased jabbering. "I want to go home now," I said. "There's something I want to do."

"Do YOU think she was genuine?" Dr. Brokaw asked.

"I don't know. I really want to say yes, but then I feel like I'm giving in to the lunatic fringe or something. Next thing you know, I'll be all California, New Age-y, and burning candles at midnight and praying to Athena."

The doc allowed herself a small smile. "You may be mixing a few cultures there."

"I want to say that it was an inspired guess. The Jacob or Jason could have been a shot in the dark. After all, most people know a Jake or a Jason sometime in their lives. But it was so… exact. The forgiveness. The wishing me happiness." I shook my head. "What do you think?"

Dr. Brokaw tapped her pen against her lips as she formulated her reply. "It could have been that she read your body language. Amazing still, if that's the case. I don't dismiss the idea that she's a genuine psychic out of turn, however. I believe there's a lot about the human mind that we don't understand. Maybe hers is more finely tuned than most people's. The important thing, though, is how it makes you feel."

I bit my lip. "Relieved. A little freaked-out. Puzzled. I mean, does this mean that Jason was there at Barnes and Noble with us? Does he follow me around? Or was he just there because she was there, passing along his message? Maybe she's just a mind reader and picked up on my thoughts. I don't know."

Leaning forward, the doc tilted her head a little. I'd had enough sessions with her that I'd learned this was a habit she had when she was about to ask something she thought was important.

"And what if it was a sham? What if she just guessed, or had prior knowledge somehow?"

"I don't think it matters," I said. "Yes, it was just what I wanted—needed—to hear, but deep down, I knew it anyway. She just provided confirmation. So if it came from Jason himself, from Danielle, or from some signal I was giving her, it doesn't matter. The message is the same, no matter the source."

Dr. Brokaw seemed pleased with that response. I was glad, because I'd come to respect her opinions and thoughts, and like a dog wanting to please his master, I sought the doc's praise.

But secretly I thought that Danielle Porter was the bomb.

CHAPTER TWENTY-FIVE

"THAT POPCORN bucket is almost as big as you are," I told Donny.

"Oh, we're starting in on the short jokes now, are we?" Donny replied, the words slightly garbled by a mouth full of kernels. We had just moved away from the refreshments counter, but of course he had to sample the popcorn right away, probably to make sure they got enough buttery slime on it. "Yes, Mr. Tall Guy, I'm vertically challenged. I'm undersized. I'm concise. A succinct package, if you will."

"In a word…."

"Oh, I have to say it? Short! Satisfied?"

He'd been teasing me all the way to the movie theater, so it was nice to give him a little back.

Donny had insisted that we go somewhere and relax, since I'd been working pretty hard all week. The art show was just one day away, and being a glutton for punishment, I'd also accepted several gigs for Connie's Catering. In fact I'd spent so much time away from home that Zach had been staying there to watch over Fantine and keep an eye on the house. Donny had volunteered to house sit, but I had my reasons for choosing Zach. For one, Zach was having his place painted, having decided that maybe purple *wasn't* the best color for a living room. And I didn't think it was the right time for Donny to be spending so much time at my place.

I stopped outside auditorium seven, which was where I thought we were going, but Donny, toting the huge bucket of popcorn, a package of Twizzlers, and an enormous cup of soda, continued on. "Where are you going?" I asked.

He turned, his face a mask of innocence. "Oh, yeah. I told you we were seeing that movie, but we're not. I got us tickets for this one." He nodded at the next entrance down from us.

"A superhero movie?"

"I've heard it's gnarly! Besides, you don't need some weepy melodrama. You need action and shit exploding. Trust me." He batted his long lashes at me as he leaned in to take a sip from his soda.

I looked at the poster outside the auditorium. "*Flamethrower Two*. I haven't seen *Flamethrower One*. Maybe I won't understand the second one."

Donny rolled his eyes heavenward. "Yeah, like that matters. First movie, he learns he can shoot fire out of his fingertips. Bad guys try to take over the world, and Flamethrower stops them. It's not Citizen fucking Kane. Come on. I don't want to miss the previews."

I followed him, feigning reluctance. In reality I couldn't care less what we saw, just as long as it wasn't my own artwork hanging up at the Stephenson Gallery, which I'd had my fill of during the week. "Citizen fucking Kane?" I asked as he pushed open the double doors and led us into the darkened theater. "Sounds like a porn film I saw once."

Donny went for seats near the middle, but I opted for something a little closer. As we settled into our chairs, Donny grinned. "Yeah, I forgot. You need to be closer to the screen. Did you bring your glasses?"

"Old jokes now? We're going there?"

He twisted to give me a kiss on the cheek, nearly spilling popcorn over both of us in the process. "Short. Old. They're just words," he said. "It's what's inside that counts."

"Very true. I…." I craned my neck, trying to see a couple in one of the front rows. "Is that… I think that's Marril and Gene."

"What? Where?"

I nodded in their direction.

"Holy shit," Donny said, sitting forward. "I think you're right. Are they on a date, do you think?"

"They're leaning close together, but they could just be talking."

Donny started to rise. "I'm going to find out."

I put a restraining hand on his arm. "Are you crazy? What if it's their first date? What if they don't want us to know just yet?"

He settled back but kept his eyes on the couple. "Oh, fuck, I think they're going to kiss!"

"Don't be sil—"

Silly or not, we both watched, gaping like fools, as Marril's and Gene's lips met. A couple of teenage boys near us must have also witnessed the sight, as one gasped loudly and another tittered. I heard one of them say, "This is probably better than the movie will be."

Gene must have heard the remark, because after the lip-lock he turned his head briefly. He was smiling an apology and seemed embarrassed but unashamed. It was one of those I-know-I-shouldn't-have-done-it-in-public-but-it-was-awesome looks. His eyes didn't pass over us, but I slid down in my seat anyway.

"Why are you hiding?" Donny asked.

"I don't know. Shut up and give me some popcorn."

I munched. On the screen the previews had started, but they weren't nearly as interesting as the drama unfolding in row three. The boys sitting in our row seemed to think so too. I heard one of them say something about fags. One of his buddies punched him on the arm.

"You don't say fags, asshole. Gays. What do you think this is, the 1990s?"

I decided I liked that kid. His friend, the one with the vocabulary problem, wasn't endearing himself to me. He had pimples, anyway.

The movie started. Not that it really mattered. What did a guy wearing red tights who could throw balls of flame from his hands have on a budding new relationship?

As THE end credits rolled, Donny and I quickly made our way to the exit. Just as Donny was tossing his trash into the receptacle, we heard our names called by a familiar voice. I turned, hoping my face showed surprise.

"Marril? Gene?" I hugged them each in turn, as did Donny. "I didn't expect to see you guys here."

"You kidding?" Marril replied. "A movie where a guy wears tights? I'm into watching bulges. I'm surprised to see you here, though. I wouldn't have thought this highbrow enough for you."

"He insisted we see this," Donny said, his delivery deadpan. "I wanted to see the Meryl Streep picture."

Was it my imagination, or was Gene embarrassed at seeing us? He was hanging back slightly, as if hoping he wouldn't be noticed.

"I thought it was good," Marril said. "Not sure that it will sweep the Oscars, but it had good entertainment value. And luckily I had someone's hand to hold on to during the exciting bits." He grabbed hold of Gene's arm by way of demonstration.

"Oh, are you guys…?" I don't think I pulled off the feigned ignorance.

Gene blushed. "We're giving it a try. Don't say anything. Not just yet. I don't want it to get back to my wife. Not until things settle down a little."

Marril smiled. "What he means is, don't expect us to be registering at Macy's just yet for wedding gifts. Give it a week or so."

We offered our congratulations, and there was some awkward shuffling of the feet from Gene. It was a big step for him, and he was just coming to terms with the changes in his life. I knew the feeling.

"Hey, you guys want to grab a bite to eat?" Donny asked. "Frank and I were going to hit the Spaghetti Factory, but if you want to try somewhere else, we can."

Marril's face mirrored that of a cat that ate a canary, or was about to. "No, thanks. We thought we'd have a quiet dinner at my place. If you know what I mean."

Now Gene was definitely embarrassed. His cheeks, always rosy, were nearly glowing in the dim light.

"Okay, but I expect to see you guys at the gallery tomorrow," I said.

We hugged our good-byes. On the way out to the car, Donny observed, "They look cute together."

"I agree."

"I always wondered if there was something between the two of them. They just gave off that vibe, you know? Like the smallest of pushes and they'd be in each other's arms."

"I guess someone pushed."

"Think they'll make it work?"

I paused to get my keys out of my pocket. "I guess there are never any guarantees. But anything worth having is worth fighting for."

Donny flashed me a questioning look, probably wondering if I was still referring to Gene and Marril.

For the record, I wasn't.

DONNY DIDN'T bother to hide his disappointment when I drove him home after dinner.

"I'd thought we'd go to your place," he said, "and... you know." He made a circle with his fingers on one hand and slid the index finger of the other hand back and forth inside the hole while making squeaking noises.

"Tempting," I said, meaning it. "But tomorrow's a big day and I'd better get a lot of rest."

"We could make it a quickie."

I arched an eyebrow his way. "A quickie for you is doing it once fast and then again much, much slower, followed by at least an hour of snuggling and cuddling before you stir out of bed."

"We can skip the last bit."

"The cuddling?"

"No, me stirring out of bed. That way you won't have to drive me home."

I chuckled.

We were parked in his driveway. Through the front window of the house I could see Aunt Rhonda, where she sat either watching TV or reading a book. Every now and then she'd twist her head to check on us. Maybe she wanted to catch us necking. I felt like I was in high school again.

Reluctantly, he put a hand on the door handle. "Well, if you're sure. I guess you've got a lot on your plate right now, so I'll let you off the hook. But tomorrow—"

"Hey, I didn't say you had to rush right inside," I said, pulling him closer to me.

We kissed, just a sweet good-bye kiss at first but one that soon morphed into passion. Our tongues met, and Donny's soft sigh became a moan as his hands grasped me tighter and tighter. A red light was visible out of the corner of my eye, and I realized I was stomping intermittently on the brake pedal and the lights were reflecting in the windows of the house across the street. I removed my foot but not my tongue.

Donny kept pressing against me until my back was uncomfortably against the driver's side door. Even then it was like he was trying to crawl on top of me. His hands were on my back, my neck, rubbing my arms and chest. Mine just held his face against my own.

"Fuck, fuck, fuck," he whispered breathlessly when we came up for air. I knew without looking that he was sporting wood. I knew I was. "How big is your backseat?"

"We don't have time," I said. "Besides, your aunt can see, and probably several neighbors."

"Fuck 'em."

"Well, if you insist."

"Come inside with me, then. Aunt Rhonda won't mind. She can turn up the sound on the TV to drown out your cries of ecstasy."

"Mine? You're the noisy one!"

He began rubbing my crotch. "Come on. I want to eat you alive."

"Cannibal. Donny, really, stop. We can't. Not right now." I'm not sure if I was trying to convince him or myself.

Donny grinned and unzipped my fly. Yeah, I could have stopped him, but you can't blame the wreck on the train. Every rational part of my being told me to put an end to his groping and grinding against me, but one part of me was overriding my brain. Guess which part.

"Blow job in the front seat, then," he said.

"I don't think—"

Too late to think, anyway. He already had my cock out and was beginning to wolf it down.

"Donny, I…."

Oh, what the hell. Feeling guilty and exposed, I glanced up at the window. Aunt Rhonda was still seated, but she was craning her neck, and I could tell she was wondering why she could no longer see Donny sitting next to me.

She'd figure it out.

Donny's mouth soon made me forget Aunt Rhonda, any nosy neighbors, and the rest of the world for that matter. The entirety of existence was just us, in the front seat of my car.

Chapter Twenty-six

I WAS sitting on the bed in what had once been Jason's and my bedroom.

Fantine sat next to me on one side, Jason on the other. He was wearing a faded Def Leppard T-shirt, torn jeans, and his favorite black canvas basketball shoes. His hair was uncombed, as usual, and he smelled faintly of patchouli.

"Hey," I said.

He smiled. "Hey."

I fidgeted a little, not sure of what to do with my hands. I wanted to hold Jason, but I didn't want to mix my signals, so I settled for stroking Fantine's back. "So, we need to have a talk."

Jason nodded. "Overdue, wouldn't you say?"

"Better late than never." I looked around the room. "There's no celebrity in here. There's usually a celebrity."

"There's Fantine."

"Maybe she'll start singing 'I Dreamed a Dream.' It would be appropriate."

Jason laughed. Music to my ears. "You're avoiding the issue."

"So I am. I'm good at that."

"A master." He leaned his head against my shoulder. "I know what you need to say, in any case. I've always known."

"You probably knew before I did."

"Everyone knew before you did," he teased.

I put my hand on his cheek. It was warm. Jason had always put off a lot of body heat. He'd been great to cuddle with on chilly nights, warming me up better than any blanket ever made. "So you know there's a new guy in my life. Donny."

"Yeah. He's great. I like him."

I felt happy, but I also wanted to cry. I thought of a lyric from the musical *The Addams Family*, about being happy and sad at the same time. It hadn't been a great musical, but that song had always been special to me. "I knew you would."

"So why have you taken so long to tell me about him?"

I sighed deeply and looked at my hands, which were now in my lap. "I don't know. I couldn't give you up, I guess. I wasn't ready."

Jason's head came off my shoulder, and he ran his hand through my hair. "Idiot," he said. He was never one to mince words. "What we had won't go away just because you're starting something with someone new. A part of me will always be with you."

"Yes, but—"

"No buts. Life is full of change. Seize the moment. You have so much love within you. Share it with someone. That's how it's supposed to work."

The tears were falling fast and furious now. "I'll always love you," I said, my voice choking.

Jason kissed me lightly on the cheek. "I know. And I'll always love you." He tapped my chest. "I'll always be in here. But leave me there." He looked around the room. "Not out here." He smiled. "Now go and enjoy your life with Donny."

I smiled sadly. "You always were one smart son of a bitch. Why the fuck did you have to go and get yourself drowned?"

That made him laugh again. God, he had a great laugh. Half bark and half horse's whinny. "Just one of those things, I guess. Believe me, if I had it to do over again…."

I took his hand in mine. "Good-bye, my love."

"Good-bye."

I leaned in to kiss him, but Jason was no longer there.

I'M NOT sure if that had been a dream, a hallucination, or if it had really happened.

And in the end, it really doesn't matter.

I DON'T know how they arranged it, but they arrived en masse. Donny was the first in the door, closely followed by Zach, Marril, Gene, Shawn, and Bob. Maybe they all came in Gene's SUV, the only vehicle owned by any of us able to hold six people comfortably. That or they agreed to wait outside until everyone arrived. Whichever it was, I was extremely happy. It was fitting that they were the first people from the public to see the show, and Donny being the first one in was a special treat for me.

The show actually wasn't officially open for another half hour, but I'd made arrangements for the gang to be allowed in early. I had told Donny that he might consider wearing the outfit I'd painted him in, but he chose to wear his suit. I was glad to see he'd bought new shoes that actually fit, although it would have been a great conversation starter if he kept losing his shoes all night.

He looked like he'd spent hours to get everything just right. There was a flower in his lapel, and his hair was combed and coiffed to perfection. With his bright, eager face, his beauty eclipsed anything hanging on the gallery's walls.

Zach was stunning in his own way, wearing a dark brown tailored suit that managed to make him look muscular rather than flabby. There was a little 1940s flair to the styling, which made him look a bit like a gangster that might be going up against Humphrey Bogart or someone similar. He also seemed a fraction taller, but I think that was just the cut of the suit, as I was used to seeing the man in heels, so tall generally wasn't an issue with Zach. Maybe it was just because he stood straight, shoulders back, exuding pride from every pore.

The rest of the guys were all in black suits and looked fantastic, although I had a vision of them walking down the street wearing dark glasses and enacting a scene from *Reservoir Dogs*. I was standing and chatting with the gallery director, Sally Jones, when they entered. I tried to look cool and detached when I turned to greet them, but Donny practically running across the room to jump into my arms ruined any chance I might have had at attempting a blasé attitude.

I kissed him, and we untangled. I caught Sally trying to hide her bemused smile. Everyone gave me a hug in congratulations in turn, and I noticed how my friends' eyes couldn't keep still. They were looking at the walls, at the sculptures on pedestals, and at the larger pieces spaced about the room.

"Where are the toilets?" Marril asked. "I was looking forward to the toilets."

"I talked him out of them," Sally said. "I didn't think he needed a gimmick to get people interested in his art. Let the work speak for itself."

In actuality, it hadn't taken much for Sally to convince me that *Life is Shit*—the infamous toilet display—was a bad idea. My mind-set was no longer on trials and tribulations. Now it was on life and all its joys.

"Where am I?" Donny's eyes were searching everywhere. "That's the one I'm dying to see."

I led the group over to the far wall, where Donny's painting was hanging, covered by a red curtain. A tug on a gold cord would reveal the painting itself. "It's in a place of honor. Ready to see it?"

"I'm gonna pee myself if you don't pull that cord soon," Donny informed me.

With a flourish, I unveiled the picture. "It's called *Donny*. Seemed appropriate."

There was silence as the curtain parted. There are times when you create something and you think it's good and hope everyone else thinks so too. With this painting, though, I *knew* it was good. I felt pride swelling in my breast as my friends gaped at my work, openmouthed.

"Wow," Donny muttered. "I'm art."

I put my arm around his shoulders. "You always were, my love."

The far background of the painting was all black, as if Donny was bursting out of the inky black nothingness of space. He could have been transported into the alley depicted, or maybe he'd always been there but had been muted. The painting, though, showed him not only coming to life in an explosion of exuberance and joy but *creating* life as well. That's what it said to me, anyway. His arms were outstretched, as if to say, "Here I am! Just try and stop me, world!" Fire and destruction were behind him, but he was rising above the explosion.

I don't know if I really knew what I was painting when I'd started. Sometimes your mind knows more than you do, if that makes any sense. Something within me knew what I wanted to convey, even if the conscious me wasn't aware of it.

"Oh my God," Zach said. "It's marvelous! The way his hair is flying around his face, the sheer joy of it… I don't know what to say."

"That's the best compliment I think an artist can get," I said.

"He looks younger in the painting," Gene said, "but older at the same time. It's weird, but in a good way."

"Well, I don't know much about art," Bob said, "but I like it."

Someone always has to say that at an art show.

THE NIGHT went by quickly for me, a whirlwind of people, champagne, and hors d'oeuvres. I shook hands, kissed people, and received hugs.

Donny rarely left my side and took pride in personally showing off his painting. People I hadn't seen in years came, and even my old art teacher from high school made an appearance. Luckily she introduced herself before I had to admit I didn't recall her face, but in my defense it had been over twenty years since I'd seen her last.

It wasn't my first art show, but it was the first in years, and I'd forgotten how tiring they were. You smile and schmooze until your lips and your schmoozer are tired as hell and your brain has long since fried. Then you just run on autopilot.

Phil, Cora, and Joy came. They gushed over Donny and his painting and seemed to like everything else as well. Phil found several paintings that were "Awesome!" and noted that quite a few of them were getting little notices up next to them, informing everyone that they had been sold.

"You must be making a fortune tonight!" he said, downing his fourth glass of champagne.

I couldn't deny it, but I've never tried to pay attention to how many works get sold during a show. You don't want to jinx things. And fortune is a relative term.

Sally obviously agreed with Phil. She came over to me at one point and announced that "we" were a success. Donny kissed me in celebration. That kiss meant more to me than all the sales that night.

Even Aunt Rhonda made an appearance. She cried when she saw *Donny*, proclaiming it to be, "Perfection! Perfection! The most beautiful thing I've ever seen!" She cried first on my shoulder and then her nephew's.

Adoration, especially so much of it, can be emotionally draining. While Donny showed his aunt around the room, I took the opportunity to grab another glass of champagne and a couple of nibbles from one of the cater waiters and tried to hide myself in a corner, somewhat shielded by a potted plant. Near me was a landscape I'd done of the Indianapolis skyline. I noticed it didn't have a sold sticker by it. I blamed the skyline.

I wasn't there long before Gene joined me. I didn't see Marril anywhere, so maybe he had gone to the restroom. Gene held a little plate loaded with hors d'oeuvres, and he talked around his chewing.

"Good crowd," he said.

I agreed.

He nodded toward *Donny*. There was a gaggle of people standing before it, one of whom I recognized as a reporter from the *Indianapolis*

Star. "I notice that one hasn't sold, although it seems to be the most popular piece in the room. Besides Donny himself, of course."

I smiled as I saw Donny across the room, surrounded by his friends and a few others. If I had to guess, they were talking about his posing for the painting. Donny was laughing and talking, enjoying being the center of attention. He looked like a grown-up and a kid simultaneously.

"It was sold before the show," I explained to Gene.

"I'm not surprised. It really is fantastic."

"Thank you." I was weary of talking about art. "How are things going with you and Marril?"

Gene grinned shyly. "Going well. Seems he's always had a thing for me as well. I guess we were waiting for each other." He swallowed another crab cake and then said, in a low, confidential tone, "My wife's filing for divorce."

"How do you feel about that?"

"Relieved. Sad. Mostly it's the kids, you know. I won't get to see them as often."

"It'll work out. Things usually do."

At least that's what we hope for.

CHAPTER TWENTY-SEVEN

DONNY WAS tipsy but not drunk. Most of his high came from the euphoria of the show.

"That was so much fun," he said as soon as we were in the house. "You should have shows more often."

His tie was off and his collar loosened even before we hit the staircase. As we'd driven to my place, he'd stated that he was "exhausted" and that he hadn't been so tired in years, but he seemed full of pep, and he took off his suit jacket and draped it over the newel at the bottom of the steps.

He was talking a mile a minute. "Where's Fantine? Usually she's all barky and greeting us at the door and—"

"She's in her kennel in the kitchen. She'll be okay for now. I'll check on her later."

Satisfied that the dog wasn't pining away, Donny went on. "That lady, Sally I think her name was, said it was one of the best shows they'd had in decades."

Donny was exaggerating. I'd been with him when she made her pronouncement, and she'd said "so far this year," not decades.

"And even Phil said that, if he could have afforded it, he'd have bought that one of the man with the dog. I sort of like that one myself. And Phil's really hard to please, so that's a hell of a compliment."

He was halfway up the stairs, and I had to reach out and hook my finger around one of the belt loops on his pants to stop him. Donny paused, midclimb, to turn to see what I wanted.

"Just wanted a kiss," I said. Well, that and some surcease from his chatter.

As he was a step ahead of me, we were fairly level, and for once he didn't have to lean up to reach my lips. While we were kissing, I loosened my own tie and took off my jacket. I tried to hang it over the handrail, but it rolled off and fell down into the hall. Oh well.

Briefly, while our lips were still pressed together, I opened my eyes to look at his face. So beautiful. So full of life and joy. His smooth, dark-tinted skin was so flawless. I wondered what I'd done to deserve him.

The little bastard must have read my mind, because when the kiss finally ended he said, "You are so lucky I came along."

"Very true."

That twinkle in his eyes. Kills me every time.

"I'm lucky too. Goes without saying."

We continued on up the stairs. Apparently his lips had to be occupied, because the litany went on. "And Aunt Rhonda! I thought she'd never stop bawling! She must have used up a whole packet of tissues from her purse! You didn't hear it, but she said you were a really special person. Had to be, she said, to see me like you do. That painting really did something to her, I can tell you—"

He'd stopped by the bedroom door and was surprised that I'd kept moving on down the upstairs hall. "Aren't we going to bed?"

I nodded. "Yeah, but I've moved bedrooms. I'm in here now." I put my hand on the door to the old bedroom.

Donny actually gasped. "We're going to sleep...."

Finally words had failed him. "Yeah. Come and see."

I opened the door and ushered him in before me.

I could tell he was surprised. Hell, it still surprised me.

The painting of Jason over the mantelpiece was gone. The photographs and drawings were down as well. I'd left one photo of me and Jason, the one with us at King's Island, but that was the only remnant of the past. I'd put a few other paintings—small landscapes—on the walls, as well as a few framed pictures of Fantine.

Donny's eyes went everywhere. "It's... it's...."

"I know."

He went over and stood before the fireplace, looking at the blank spot on the wall. "Looks kind of bare now."

"Well, I've got an idea for that space, but I'm leaving it up to you. I thought we could put your painting up there. *Donny*. Although you may not want to be looking at yourself all the time. I mean, that space is pretty visible from our bed."

My choice of pronoun wasn't lost on him. "*Our* bed?"

"I know Aunt Rhonda would miss seeing your smiling face every day, but if you'd like—"

He blinked. "Are you asking me to move in with you?"

"Yeah, I—"

I didn't get to finish because Donny covered the few feet between us with a speed that would make a sprinter shake his head in wonder. He practically tackled me, and with him whooping and laughing, we toppled to the floor. After a little wrestling around, I ended up on my back with him on top of me, our noses touching.

"You're sure?" he asked breathlessly.

"Absolutely."

I'd have said more, but the one word was hard enough to get out as Donny smothered me with kisses on my nose, mouth, cheek, back to the mouth, other cheek, chin, mouth again, eye—closed it just in time—eyebrow, nose, mouth, and then he gently bit my neck while trying to sound like a tiger. Eventually he sat up, straddling me and holding my hands above my head.

He grinned. "I've got you pinned."

"So you do. What now? Am I supposed to give up? Say uncle?"

Donny released my hands so that he could undo the top button on my shirt. "Oh, you're going to say uncle all right."

I smirked, just to show him he wasn't the only one who could. "I have a headache."

"Take a fucking aspirin." The second button went, followed by the third.

I looked up at that gorgeous face. "Te amo mas que la vida, Donny."

"That's the worst accent I've ever heard," he said, leaning down to kiss me again. "But the intent is divine."

"Hey, I've worked all week on that!"

He rolled his eyes. "And it showed." He ran his index finger along my lower lip. "I love you more than life too, Frank."

"So I got it right?"

"Hard to tell with that pronunciation."

I'm pretty sure he was just kidding me, as I'd been coached on the phrase by one of the bartenders at Dixon Street, whose parents had been born in Mexico. I guess it didn't matter. I smiled and reached over with my right hand to pinch my left arm. "Ouch," I said.

"What did you do that for?"

"Just wanted to make sure I wasn't dreaming."

"Satisfied?" He had to scoot down to undo the rest of my buttons. He started on my belt next.

"Yeah. I should have known, anyway. I couldn't have dreamed you up."

"Are we going to chatter all night or get to the—hey. Those dressers are new. You got new furniture."

"You just now noticed?"

"I was too amazed at the walls before to take in the rest of the room."

"I thought it was best to make a fresh start." I propped myself up on my elbows and gazed into his eyes seriously. "Look, I don't know if this will work out or not. I'm not saying I'm never going to make mistakes, or every now and then pine over Jason, or what. We've got some obstacles still. The age gap, for one. What I'm saying is, I'm willing to give it my all. You've… done something to me. Woken me up, shaken me. I don't know just what, but I know that I can't imagine not having you in my life now."

He kissed me briefly. "We'll get through it. I know we will."

"I wish I had your confidence." I caressed his cheek. "And skin. Honestly, how the hell do you keep it so smooth? Do you not have to shave? Do you moisturize hourly? What?"

"It's a secret. Only Hispanics are allowed to know. Sorry. Are you comfortable down here? I mean, there's that nice, comfy bed over there. Just saying." He looked over at it. "Is the bed new too?"

I nodded. "Shall we break it in?"

"I think we should. Be a shame not to."

We broke it in. Oh, how we broke it in.

CHAPTER TWENTY-EIGHT

WE SAT, our chairs as close together as possible without actually touching. Donny's left leg had the jitters and was bouncing to beat the band. His hands were clutching the armrests tightly.

"Are you nervous, Donny?" Dr. Brokaw asked.

"Not really."

She raised an eyebrow.

"Maybe a little. I've never been to therapy before."

The doc smiled. "It's perfectly understandable to be anxious. Couple's therapy is—"

"See, it's like I was telling Frank when he suggested this," Donny blurted out.

I had warned Dr. Brokaw that once he started talking she might not get a word in edgewise.

"I'm not sure we need this. We're good. We've been living together for weeks and we've not even had our first fight yet, unless you count that time I ate the last of the Wheaties and he came down all grumpy and…."

He actually went on for several minutes, not really saying much of anything, but talking seemed to calm him down a little.

Dr. Brokaw let him run on, and when he'd finally finished, she said, "Your concerns are certainly valid. It does seem odd to seek therapy when there doesn't seem to be a problem. Our goal here is to make sure that things continue to run as smoothly as possible and not to let those little aggravations and annoyances fester and become big problems. And I'm not talking just about problems between you and Frank. Outside influences can have a bearing on your relationship as well. For instance, how do your friends feel about you and Frank being together?"

Donny fidgeted some more. "They're good. Real good. Especially Joy and Cora. They love Frank. Phil, well…. Phil's a little difficult sometimes."

"How so?"

"He can be kind of negative."

"In what way?"

Donny flashed me a quick glance, which I read as "Is she always like this?" But then he looked down at his hands and replied, "Well, he did say he didn't think Frank and I would last. The age thing. Not that he doesn't like Frank. He does. Just thinks that… you know."

"And how did that make you feel when he said that?"

Donny and I shared a smile. On the car ride downtown to see Dr. Brokaw, Donny had predicted that she'd use the phrase "how did that make you feel" at least twice. He answered her question honestly, though.

"Kind of mad. I mean, I know he's just trying to look out for me, but geesh! Give me a chance! It's like he doesn't want me to be happy."

Dr. Brokaw nodded. "Do you think he might be jealous?"

"You mean, like does he want Frank for himself?"

"Or you."

Donny's face went slack. "Oh, shit. I never thought about that. Phil having a crush on me? No. I don't think so." He thought hard about it. "At least, I'd never really considered it before. Maybe he does. I don't know."

"It could explain his feelings about you and Frank. Or it could just be concern over you dating an older man. Something to think about, anyway. I'd also like to ask you about another matter. You know, of course, that Frank has been seeing me about his grief over the death of his former lover, Jason. He's been making progress—"

"Slowly," I interjected.

The doc smiled. "I wouldn't say that. But Donny, I'd like to get your take on it. I only see Frank during my sessions with him. You see him quite a bit more. Do you feel like he's coping better?"

Donny made sure his reply was well thought out. He started to speak, stopped himself, and sat back in his chair, pensive. Finally he said, "I think I was afraid at first that I'd move in and feel like that chick in *Rebecca*. I didn't read the book or see the movie, but Frank told me about it. You know, living in the shadow of the first Mrs. de Winter, so to speak. But it hasn't worked that way. Jason hasn't come up any more than Kevin has. Kevin's my ex, in case Frank's never mentioned him. Anyway, it's been pretty normal. I have caught him looking at old photo albums and looking all sad, but—"

"Once," I said. "I was moving some stuff around, and the album was there, so of course I had to—"

"I didn't say it was a bad thing! I just hate to see you like that. But I guess it's going to happen every now and then." Donny looked at Dr. Brokaw. "I can cope with that."

"And Frank, how has Donny's presence in the house affected you?" I noted the slight censure in her tone. The doc hadn't been overjoyed when I'd told her that I was asking Donny to live with me. She thought I might be pushing things, going too fast.

I sighed and struggled with how honestly I should answer, especially with Donny sitting right there next to me. I thought it would have been a better question for one of our private sessions, but I assumed Dr. Brokaw knew what she was doing.

"Overall, it's been good. There have been a few moments when I've had to stop myself from pointing out that Donny was sitting in Jason's old chair, or that he was using the same coffee mug that Jason used—"

"That mug's that old?" Donny made a sour face. "You should have told me."

I knew he was just trying to lighten the mood, but I ignored him. Maybe the doc was right. Maybe Donny did need to know that it wasn't always easy for me. "And sometimes, when he comes in the front door after coming home from work and he calls out my name, I think immediately of Jason, because he'd do the same thing. The Ricky Ricardo 'Honey, I'm home!' It doesn't *bother* me, which kind of surprises me, but it does give me a pang. Just a mild one. And then I see Donny's face, and everything is right with the world again."

He smiled at that and reached out and grabbed my hand. It felt right, sitting there holding hands.

"Well," he said, "I won't be saying *that* again."

"No, it's okay. Things are going to remind me of him. More so at first. Over time—and I hope we're together a long, long time—even those memories will fade. Like they should. He'll never be entirely gone, but I wouldn't want him to be. But he's becoming more and more of a memory and not... I don't know how to express it exactly... real. I think it's finally hitting me that he's really dead. I mean, I knew he was. I think what I'm saying is that now I'm coming to terms with the fact."

Dr. Brokaw nodded slowly and then let out a sigh of her own. In a weird sort of way I wanted her to say that she was proud of me and how far I'd come, but she didn't. Maybe she was too cautious. And maybe she had a right to be. I was determined to prove to her that I could do this, though. I could make it work.

"I'd like for each of you to tell me something that frightens you. Your biggest fear. Pretend your partner isn't in the room, if that helps. Just honestly tell me what scares you the most." She looked at Donny first.

He bit his lip. "That's a tough one. Let's see. Spiders. Hate them, all the legs. Especially the furry ones. They're just wrong. But I wouldn't say they scare me the most."

"Take your time," Dr. Brokaw said.

"Um… well." Donny looked at me, then at the doc. "Like he's not in the room, right?"

"Right."

Donny flashed me a thin smile. "You're not here, so you have to pretend you can't hear this." He turned to Dr. Brokaw. "I'd say my greatest fear is that Frank will give up on me too soon. He'll hit a snag somewhere along the way, and rather than deal with it, he'll just give up. And he'll leave me. I couldn't bear that."

I squeezed his hand.

"Very good," Dr. Brokaw told him. "Frank?"

"I think I'm afraid that this is all a dream," I said, drawing Donny's hand close enough so that I could kiss the knuckles. "He's given me a new lease on life. Woken my sleeping demons up. And I'm afraid that someday I'll open my eyes and he won't be there any longer."

Donny grinned. That old cheeky grin. "I'm not going anywhere."

"Please don't."

And he leaned over to kiss me. When our lips met, I felt an electric jolt hit my spine, as I often did. It was a brief kiss, with Dr. Brokaw sitting there watching us, but it was a sweet one. And it spoke volumes. We were going to make it as a couple or make a damn good try at it. We'd have our ups and downs and obstacles to conquer, but we'd survive.

I knew we would.

CHAPTER TWENTY-NINE

IT WAS Christmas.

Well, technically, it was two days before Christmas, but we were having a party at our house to celebrate the season. Donny had been in the kitchen all day, cooking. Enticing smells had reached my nostrils for hours, but every time I went in to see what he was doing, he threatened to beat me with a wooden spoon and shoved me back out. Whatever he was making, it was spicy.

When he'd first moved in, I'd done the lion's share of the cooking, but apparently he found my cuisine too bland. He'd come home from a trip to Barnes and Noble loaded with cookbooks, mostly with a Mexican flair. In the months that followed he'd become quite the chef, but I was never allowed in the kitchen when he was concocting his dishes, which worried me slightly. I'm sure it was just because he was a slob at heart and he knew the sight of dirty pots and pans everywhere would drive me crazy, but I did wonder if some of his cooking techniques left something to be desired. Donny was a strong proponent of the five-second rule, and the thought of food hitting the floor and then being put back into a pan filled me with dread.

The Christmas tree had been up for over two weeks, and he'd made fun of me while we'd decorated it, asking if I needed a ruler to ensure the bulbs were just the right distance apart. I refrained from telling him that Jason had always used the same joke. Donny had to concede, though, that when finished it was one kick-ass Christmas tree.

Mistletoe had been hung in the archway leading into the living room, there was a fragrant wreath over the fireplace, and the lawn was festooned with reindeer figures, a blow-up Santa, and Snoopy on his decorated doghouse. For the occasion Fantine was wearing bells on her collar, and Donny and I donned our best—or worst—Christmas sweaters.

Knowing our guests were due to arrive at any moment, I went to the kitchen door and knocked lightly. "You nearly done in there?"

"Nearly!"

"It's just that it's about time, and I wondered if people were actually going to be able to eat anything other than pretzels and potato chips."

The door opened just a fraction. I could see one of Donny's eyes, nearly obscured by the hair falling across his forehead. "Shush," he said. "You can't rush perfection." And then he firmly closed the door.

"Perfection," I muttered to myself. "Good to know."

The doorbell rang. I left the Mexican American Gordon Ramsay to his cooking—reluctantly, as the sound of something crashing to the floor followed by Donny yelling "Shit!" came through the door—and went to answer it. It was Zach, wearing a big red overcoat with a faux-fur collar.

"It's cold out tonight," he said as he came in, stamping his feet on the mat. "Maybe we'll get some snow and have a white Christmas."

"They're calling for it," I said. Eying his coat, I added, "My aunt Myrtle had one just like that."

"Where do you think I got it, honeychild?" He sniffed the air as he took off the outer layers. "That does not smell like turkey."

"Enchiladas," I informed him.

"Not very Christmasy."

"He's serving cranberry sauce on the side."

Zach smiled and nodded. "That's all right, then. Am I the first to arrive?"

"As always."

We hadn't even made it to the living room before the doorbell chimed again. This time it was Shawn, on his own. He and Bob had split up at the end of summer, but he seemed to take the breakup well, with the help of Dr. Brokaw. It had taken a lot of persuasion to get Shawn to see her, but once he'd agreed he'd become one of her biggest fans. Hopefully there would be no more suicide scares in his future, accidental or otherwise.

Shawn had brought a bottle of wine, and he handed it to me as he took off his coat.

"I figured white would be best, as I expected turkey." His nose twitched. "Apparently not."

"Enchiladas," Zach said. "Surely you know it's the traditional Christmas fare of Cabo San Lucas."

Gene and Marril came soon after that, wearing matching Rudolph the Red-Nosed Reindeer sweaters. They were now living together, and Gene often said it was due to Donny that he mustered the courage to make changes in his life. "That little bugger is just so full of life, he makes you want to live yours to the fullest," he'd said on more than one occasion.

Amen to that.

Donny's friends were the last to arrive. Joy had tiny candy canes dangling from her ears, and Cora's green pants and red top made her look like some sort of weird elf. Phil was dressed more conservatively, the only concession to the season being a Santa hat perched on his head. I got everyone settled into the living room and enjoying some libations and nibbles before heading for the kitchen.

I knocked again. "Everyone's here."

Donny sounded slightly frustrated. "Yeah. Great." Something clattered, maybe some silverware falling to the floor. "Entertain them. It'll be about five minutes more."

"Real five minutes or Donny five minutes?"

"I'll let you know."

I could hear Fantine padding around the kitchen restlessly. I hoped he wasn't testing out his cooking by having her sample it. She didn't need any spicy food. I heard Donny mutter a few expletives.

"Donny, it's just our friends. We don't care if everything is perfect."

"Yeah. Sure. Five minutes."

It was closer to fifteen, but no one seemed to care. Once Donny announced that the food was prepared, we adjourned to the dining room and took our seats.

The food was divine, and he really did have cranberry sauce. I had actually been kidding, but maybe he overheard me and felt he had to oblige.

Whenever anyone complimented the food, Donny blushed. He sat at one end of the table, I at the other, because he said that was the proper way to do it. I watched him drink some wine, his cheeks flushed from praise given by Marril, and thought I couldn't hope for a more loving, adorable companion. I loved him unequivocally.

In fact, I was so engrossed in gazing fondly at my lover that I missed something Cora said to me.

"I'm sorry," I said. "What was that?"

"I was saying that Christmas was a good time for ghosts and ghost stories." She paused to swallow some wine. "Although Shawn seems to feel that's silly."

"I didn't say it was silly," Shawn protested. "I just said that I didn't believe in ghosts. But ghosts and Christmas obviously go together.

Dickens and all that. The ghost of Christmas past, present, and future. But they're just stories."

"Are they?" Joy asked with a sly smile. "There are lots of ghostly legends associated with Christmas. They must have *some* basis, having stuck around for so many years."

"Well, that doesn't necessarily follow," Shawn grumbled to himself.

Gene sniffed and patted his lips with a napkin before entering the conversation. "Aren't you confusing Christmas with Halloween? That's the time for ghosts."

"If you think about it," Donny said, "Christmas is a time to celebrate not only the present but the past. Don't you give a few minutes each Christmas thinking about those you've lost over the years? Ghosts might be drawn to that energy."

Shawn frowned. "Are we talking actual ghosts here, or just memories?" He narrowed his eyes at Donny. "And how many people could you possibly have lost over the years? What are you, twelve?"

Ah, I preferred the days when Shawn was with Bob. He'd been definitely less snarky then.

"But even if you don't believe, the legends can be fun," Cora said. "There's a story I heard once, that if you look out the window and down the garden path at midnight on Christmas Eve, you get to see the faces of those that love you the most in your life."

"Sounds very Victorian," Marril said.

Phil seemed dubious. "I've never heard that legend. Are you just making it up?"

"Read it in a book. An old one," Cora said, as if the age of the tome gave it veracity.

"Who has a garden path these days?" Zach asked.

I blinked. "We do."

Donny smiled. "That's right. There's that little footpath out back. And if you look out the kitchen window, you've got a perfect view."

"I guess I know where I'll be at midnight on Christmas," I joked.

Or was it really a joke?

I WAS sure Donny had forgotten about the legend, but I certainly hadn't. So on Christmas Eve I waited until nearly midnight to volunteer to wash the days' dishes. I didn't really expect anything to happen, but you never know.

We'd spent the evening listening to music, holiday albums from Barbra, Frank, and Andy Williams, and watching Alastair Sim as Ebenezer Scrooge while downing eggnog, which Donny insisted was an integral part of viewing *A Christmas Carol*. I left him and Fantine on the couch in the living room, both of them nearly asleep.

I was washing a glass at midnight, and feeling slightly silly, I gazed out the back window. There was too much light in the kitchen to really see outside, so I flicked the light switch.

A dusting of snow had fallen, and it gleamed and sparkled on the grass and bushes. Straining my eyes, I could make out the little footpath. There was no movement anywhere, of course. How absurd to think there could be—

At the end of the path. Was that a figure? Someone tall, someone....

He was walking away from the house, but before he disappeared from view he turned so I could see his face. I couldn't forget that face if I lived to be a thousand. Those eyes. Hell, he was even wearing that idiotic belt.

Jason.

He smiled, gave a little wave, and then promptly vanished.

I don't know how long I stood there, in a darkened kitchen, staring out of a window at nothing. Eventually I realized I still had a soapy glass in my hands. I shook my head, dismissing what I'd seen. Daydreams, that's all.

I looked up, and there were other faces reflected in the window. I gasped but quickly realized it was Donny's face. He'd come into the kitchen so quietly that I hadn't heard his approach. He was holding Fantine in his arms, and I could see both of their faces clearly in the glass. Donny's smile was a tired but happy one.

"Why are you in the d— Oh." He put Fantine down and came up behind me and encircled me with his arms. "See your loved ones?"

"Yeah," I chuckled. "You and Fantine."

"See? Some legends do come true."

"They do indeed."

"Were you really washing dishes in the dark?"

I flicked the lights back on. "No, I just switched them off to see if Cora's story had any veracity."

He kissed the back of my neck. "Coming to bed? We've got to get up early tomorrow. We've got to unwrap presents early so that we can head out to Aunt Rhonda's for lunch and then hit Kokomo to see your parents for dinner."

"You go on up," I told him. "I'll finish here and be up in five minutes."

"Real minutes or Frank minutes?"

I turned and kissed his forehead. "Real ones. Now get going."

He kissed me on the lips. "Merry Christmas, Frank."

"Merry Christmas."

He and Fantine left, and I turned the water back on to rinse off the glass. I glanced out the window. There wasn't much of a moon, so there was little to see. I squinted. No, no movement. No one out there.

Just the way it should be.

STEPHEN OSBORNE lives in rural Illinois with Christine, a Border terrier mix with a diva complex. In addition to writing, seeing musicals in Chicago, and losing at Monopoly, Stephen sometimes spends cold, shivery nights in haunted locations—just because he likes to.

Facebook: www.facebook.com/stephen.osborne2
Twitter: @southbendghosts
E-mail: leftyIN@yahoo.com

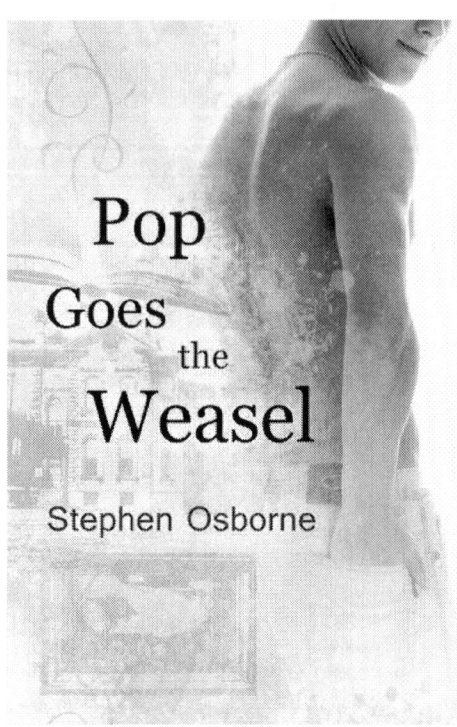

Pop
Goes
the
Weasel

Stephen Osborne

Patrick Weasley, aka Weasel, is a fun-loving college student with a wealthy homophobic jerk stepfather and a best friend, Jake Winston, who's just as gay as Weasel. When Jake's aunt dies, many from the publishing world—including Jasper, Weasel's weasel of a stepfather—gather at Winston Manor for the reading of the will, and Weasel is obligated to tag along.

Turns out all he has to do is three things: 1) swap the wills so Jake's uncle inherits the house instead of the gardener, who's also an old enemy of Weasel's; 2) secure a publishing contract from author Cecily Talbot; and 3) hook Jake up with his deceased aunt's male nurse. But what he ends up doing is 1) falling for Tony, one of the food servers; 2) accidentally affiancing himself to Cecily; and 3) fighting with Jake, who thinks he was making a play for the nurse.

To make matters worse, every time Weasel and Tony start to get intimate, Jasper is right around the corner. So when burglars come to steal a valuable piece of art, Weasel must 1) use all his ingenuity to keep the painting safe; 2) dis-engage himself from Cecily; 3) unite Jake with the nurse; and most importantly, 4) pursue Tony to an elusive happy ending.

www.dreamspinnerpress.com

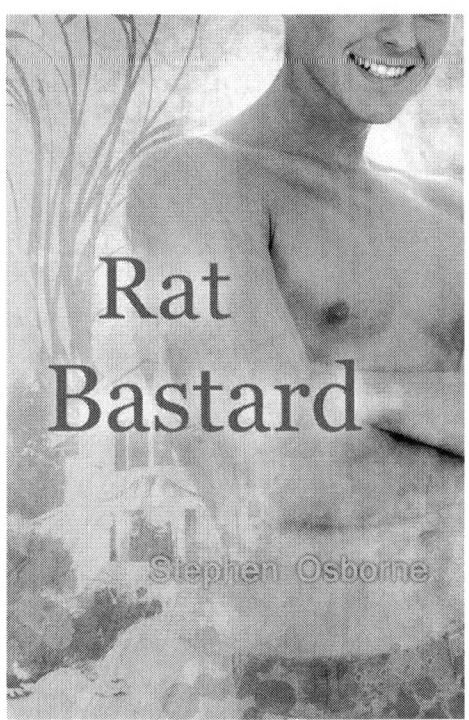

Rat Bastard

Stephen Osborne

Sequel to Pop Goes the Weasel

Patrick "Weasel" Weasley is worried he's not spending enough time with his new boyfriend Tony, now that they are living and working in different towns. He decides the best way to cement the relationship is to buy Tony a ring for Christmas. Unfortunately, Weasel's evil stepfather—a rat bastard if ever there was one—has cut him off without a cent, and he is left with no other choice. He must (gasp!) get a job!

Weasel wouldn't mind working at the Phantom Lady Inn if it wasn't for Tony's ex-boyfriend Gates Stumpenhorst, who wants to beat the stuffing out of him, or Cicely Talbot, a writer who believes she can prove to Weasel that he's not really gay. As if that wasn't enough, the deputy sheriff thinks Weasel is the local arsonist. Adding to their troubles is a rumored Phantom Lady haunting the inn and pilfering trinkets. With all this going on, Weasel might not live to survive Christmas, much less find time to go on a date with Tony!

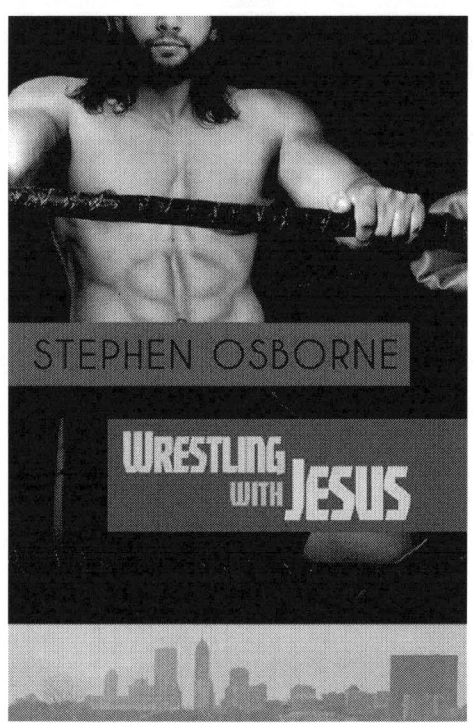

Bookstore owner Randy Stone is smitten. His new boyfriend, Kyle Temple, is sweet, hot, attentive, and great in bed. But introducing Kyle to his family takes courage, because Randy's parents can be a little judgmental, and Kyle is ten years younger than Randy, a small-time pro wrestler, and dumber than the proverbial sack of hammers. Needless to say, Randy's parents aren't exactly thrilled, and even his best friend is skeptical.

Despite the challenges, Randy is determined to tough it out for Kyle. After all, enduring a few scornful comments from his mother is nothing compared to what Kyle's going through trying to quit smoking for Randy. When a hypnotherapy session designed to help with Kyle's cravings leaves him quoting Jesus Christ—in Aramaic—Randy's parents are suddenly the least of their problems. Once word gets out, their privacy is destroyed. News crews follow them everywhere, and everyone who knows Kyle seems determined to make a buck. It's a mess that could make Kyle's dreams of wrestling in the UWE come true—but what about his dream of being with Randy?

www.dreamspinnerpress.com

Private detective Duncan Andrews's best friend Gina is a witch. His dog is a zombie. And his dead boyfriend, Robbie, is a ghost. So it's hardly any wonder that he uses his connection to the supernatural to help him solve cases. Good thing, too, because Duncan has his hands full. Janice Sanderson, the richest woman in Indianapolis, wants him to find her stripper daughter, Brenda, and another client is having some trouble with a specter haunting her family home. On top of that, Duncan has decided to add dating into the mix, though after Robbie's death, he's not sure he's ready.

When Duncan meets Nick while tracking down a lead on Brenda's boyfriend, he shelves his doubts and agrees to a date. Robbie doesn't make it easy on him, showing up to spoil his chances, but that is the least of Duncan's worries—because one of his clients' husbands is missing and there's a serial killer on the loose—one Duncan fears isn't human.

www.dreamspinnerpress.com

Sequel to *Pale as a Ghost*
A Duncan Andrews Thriller

Private detective Duncan Andrews has the home-team advantage when it comes to solving paranormal crimes: His best friend, Gina, is a centuries-old witch. His dog is a zombie. And his boyfriend, Robbie, is a ghost.

Duncan certainly has his work cut out for him with this case. Someone's been using the skull of a powerful wizard to control animals, and whoever it is, they're not out to set up a petting zoo. For Gina, the case hits close to home—she knows just how dangerous it is, since the wizard was her father.

Just when he thinks they're close to breaking the case, tragedy strikes, leaving Gina in a coma. Then, after years as a ghost, Robbie finally decides to move on, leaving Duncan to protect young Ashton Marsh, the victim of several strange animal attacks. Suddenly Duncan is working without his supernatural safety net. Without his friends, can Duncan defeat the power of Eleazar's skull and keep Ashton alive? Or will the struggle for his life end in broken bodies as well as broken hearts?

www.dreamspinnerpress.com

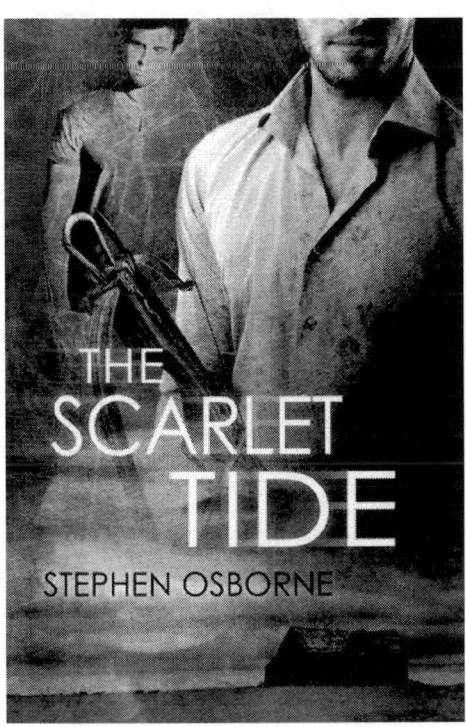

Sequel to *Animal Instinct*
A Duncan Andrews Thriller

Duncan Andrews, a private detective who specializes in paranormal cases, is back, along with his usual gang. Robbie Church, his boyfriend, is a ghost. Gina, a centuries old witch, is his best friend. And Daisy, Duncan's bulldog, just happens to be a zombie. Odd man out seems to be Nick, a history teacher. He's a normal, living human.

Duncan's latest case leads him to a rock band in Indianapolis called The Scarlet Tide. It doesn't take Duncan long to realize all of the band members are vampires. He sets out to destroy them, but runs into trouble with the charismatic leader of the band, Dominic Hunt. Duncan ends up under Hunt's psychic control, and is forced to examine his relationships with Robbie and Nick, as well as his attraction for Hunt. Can Robbie and Gina help Duncan break Hunt's psychic grip? Is there any hope the vampire can be destroyed once and for all?

www.dreamspinnerpress.com

Sequel to *The Scarlet Tide*
A Duncan Andrews Thriller

Duncan Andrews's best friend Gina is a witch, his bulldog Daisy is a zombie, and his boyfriend Robbie is a ghost. Duncan himself is just your average private detective, who happens to specialize in paranormal cases.

Robbie's cousin, Jason, has a problem. The house he's living in is haunted by the ghost of serial killer Dr. Stanley Moore. Duncan thinks banishing the spirit will be an easy task, but when confronted, the ghost nearly kills Duncan.

If that's not bad enough, a witch-hunting group called the Order of Cotton Mather have tracked Gina down and are bent on destroying her. And Robbie and Duncan's relationship may be nearing an end, as Robbie feels he's holding Duncan back from having a lover he can actually touch.

Duncan must rid Jason's house of the evil Dr. Moore, save Gina, and somehow manage to hold onto Robbie in the process.

www.dreamspinnerpress.com

Also from Dreamspinner Press

BEYOND   BSESSION

JohnSIMPSON RobertCUMMINGS

www.dreamspinnerpress.com

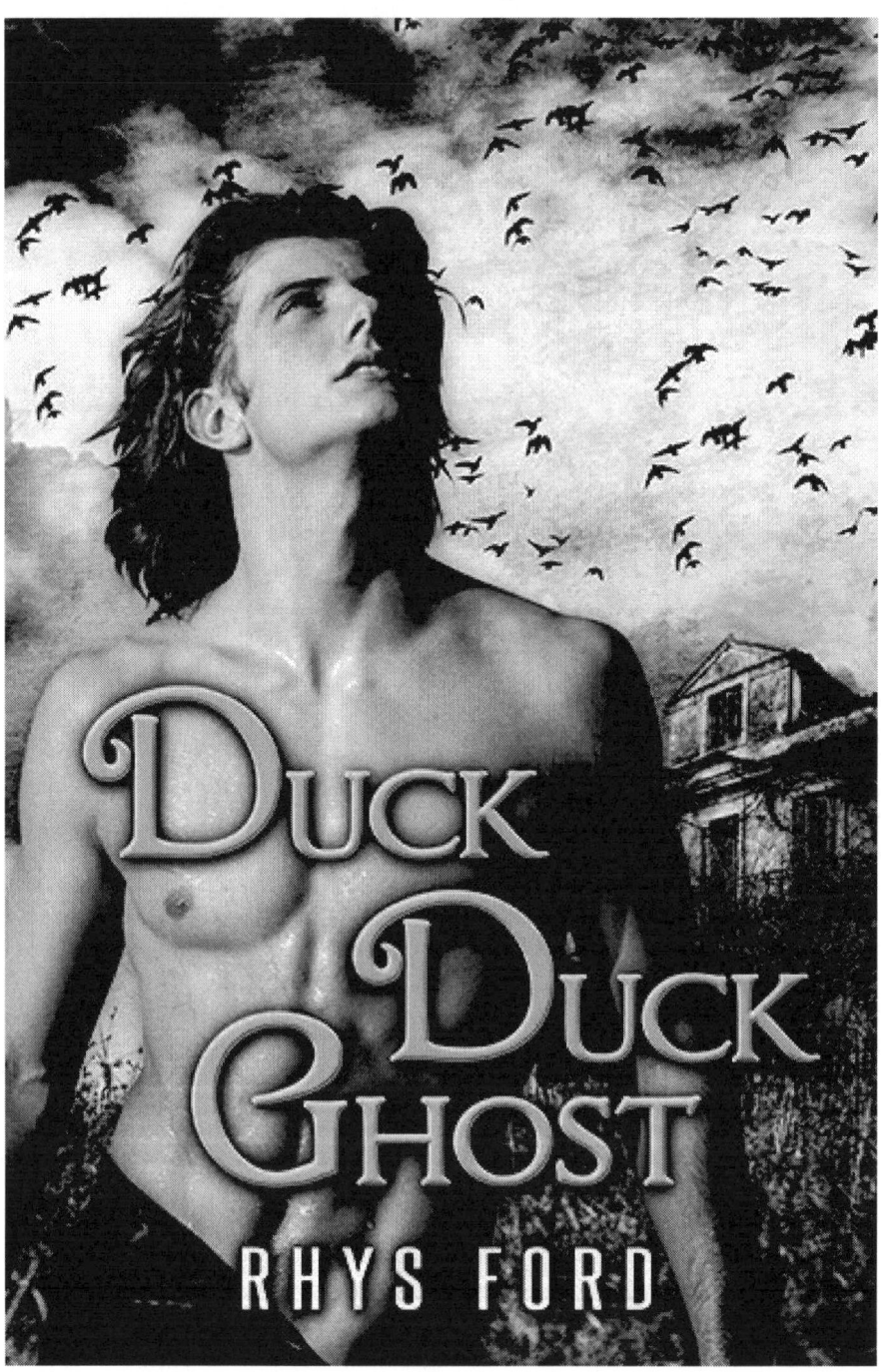

Also from Dreamspinner Press

Also from Dreamspinner Press

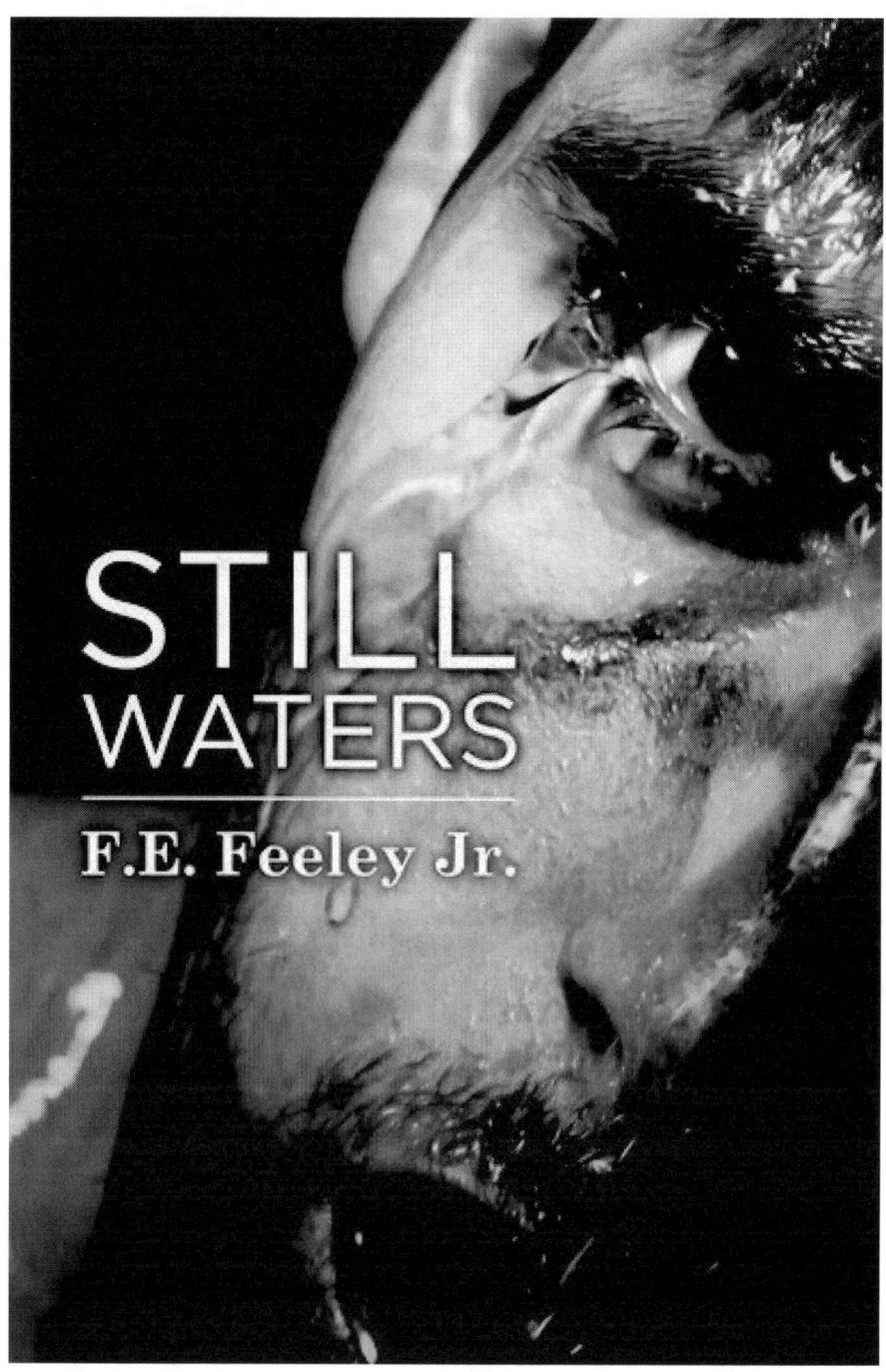

STILL
WATERS

F.E. Feeley Jr.

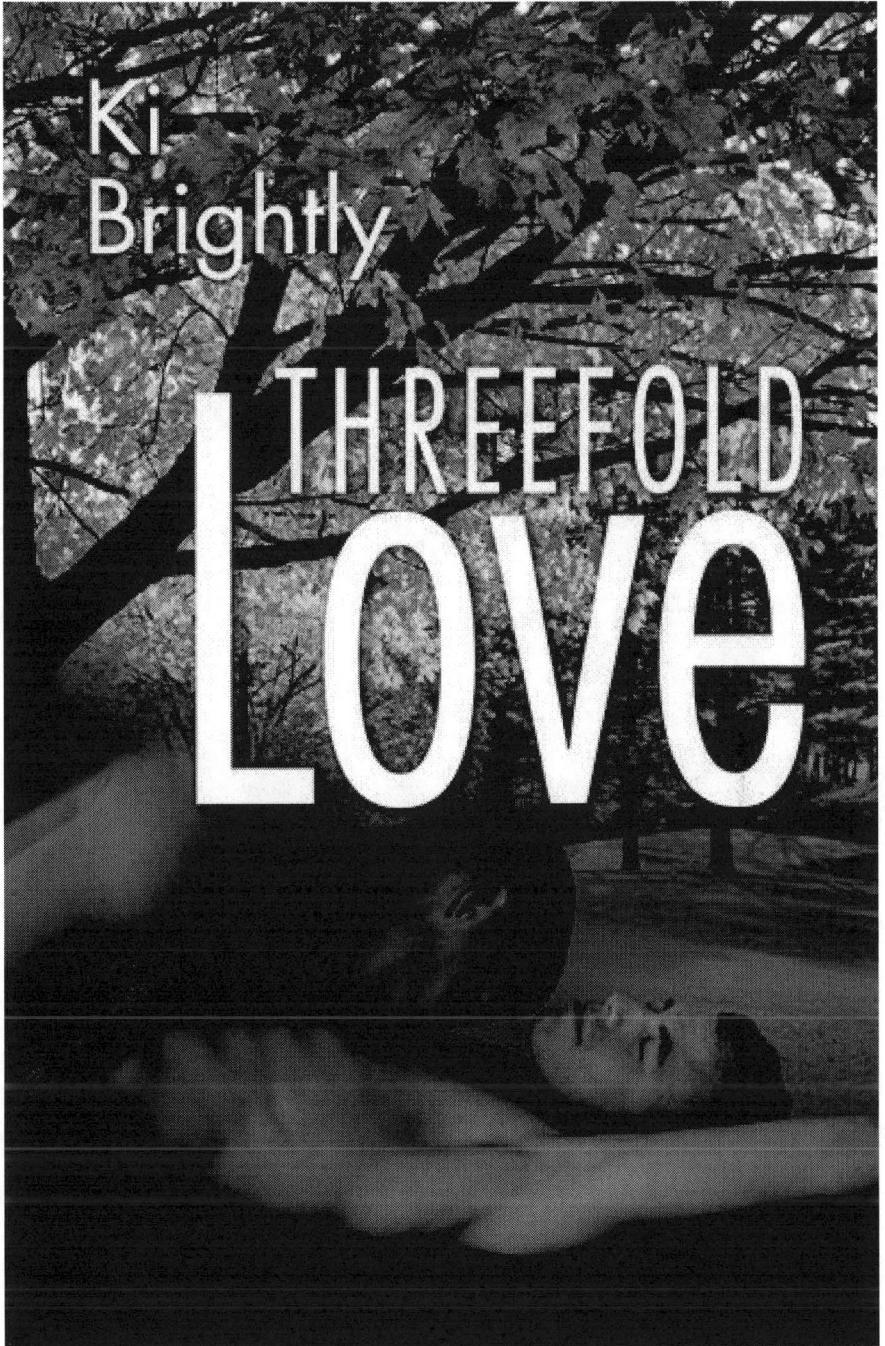

Made in United States
Orlando, FL
05 November 2023